'What is funny?' Hugo asked.

She took a deep gulp of air and turned her gaze back to him, only to be caught by the passion in his face. His lips were curved, their well-defined outline begging to be traced by her finger…by her tongue.

'Funny?' he reminded her.

'You. Me. The feelings you create in me.' The words tumbled from her mouth, making no sense. 'Both safe and yet scared.'

'As though this is completely new?'

She nodded. Was he going to kiss her? Would he stop with just a kiss? Did she want him to? She no longer knew what she wanted.

'I am going to kiss you, Annabell. If you don't want that, then tell me now.' His voice was low and urgent.

Her eyes fluttered shut. Fool that she was, she wanted his kiss, his touch. 'Please…'

Georgina Devon has a Bachelor of Arts degree in Social Sciences with a concentration in History. Her interest in England began when the United States Air Force stationed her at RAF Woodbridge, near Ipswich in East Anglia. This is also where she met her husband, who flew fighter aircraft for the United States. She began writing when she left the Air Force. Her husband's military career moved the family every two to three years, and she wanted a career she could take with her anywhere in the world. Today, she and her husband live in Tucson, Arizona, with their teenage daughter, two dogs and a cockatiel.

AN UNCONVENTIONAL WIDOW features characters you may have already met in THE LORD AND THE MYSTERY LADY.

Recent titles by the same author:

THE RAKE*
THE REBEL*
THE ROGUE'S SEDUCTION*
THE LORD AND THE MYSTERY LADY

novels have linking characters

AN UNCONVENTIONAL WIDOW

Georgina Devon

MILLS & BOON®

*First published in Great Britain 2004
Harlequin Mills & Boon Limited,
Eton House, 18-24 Paradise Road, Richmond, Surrey TW9 1SR*

© Alison J. Hentges 2004

ISBN 0 263 83989 3

*Set in Times Roman 10½ on 11¼ pt.
04-1204-87127*

*Printed and bound in Spain
by Litografía Rosés S.A., Barcelona*

AN UNCONVENTIONAL
WIDOW

Chapter One

Annabell Fenwick-Clyde, Lady Fenwick-Clyde, stood up, clenched her hands, pressed them into the small of her back and stretched. She looked skyward as she enjoyed the loosening of muscles made tight by bending over the shards of tiles found in this destroyed Roman villa she was excavating.

Clouds scuttled across the late April sky, promising rain later today. She would have to be sure the exposed portions of the villa were well covered before she left.

'Ah,' a raspy baritone voice said. 'A nymph, and a very interestingly dressed one.'

Annabell started, dropped her hands and whirled around. She had been caught up in her work and not heard anyone approach. A man stood not ten feet away, studying her. A very attractive man.

Tall and lean with long legs and broad shoulders, he let his gaze run over her in a way that made her blush. His brown hair was longer than the fashion and dishevelled, as was the brown jacket and white shirt that opened at the collar to reveal a light curling of brown hair. His eyes were a startling clear green and seemed to see through her clothing.

She took a step back, irritated at the heat suffusing her

face, but unable to stop it since he continued to look at her as though she were a tasty morsel he intended to devour. 'I did not hear you approach,' she said, her voice breathless, which added to her discomfort and ire.

He smiled and her knees nearly melted. His mouth was wide and well formed, the lips sharply delineated. His teeth were strong. He radiated a predatory interest.

'You were engrossed in something in the dirt. I was engrossed in something much more appealing.' His gaze dropped to her hips.

Her blush deepened. 'I beg your pardon, but a gentleman would not stare as you do.' Thankfully her voice was cold and pointed instead of the breathiness of seconds before. 'Nor would a gentleman continue to do so,' she added when his attention moved to her torso.

He shrugged. 'A lady does not wear clothing that is very similar to that worn by the women in an Arab sheik's harem.' He cocked his head to one side. 'Although it is a delightful contrast to the chip straw bonnet that is so very English and the starched and buttoned-to-the-ears shirt. Which, unless I mistake the tailoring, is a man's garment.' His gaze moved to her face. 'Altogether charming.'

Her skin flamed, the heat spreading down her neck. Drat the man and drat her response to him, a reaction she could not explain. She was used to meeting men head on and holding her own, even dressed as she was. Her two brothers, Guy, Viscount Chillings, and Dominic, had first been scandalised by this mode of dress, then vocally adamant that she was to wear the clothing of an English lady and then, when she continued to go her own way, *nearly* indifferent. A smile curved up one corner of her mouth. Now, when they saw her dressed this way, all they did was glare.

This specimen of the species, however, was doing much more than glaring. He was mentally undressing her, unless she missed her mark, which she did not think likely. Her deceased husband had taught her what it felt like to have a male undress you with his eyes. But instead of the nausea the previous Lord Fenwick-Clyde had always made her feel, this man made her as unsure as a Miss just out of the schoolroom.

'I have had better compliments,' she said tartly, the words out before she considered them.

He took several strides towards her, his well-muscled legs encased in buckskin breeches eating up the distance. 'I am sure you have,' he murmured.

She clamped her lips shut before she said something else suggestive. Her eyes narrowed as he took another step in her direction.

The sun chose that moment to break through the clouds and shine down on them. She noted that his eyes were deep set and heavy lidded, with lines of dissipation radiating from the outside corners. He looked to be in his late thirties, a man who had lived a hard life. And noting the gleam in his eyes as he watched her study him, he had enjoyed every minute of his dissipation. Most likely, he was a rake of the highest magnitude. Well, that was nothing to her and nothing she had not encountered before. In fact, her younger brother was a libertine and she handled him quite well. Of course, Dominic's interest was never aimed at her.

'Now that you have studied me like one would a specimen pinned to a board, please be on your way. I,' she said pointedly, 'am busy.'

His eyelids drooped over speculative eyes and his mouth turned sensual. 'I warrant you are.' He closed the distance between them. 'But you are busy on my property, and I think, what with life's trials, tribulations and...' his voice turned husky '...temptations, you owe me a forfeit for trespassing.'

'I owe you nothing,' she said indignantly, moving to one side. 'If you are Sir Hugo Fitzsimmon, your steward has given me permission to be here.'

His smile lost none of its anticipation as he moved to

block her. 'Then he did not ask me before granting you leave.'

'That is your problem,' she said sharply. 'Not mine.'

She dodged to one side as he continued to close the distance between them. Sir Hugo or not Sir Hugo, she did not know him. No matter that her body screamed she did know him and wanted to know him better, her mind was adamant. She did not know this man.

She was too slow. He caught her and drew her inexorably toward him. Her face inches from his, she noted that he had the swarthy complexion of a man who spent much of his time outdoors. The muscled strength of the arm holding her pinned to his chest suggested that he was a sportsman, possibly a Corinthian.

All of this observation, she knew, was a wild attempt on her part to ignore the tension that started in her stomach and was spreading outwards through her body in waves. There was something about this man that ignited sensations she had never known she possessed. But no matter what that something was, she did not appreciate her body doing things her mind did not want it to do.

His smile widened as though he could read her thoughts and found them amusing. With his free hand, he caught the cherry-coloured satin ribbon tied into a bow beneath her chin and pulled. Her wide-brimmed bonnet toppled off the back of her head.

'How dare you.'

His grin turned wolfish. 'I dare a lot. As you shall see.'

Then his mouth was on hers. She expected him to be rough. She was prepared for rough. He was persuasive.

His lips moved provocatively over hers as his free hand burrowed into the hair at her nape, and held her still for his exploration. His arm around her waist tightened so her breasts pressed against his chest, making her aware of him in ways she had never experienced before.

When his tongue glided along her bottom lip, skimming

her skin so lightly that he was like a treat held just beyond reach, she wondered if she would disgrace herself by following his oh, so clever tongue with her own. He saved her that indignity by taking her small gasp of surprise and using it to slip inside her mouth.

Sensation coursed through her, sensual and warm and arousing. Her eyes closed slowly, as she sank into his embrace. A shudder of delight rippled down her spine.

She gave herself over to his seduction without conscious thought. Her body reacted as her mind slid away.

'Ahh…' he breathed, taking his lips from hers, his voice a rasp. 'You have rewarded me well.'

Her eyes snapped open, and her mind seemed to get back into working order. What had she done? She had acted like a wanton, like a loose woman. And she did not even enjoy the carnal relationship between a man and woman. Her past husband had told her that frequently enough—and she had agreed wholeheartedly with him.

She splayed her palms against this stranger's chest and pushed. Hard.

'Let me go.' Her former blush returned with a vengeance.

He laughed, but did not release her. 'And what will you give me if I do?'

Her eyes sparked. 'What will I give you if you do not, is the better question, sirrah!'

His laugh deepened, so that lines carved into the skin around his mouth. His hair, too long and too long from a razor, lifted in the breeze.

'Threats or promises?' He leaned back and gazed down at where their bodies still met. 'I choose to believe promises.'

'You are no gentleman. Nor are you very intelligent.' Annabell tried desperately not to sputter in her anger at his arrogant assumption of her willing compliance. Although, in all honesty—and she always tried to be honest with herself—he had every reason to think she would succumb to him.

'No?' he drawled, his eyes narrowing dangerously, all hint of humour gone. 'I think I understand you perfectly. Shall I prove it again—to your satisfaction and mine?'

'You have gone too far already.' She sputtered in her fury. 'I may have let you kiss me—'

'Let me? You kissed me back.'

'Let you kiss me, but I was not willing.'

He laughed outright. The sound was full and rich with resonance. It sent shivers cascading down her spine. But enough was enough. She pushed hard at him and hooked her lower leg behind his knee. He released her waist just before he fell to the ground like a stone. Surprise widened his eyes seconds before they narrowed.

Instead of jumping to his feet as she had expected, he rose up on his elbows and studied her with an insolence that made his countenance cold. 'I see you are a woman who can defend herself.'

She returned his appraisal; hands on hips. 'I learned early with two brothers that sometimes fighting unfairly is the only way a woman can protect herself.'

A twinge of guilt narrowed her eyes. Guy and Dominic had never abused her as her husband had. If truth be told, the late Fenwick-Clyde had taught her more about unfair fighting than either of her brothers. But that was something only she knew or needed to know.

The man who called himself Sir Hugo got to his feet in one lithe movement that told her clearer than words that, if he really wanted to do something to her, he could. Instead, he carelessly straightened the handkerchief knotted at his neck, similar to those worn by prizefighters.

'Women are not the only ones who often need an advantage to protect themselves. But that is neither here nor there.' He slid out of his loose-fitting jacket and shook it to get off some of the dirt from the excavation. Instead of putting it back on, he folded it across his arm. 'You are on my land without my permission. I could have you arrested for trespassing.'

Annabell's deep blue eyes sparked in a way both her brothers would recognise as the first warning of a verbal attack. 'If you are unaware of my presence then it is the fault of your steward, who agreed to our excavation.' Her mouth thinned. 'Perhaps he could not reach you. And furthermore, you could try to arrest me for trespassing, but you would be unsuccessful. Everyone around here knows who I am and that I am invited.'

'Perhaps.' His voice grated.

She smiled sweetly while venom dripped from her words. 'I assure you, Sir Hugo, I have a letter from your man authorising me to be here.'

His jaw sharpened. 'I am sure you do, Miss—'

She notched up her chin. '*Lady* Fenwick-Clyde.'

For an instant only, his pupils dilated. He made a curt, mocking bow. '*Lady* Fenwick-Clyde.' He waved his long-fingered hand to encompass her work area. 'Until I check into this further, please feel free to do with my land as you please.'

She ignored the sarcasm in his voice. 'I shall do just that, Sir Hugo.'

He gave her one last, long look. This one did not go below her neck. It was as though he were reassessing her. Then he spun on his well-shod heel and strode to where a chestnut mare stood patiently waiting, eating the vibrant spring grass.

It was not until he walked away that she noticed his limp. The catch in his gait was so minor as to be nearly indiscernible. Nor did it mar his natural predatory grace.

She watched him mount the horse and disappear into the smattering of trees separating the site from the nearby dirt path that substituted as a road. He rode with the same easy grace that he moved. No wonder he had a reputation with women.

He was one of the handsomest men, albeit in a disreputable way, she had every seen. Her brothers were considered very good specimens, but to her mind Sir Hugo surpassed them.

Unconsciously, her fingers went to her lips. She could still feel the tingle of his mouth on hers. Ridiculous.

She had things to do. This was a valuable site of Roman occupation. Her goal was to preserve it for posterity. She had thought she had months to do so. With Sir Hugo in residence, she had very little time. Not even a widow's reputation was safe when linked with the Wolf of Covent Garden.

A rueful grin twisted her mouth. Funny she should remember that name for him. Her younger brother Dominic had thrown it at her in one of his tirades when he discovered exactly where the Roman villa she was excavating was located. He had called Sir Hugo dangerous. He was probably right.

She unconsciously rubbed her still swollen lips.

And the way the man had looked at her. It had been nothing short of indecent. She might be dressed unconventionally, but she had every right to wear what she chose. Men did.

But, perhaps, with him in residence, it would be better to dress more conservatively. Much as she had denied the attraction he exuded, she had been unable to resist him. What if he chose to take advantage of her again?

Her body heated and she sank to the ground.

Tomorrow she would wear a proper English skirt. Her spine stiffened and she pushed herself back up to her feet.

No, no, she wouldn't. His bold disregard for the proprieties would not make her skittish. She would do as she wished and was practical. As she always did. No man, and especially not one as disreputable as he, would alter her actions.

That settled, she bent back to her work, forgetting that her bonnet lay in the dirt several feet away where it had fallen.

Hugo moved easily in the saddle despite the twinge in his left thigh and the sharp pull that radiated to his groin. He was not a man to pity himself. He had taken a musket ball during Waterloo. Many others had taken worse.

He had even been given a knighthood for bravery. His mouth twisted. He had only done what needed to be done. Still, he had accepted the knighthood for his father's memory. His father had spent his life trying to get a title bestowed on his only child and failed. Hugo knew logically that his father was gone and the knighthood bestowed too late to make his father feel better, but his heart had told him to accept and trust that somehow his father knew.

He resisted the temptation to look back at Lady Fenwick-Clyde. He was not sure if he would feel desire or pity, and did not want to find out. Instead, he urged Molly into a canter.

He remembered Fenwick-Clyde as a lecherous old sot with a reputation for roughness among the less privileged prostitutes. He scowled. No sense sugar-coating it to himself. Fenwick-Clyde had been abusive. He had heard rumours the man was the same with his young wife. He had been repulsed by Fenwick-Clyde and so never met the wife who had kept to herself and avoided most of the *ton*'s activities. He wondered if she still stayed away from society now that she was widowed.

It was none of his concern.

He noticed the ground change. They were on the fine gravel driveway leading to Rosemont, named for the profusion of roses that came into bloom during the late spring and summer. Hugo urged Molly into a run for the remaining distance.

Minutes later they came to a halt, dirt and rocks flying behind the mare's back legs. With a laugh of pleasure, Hugo slid to the ground. Home at last. It had been nearly a year.

He breathed deeply of the fresh air, redolent with growing life—freshly scythed grass, flowers and the hint of stables. His mouth twisted into a wry smile. He had missed this place more than he cared to admit.

In front of him were the steps to the entrance, situated in the middle between two wings. Rosemont was an H-shaped Elizabethan manor house, built from red bricks and thick oak beams. He had been born here in the house-keeper's room thirty-six years ago.

The front door opened and Butterfield came out. The old butler was tall and stick thin, holding himself with more dignity than anyone else Hugo knew, with the possible except of the Iron Duke. Wellington was well-known for his good self-image. And Hugo knew it well. He had served as one of Wellington's *aides-de-camp* for the past year. He had been one of the few to survive that duty.

'Butterfield,' Hugo said, hugging the butler in spite of the old man's attempt to hold himself aloof.

'Sir Hugo,' Butterfield said, his voice warm even through the tone of censure. 'You mustn't do that.'

Hugo took pity on his old retainer and released him. 'You did not always feel that way.'

Butterfield's old rheumy eyes softened. 'Aye, but you were a young buck in leading strings then. Now you are the lord here and a man with a reputation for bravery, too.'

Hugo waved him to silence. 'None of that.' He strode forward. 'The carriage with my baggage will be here later. We ran into rain and, subsequently, muddy, pocked roads.'

He strode past the running stable lad come to fetch Molly. The boy pulled his forelock and grinned from ear to ear. Hugo smiled, but kept going. Now that he was here at last, he wanted nothing more than to be inside, seated in the library with a snifter of good French brandy that had not been smuggled. The Lord knew he and others had fought long and hard to defeat Napoleon and gain access once more to a France under Bourbon rule. He hoped they would never forget all Britain had sacrificed.

He entered the foyer, unconsciously absorbing the presence of the wooden plank floor and various suits of armour and the accoutrements that went with them. Shields of every shape and size hung from the oak-panelled walls. Muskets alternated with lances. Everything was polished to mirror brightness. He expected nothing less from his staff with Butterfield in charge. But the butler was ageing. He would have to hire a housekeeper soon, whether he wanted to or not. He had never wanted another housekeeper after his own history. Not that he would repeat his father's indiscretions.

Hugo waved off a footman who had come to get his jacket. 'No, Michael, I will keep it with me.'

The young man, short and thin, the antithesis of most footmen who were often hired for their looks so as to enhance their employer's standing, stepped back. A smile curved the youth's mouth at being remembered. Unlike some of the aristocracy, Sir Hugo always knew the names of his servants and called them by their given names. Some of his peers named their staff for the jobs each servant did, regardless of the servant's actual name.

The footman bowed. 'Yes, Sir Hugo.'

Hugo continued to the library. It was the room at Rosemont where he felt most at home and relaxed.

With a sigh of satisfaction, he entered the room. Huge multi-paned windows covered the outside wall, allowing the late afternoon sunlight to enter in myriad prisms. Colours danced off the polished wood floor and flashed from the glass that enclosed floor-to-ceiling bookcases. A fire roared in the massive grate. Even this late in the year it was cold inside a house this old.

He went to his desk and picked up a full decanter of brandy and poured himself a healthy portion. He drank it down in one long, satisfied gulp.

'Ahem,' a female voice said. 'I don't believe you belong here.'

Hugo swallowed a less than gracious retort. Instead of looking in the direction of the voice, he poured himself another brandy. He had a feeling he was going to need it.

'This is a private home, young man, and the owner is not about.' The woman's voice was sharp yet breathy, as though she struggled for oxygen. 'I suggest you leave before I call a footman and have you ousted.'

Taking another long drink, Hugo pivoted on his heel and faced the woman. She was tall and thin to the point of near emaciation. Her chin was pointed and her brown eyes seemed too big for her face. Pale blonde hair, streaked with grey, was pulled back into a tight bun. Her mouth was pinched with irritation at the moment.

'I don't believe I have the pleasure of your acquaintance, ma'am,' he drawled, finishing the brandy.

She drew herself up. 'Nor do I have yours. Nor do I wish to.' She crossed to the pull by the fireplace and yanked the velvet strip.

'You must be here with Lady Fenwick-Clyde.'

'Yes.' Her back was ramrod straight in its pale lavender kerseymere.

He set the empty glass down, resigned to another confrontation and one not nearly as pleasant as the last. He made her a short bow. 'Allow me to introduce myself then, since I doubt I will be seeing the last of you for some time.' He ignored her indignant gasp. 'I am Sir Hugo Fitzsimmon—your host.'

Her pale blue eyes widened and a scarlet flush mounted

her cheeks. 'Oh, dear. How very inconvenient,' she muttered.

Hugo choked back a laugh, grateful he was not drinking the brandy. It would have spattered over everything.

'How gracious of you,' he replied. 'You must be Lady Fenwick-Clyde's companion.'

'Yes, I am, and I can tell you, sir, that we certainly did not expect you to return as you have.' She shook her head. 'Your reputation is such that not even a widowed lady with a chaperon is safe with you in attendance.'

He shrugged with true indifference. 'Then you must relocate to the inn nearby. Their rooms are clean and their food passable.'

'You could much easier go back to where you came from for a while.'

Hugo wondered if his hearing was going bad or if she had just attempted a joke. One look at her serious, clearly affronted countenance told him neither was correct. She meant exactly what she had said.

'We, after all,' she continued, 'have express permission from your steward to lodge here and be at liberty on your land for as long as it takes Bell and her team to excavate the Roman villa.'

Hugo wondered if he had actually died at Waterloo and gone someplace that was not heaven. This situation was surreal.

'I think not,' he said, pouring another glass of brandy and gulping it down. 'I shall leave you here while I go to my rooms. When I come back, I shall expect you to be gone.'

Before she could do more than open and close her mouth, he was out of the room. His one refuge in this house, the one place he felt completely at liberty, and she had invaded it.

'Sir Hugo,' Butterfield said, coming toward the library. 'Oh. Miss Pennyworth must be in there.'

Hugo halted. 'Miss Pennyworth? A tall, thin woman who thinks she owns Rosemont?'

Butterfield nodded.

'I am going to my rooms, Butterfield. Get Tatterly and tell him I expect him to meet with me on the hour. In the library. Without Miss Pennyworth or anyone else for that matter.'

'Yes, m'lord,' Butterfield said to Hugo's back.

Chapter Two

Annabell strode into the foyer to the sound of male voices raised in irritation. They came from the library, her favourite room. Much as it pained her to admit it, she recognised one of the voices as belonging to Sir Hugo. A meeting lasting only minutes, and his voice was now imprinted on her senses. What was happening to her?

'Tatterly,' Sir Hugo said, his tone low, 'see that Lady Fenwick-Clyde and her chaperon are out of here by tomorrow. Tonight if possible.'

Hearing her name, Annabell did the unthinkable. She moved closer. Better to know in advance what was being said about her than to find out when it was too late to do anything about it. She all but put her ear to the oak panel.

'Yes, Sir Hugo, but—'

'No buts. I am home and intend to stay here until I decide to leave, not until some rumour-monger forces me to leave in order to save that woman's reputation.' There was an ominous silence. 'And that chaperon. She would drive me to mayhem.'

That was enough! How dare he speak that way about Susan. Annabell found herself fully as angry as Sir Hugo. She marched through the library's open door and stood just past the entrance, feet apart.

'You, Sir Hugo, should ensure the doors are closed before you go on about unwelcomed guests.'

The object of her censure turned slowly to face her. 'I should not have to pay attention to what I say in my own home, Lady Fenwick-Clyde.'

He was right and she knew it, but still... 'You may not have expressly invited me, but Mr Tatterly said it would be acceptable for Miss Pennyworth and me to stay here as long as necessary to excavate the Roman villa.'

Sir Hugo took one step towards her and stopped as though he did not trust himself any closer. 'As long as I was on the Continent it was. I am not there now. Nor do I intend to move into a room at the village inn. So, you had best go. Your reputation won't be worth the breath used to shred it if it becomes known you are sleeping under the same roof as I am.'

She notched her chin up. 'I am a widow. Widows may do as they please.'

His eloquent mouth nearly sneered. 'Widows of a certain ilk, certainly. Somehow...' he ran his gaze insolently up and down her body '...I don't believe you want to be in that category in spite of your unconventional dress. But correct me if I am wrong.'

'Leave my clothes out of this,' she said, barely able to contain her ire at his insinuations. 'Until you arrived unannounced, my reputation did not need preserving.'

He shrugged and turned his back to her. 'I am here now, this is my home, and that is that.'

'Sir Hugo—' Tatterly said, his strong, solid face agonised.

'Not another word, Tatterly.'

Annabell took pity on the man. It was not his fault. 'Mr Tatterly, don't worry. You are not to blame for any of this. None of us believed Sir Hugo would forego his pleasures so quickly to rusticate.'

Sir Hugo's shoulders shook and Annabell heard what

sounded suspiciously like a snort. Yet, when he turned around, his face was unreadable. 'I take my pleasures where I find them, Lady Fenwick-Clyde. For the moment, I find them here.'

Annabell bit her lip, a bad habit she had when confronted with a problem to which she did not like the solution. 'Very well, Sir Hugo. Miss Pennyworth and I shall move to the inn.' She turned her brightest smile on the steward. 'If you would be so kind as to procure us rooms, Mr Tatterly, I would be forever in your debt.'

Mr Tatterly turned brick red. 'Of course, milady. It would be my pleasure.' He started for the door where Annabell still stood, but stopped in time to ask his employer, 'May I be off, Sir Hugo? The sooner this is done, the sooner everything is solved.'

Sir Hugo nodded. 'By all means, Tatterly. We wouldn't want to inconvenience Lady Fenwick-Clyde any more than necessary.'

Annabell stepped to the side so Mr Tatterly could pass. She pointedly did not look at Sir Hugo, who had moved to stand by one of the many windows. His sarcasm in dismissing Mr Tatterly had increased her irritation, which was decidedly unlike her. All the years of her marriage she had managed to ignore Fenwick-Clyde's snide remarks and disparaging words. Although, in all truth, Sir Hugo was not disparaging or snide, he was sarcastic and sensual and hard to ignore.

'Do you have a maid?' Sir Hugo asked without taking his attention from the scene outside. 'If not, I will have a maid sent to help you pack.'

'That won't be necessary. I can take care of myself, Sir Hugo.'

He turned and gave her an appraising study. 'I believe you can, but why would you when it isn't necessary?'

She raised one black brow. 'Because it makes me self-sufficient.'

'As you wish.'

She thought his mouth thinned, but if so it was so slight she immediately decided she had been mistaken. And even if she was not, it did not matter. After life with Fenwick-Clyde, she did not care what a man thought of her or her need for independence.

'I won't impose on you a moment longer than absolutely necessary.' She pivoted on the heel of her boot and stalked from the room. The sooner she was gone, the better for all of them.

Hugo watched her stride from the room and shook his head. She looked cool and composed in her outrageous clothing—a woman who thumbed her nose at the world— but in truth she was anything but cool. She was a spitfire for all that her hair was as silver as the full moon. And undoubtedly a bluestocking, determined to prove she did not need a man for anything.

Before he realised it, his mouth curved into a devilish smile. It would prove interesting to show the very independent Lady Fenwick-Clyde that men were good for many things. His smile deepened and his green eyes darkened. His body responded.

His laugh filled the empty library. Oh, yes, it was good to be home.

Annabell turned to her travelling writing desk and made sure the quills were in place and the ink securely stoppered. Without her volition, her fingers strayed to the leather writing portion. Many years of use had made the fine cowhide smooth as satin. In one corner was an ink stain. In another were initials she'd carved into the mahogany wood years ago. She could still remember when.

She had been married several years and miserable. Guy, her older brother, had given her the money to get away from Fenwick-Clyde not knowing she intended to go to Egypt. He had thought she just wanted to go to Scotland or Ireland or even Italy, places acceptable for a married woman with a chaperon to go. Guy had been furious when he learned where she had really gone, but it was too late by then. She was at her destination and fascinated.

The Egyptian desert with its exotic heat and plants had intrigued her, but the pyramids had caught her imagination. It was the start of her love for antiquities. Prior to that she had been interested, but it had been academic. Now it was nearly a passion.

Her Egyptian guide had been a native of the region who taught her to enjoy strong coffee and to appreciate the harsh beauty of the desert. If she concentrated hard enough, she could still imagine the feel of the dry, hot winds against her skin.

The trip had been a turning point for her.

She had always been interested in everything ancient, since first studying the classics with her brothers when they prepared for university. This trip showed her she could participate in the discovery of the past, not just read about it.

Fenwick-Clyde had threatened to banish her to the country when she made her first trip to Egypt against his orders, but she had not cared, she had gone anyway. A wife who openly defied her husband—he had made her pay in ways polite society would never know about. Fenwick-Clyde had died shortly after that, overtaken by too much drink, women and general dissipation.

Annabell snapped shut the lock on her portmanteau as someone knocked on the bedchamber door. 'Come in.'

'Lady Fenwick-Clyde,' Tatterly said, his tone slow and stolid, yet managing to draw her back from her reverie. 'Excuse me, but there is a problem.'

Still fiddling with her packing, she looked at him. 'Yes?'

His large fingers played slowly against the smooth wood of the doorjamb. He was a wide man, not particularly tall, but solid. Like a man who made his living at physical labour even though he was a gentleman and had been educated at Oxford.

'Yes, my lady.' He took a deep breath. 'The inn is filled completely. There is a prizefight in the area this coming weekend.'

'Does Sir Hugo know?'

'No, my lady. He is riding the grounds, letting the tenants know he is back.'

In spite of herself, she was impressed. Very few men of her acquaintance would take the time immediately upon arriving home after being gone for nearly a year to reacquaint themselves with their landholders.

'He is a conscientious man.'

'Very much so, my lady.' Tatterly still stood on the threshold of the room, his stance tense. The problem of her quarters was not resolved. 'What do you want me to do, Lady Fenwick-Clyde? There is another small village, but it is more distant and would take you at least an hour in travel each way. And that is if the weather is good.'

Annabell frowned and stopped what she was doing. Things were definitely not getting any better. 'Tell Sir Hugo I would like to meet with him immediately upon his return.'

'Yes, my lady.'

She smiled at the still-tense man. 'And thank you for everything you have done, Tatterly.'

'You are welcome, Lady Fenwick-Clyde.'

He stayed where he was, radiating uncertainty. Now his fingers were motionless against the door. Annabell glanced at him and raised one brow.

'Yes, Tatterly?'

'Um…if you permit, I thought I would tell Miss Pennyworth you won't be leaving immediately. I saw her in the morning room.' His fair skin turned russet. 'That is, if you don't think she would mind.'

Annabell smiled. The man was transparent. 'Please do

that for me. I would appreciate not having to stop what I am doing to inform her.'

He cleared his throat so that his Adam's apple bobbed. 'My pleasure.'

I don't doubt that, Annabell thought, watching him leave without closing her bedchamber door. If they stayed here too long, she might lose her companion. She and Pennyworth had been together a long time. They met on Annabell's first trip to Egypt, on the ship coming back from Gibraltar. Miss Pennyworth had been escorting a young girl from India back to England for school. Annabell had offered her the position of her companion when her commitment to the girl was finished. Miss Pennyworth had accepted. Now Tatterly, unless Annabell missed her guess, was interested in offering Miss Pennyworth a new position as wife. If that was what Pennyworth wanted, she would not begrudge her the chance for happiness, even though she would miss her sorely.

But for the immediate future, she had other problems. She was not travelling an hour each way every day in order to excavate the Roman villa. And longer if the weather turned bad.

She started unpacking.

Hugo breathed deeply of the cool air, filled with the hint of moisture. The scent of live things permeated everything. He heard the sound of movement in the underbrush and saw the flip of a wing overhead. He had missed England. He had missed Rosemont. He had not expected to miss either.

His hands tightened on the reins so that Molly shied. 'Easy, girl,' he murmured, leaning forward to stroke her glossy neck. 'Nothing is wrong. Not really.'

He reined Molly to a stop. The remains of the Roman villa stood in stark contrast to the green grass and trees surrounding it. He could make out bright shards and pieces of earthenware pottery. She had done a good job of preserving the site. Antiquities had interested him since his Oxford days. It was intriguing that she was fascinated by them as well.

He might not want her in his home because of all the problems her presence would create, but he did want to see this villa preserved. If possible, he would like it restored to its former glory, or as near as possible without compromising its integrity.

That was why, when Tatterly had written to tell him one of the farmers had dug up a Roman antiquity while ploughing near the orchard, he had told his steward to arrange for someone qualified to come and excavate the site. He had thought the expert would be male.

His mouth quirked. Never in his most fantastical dreams would he have imagined a woman interested and qualified to do what Lady Fenwick-Clyde was doing.

This interest was a strange thing to have in common. But his concerns over the excavation were not enough to allow her to remain in his home, given the possible ramifications. She could easily be ruined, or he could be pressured to marry her. Neither possibility was acceptable.

Unless she chose to stay, understanding that, no matter what happened, marriage was not an option.

Annabell found him once more in the library, his legs propped on an ottoman, a book in one hand and a brandy in the other. He looked perfectly content. For a man of his reputation, he seemed to spend a lot of time in a quiet room. She would have thought he would be gambling or wenching in the nearby tavern, the one he had wanted her to relocate to.

When the footman moved to announce her, she waved him away. Better to have the advantage of surprise. It had always worked when dealing with her brothers—no matter that it had not been effective with Fenwick-Clyde. Somehow she thought Sir Hugo was more like her younger sibling than her previous spouse.

'Sir Hugo,' she said firmly, entering the book-shrouded room. 'I need to speak with you.'

He said something she could not make out. He did not bother to stand or to even look back at her. He ignored her.

'I said I have something to talk to you about.'

She stopped to the side of where he sat and scowled down at him. It was a mistake.

His hair was tousled from his ride, the heavy curls falling across his wide forehead. His eyes were greener than she remembered and held a hint of emotion she could not name. His mouth, that generous yet firmly moulded mouth, caught her attention.

She knew what his lips felt like pressed to hers. She knew his mouth was as skilled at kissing as it was beguiling to look at. The urge to reach out and trace the curves of his lips nearly undid her. She curled her fingers into fists and held them securely at her sides. Better to look anywhere else than at his mouth. It made her remember sensations better forgotten.

Her gaze dropped. His shirt was loosened at the neck and the handkerchief that had been knotted around his throat earlier was gone.

He was a very disturbing man.

He laid down the book he had been reading, one of Jane Austen's. 'I thought you would be gone by now.'

'The inn is full.' She made it a flat statement of fact, unarguable.

'That is too bad.'

She waited, but he didn't say anything else, just sipped his brandy. 'You drink a lot of that.'

She was trying to be deliberately provoking. For some reason he brought out the worst in her.

He nodded. 'Yes, but not as much as others. Where are you going to stay now?'

Her mouth opened to tell him in no uncertain terms that she was staying here. She clamped it shut so hard her teeth clicked. This was his house. He could order her out even if she had nowhere else to go. She had been on her own and answerable to no one for too long when her manners went begging like this.

'May I have a seat?' She kept her voice mild and reasonable.

He waved a negligent hand at the nearest chair, a big, stuffed chintz she often sat in. There was nothing nicer than sitting in here before a roaring fire, having tea and reading a good book. Sometimes eating buttered toast. He had an extensive collection, everything from the classics to Jane Austen. She wondered if he had read them all, but doubted it because there were so many.

She sat down and ran her hands down her lap, smoothing the skirt of the high-waisted kerseymere she had changed into. 'The next closest inn is at least an hour's ride each way. That will make it very difficult for me to have a productive day.'

He turned to watch her, but said nothing. She found his perusal unsettling, to say the least. It made her flush and her stomach twitch. She wanted him to look elsewhere—anywhere but at her, which made her uncomfortable.

'Have I a smudge on my nose or chin?' Her voice was more tart than she had intended.

His mouth curved into a rakish grin. 'Not that I can see, and I am looking very hard for flaws.'

Her eyes widened and she leaned away from him. 'I beg your pardon, Sir Hugo.' Embarrassment was a wonderful cure for self-consciousness, she found. All thought vanished of trying to talk reasonably in order to convince him to let her stay here. 'I did not come here to be flirted with.'

His smiled widened. 'No, I imagine you didn't. You came to wheedle me into letting you stay here at Rosemont.'

'I didn't come here to *wheedle* you. I came here to explain why I need to stay here at least until the village inn has room, which should be early next week after everyone who has come for the prizefight has left.'

'Ah, I understand now.' He took a long drink of his liquor. 'You don't much care about your reputation. You think that being a widow with a chaperon will protect you from the gossips. You are more concerned about your convenience and comfort.'

She eyed him with dislike. Her body might respond to him and her eyes might take pleasure in looking at him, but she did not have to like him as a person.

'I am an adult woman. I can do as I choose. Men do it all the time. I choose to stay where it is convenient for me to accomplish my work.' She took a deep breath. 'Were you in my position, you would do exactly that.'

He laughed outright, but it wasn't a mirthful sound. 'You are either naïve or delusional. Women, *like men,* should value their good name. For you, much of your good name is locked up in your reputation. Nothing would protect your reputation—or any other woman's for that matter—from the gossip-mongers. Particularly since my conduct among the fairer sex is disreputable to say the least, as you so willingly informed me this afternoon.'

'You were insufferable,' she retorted without thinking. When his smile became self-satisfied, she knew she had played right into his hand. 'Not that I can't handle you.'

A different look moved over his face. 'I am sure you can.'

Now she'd made the situation worse. And he did have a valid point. In many ways, she knew him to be right, which only increased her irritation with the entire situation. It was the way of their world to constrain women and to put name and background before individual happiness. She had done that once by entering into an arranged marriage. Never again. She was tired of the world she came from. She wanted freedom to be herself, hard as that might be.

Her voice was waspish as a result of her thoughts. 'Let us not mince words, Sir Hugo. You are a rake and a libertine. I know that, and I am prepared to take the risk of ruining my reputation.'

He shook his head and set the empty glass down. 'Is this excavation so important that you can't wait a couple of days? Move to the distant tavern or go back to London until the village inn has room.'

She raised her chin up and squared her shoulders. What he said had merit, but not for her. 'I could do that, and that would be the reasonable thing to do. But I don't choose to do so.'

'May I ask why?'

'You may, and I will even tell you.' She took a deep breath. 'I choose not to do the respectable thing because I am sick of what society says is acceptable for a woman. Men may do as they damn well please, but women must do as they are told. Well, I will do as I see fit. If that ruins me in the eyes of the *ton,* then so be it. It is a small price to pay for being able to decide what I do, when I do it and with whom I do it.'

She stopped, realising she had very nearly launched into a tirade. Ever since Fenwick-Clyde had dominated her in every way possible, she had taken every opportunity to defy anyone and anything that tried to dictate to her. And, truth be told, she had always been rebellious. That trait had just worsened after her marriage.

He refilled his glass, picked it up and saluted her. 'I believe I understand perfectly. You are a bluestocking and a revolutionary. I congratulate you on your courage. Make yourself at home. It does not matter to me if it does not matter to you.'

She gaped. Her victory was too easily won. But then they had not been in battle.

'Why have you changed your mind? Earlier today you were adamant that I was to leave.'

'Earlier today I felt like following society's dictates. Now I see you do not care, so I leave the responsibility for your welfare to you. I came home to rest and recuperate, not fight with a woman I don't even know.' He drank the brandy in one long gulp, his Adam's apple moving just above the white collar of his shirt. 'Besides, I admire your courage.'

She nearly fell over from shock. 'Admire my courage?'

He nodded, a mysterious gleam in his green, green eyes. 'Yes, courage. That is a rare commodity in any person and one to be preserved. If you are not afraid of anything, then so be it.'

'You are letting me stay because you think I have courage?' He nodded and she blinked. 'I also have stubbornness.'

He shrugged. 'That too. Besides which,' he added, 'my stepmother has written to inform me that she and my brother and sister will be here shortly. She started from London as soon as she heard I was in the country.'

'Ah.' That explained his change. 'An impeccable chaperon.'

He shrugged. 'Perhaps to some.' He slanted a speculative look at Annabell, his gaze traveling from her smooth hair, which she had pulled primly back into a bun, to her lap where her hands lay still. 'I believe she is your age or younger. My father married late in his life.'

'Hah! Yes, she will be the perfect protection for my honour. How like society to determine that your stepmother, even though she may be younger than me, can be depended upon to be a buffer between your lascivious urges and my widowhood. That is exactly what I meant about freedom.'

'You are right, but that is the way of things.'

He continued to watch her as he said the irritating words. Annabell wondered if he said them merely to goad her, to see what she would say. Her brothers would have. But she had been on her high horse long enough, and it was late and she wanted to take one last look at the site before finishing for the day.

She stood abruptly. 'Well, now that we have resolved everything, I will leave you to your pleasures.'

He nodded. 'Yes, I do like my pleasures.'

She gave him a narrowed look, suspecting him of innuendo, but saw his countenance was noncommittal. 'Yes, you do, Sir Hugo.'

She looked pointedly at a nearby brazier that added its warmth to that from the fireplace. Then there was the fine cashmere rug he had over his legs and the supple leather slippers he wore that seemed soft as a second skin.

He smiled up at her, not in the least discommoded. 'Life is short. I live it to the fullest and the devil take the hindmost.'

'A hedonist.'

He smiled, thinning his lips. 'Exactly.'

'Someday you will tire of living only for pleasure.'

'I doubt that.'

'Wait and see.'

She was always one to give as good as she got and she never backed down from anything. She had often confronted Fenwick-Clyde, usually to her regret in the long run. But she had been determined to stand up for herself, even when performing the duties expected of a wife. She shivered.

'Are you feeling unwell?' Sir Hugo stood so that he was nearly touching her. 'You suddenly paled.'

She blinked and realised her hands were clenched. It had been ages since she thought of what Fenwick-Clyde had required of her. Why now?

'I am fine. Just old memories.' She would have sounded more convincing if her voice hadn't trembled. Sometimes she disgusted herself. 'Perfectly fine. I must be on my way.

Thank you so much for allowing Miss Pennyworth and myself to remain here.'

He watched her, the look in his eyes telling her as clear as spoken words that he didn't believe her. But he said nothing further about that.

'One last thing,' he drawled, his voice stopping her. She looked back at him. 'If your reputation is shredded, Lady Fenwick-Clyde, don't look to me to remedy the situation.'

She stared at him, not sure she understood. 'Exactly what are you trying to say?'

He sipped his brandy. 'That I won't marry you to preserve a name you are determined to sully.'

The urge to stalk across the room and slap him for his arrogance was strong. Somehow, she managed to resist.

'Be assured, Sir Hugo, I won't require that sacrifice from you. Ever.'

Annabell made her exit before he could reply. Goodness only knew what he would say given the opportunity. And goodness only knew what she would do if he continued to goad her.

Sir Hugo watched her go and wondered if he had made a colossal mistake by allowing her to stay. Her slim hips swayed in spite of how stiffly she held her shoulders. Wisps of her blond, nearly silver hair escaped the severe bun and wafted behind her like moonbeams. He scowled. He was not a poet and had no aspirations to be one, yet here he was describing her in flowery words. Sometimes his libido got the better of him.

He sank back into his chair.

Juliet might be coming and bringing his half-brother and half-sister, Joseph and Rosalie, but he doubted they would make good chaperons. Still, society would be appeased. He would nearly have a house party.

His mouth curled into a sardonic grin. The perfect setting for a seduction.

And he had warned her that he would not marry her, no matter what happened. His conscience was clear.

Chapter Three

Hugo sprawled leisurely in his chair and watched the other three people at the dinner table. Lady Fenwick-Clyde sat on his right, Miss Susan Pennyworth on his left. Beside Miss Pennyworth was Tatterly, still as a church mouse as he listened attentively to every word Miss Pennyworth uttered, which was many. The man was transparent, but Miss Pennyworth seemed unaware of his infatuation. Of course, Hugo decided, Miss Pennyworth was a ninnyhammer and very likely unaware of many things.

'Lady Fenwick-Clyde, was your archaeological site safe when you checked it earlier?' He had to find conversation of some substance or banish the nattering companion from the room.

She looked at him as though she suspected him of teasing her, which he was. He found her interest in scientific matters fascinating. He also enjoyed watching the emotions flit across her face. She was totally unaffected. For an instant, he wondered how she had ever survived Fenwick-Clyde. Then he pushed the thought away. It was none of his concern.

'Yes, Sir Hugo. Tomorrow I shall start removing the top layers of dirt and debris in the area I was exploring today. I believe there is a nearly intact mosaic.'

'Really,' he drawled, more interested in her than her words.

The play of enthusiasm and interest across her delicate face caught him, made him wonder how she would look beneath him, with him buried inside her. An interesting possibility.

'What do you intend to do with your find? It is, lest you forget, on my property.'

She blinked and bit her bottom lip. The actions made her eyes sparkle and her mouth blossom a deep, rosy hue that beckoned to him. He doubted she realised how enticing she was. But she would know if he stood up. His reaction to her was strong and intense, unlike anything he had experienced in these last ten to twenty years.

'Well, I had thought you would preserve it. It is a fine example of Roman life here. A wonderful bit of history. Otherwise, why would you have commissioned the dig?'

He wondered what she would do if he continued to bait her. The urge to find out was irresistible. He had always been curious, even as a child. The trait had often ended with him covered in mud or dirt, or finding himself in a situation that was potentially dangerous. Like the time he had found a colony of bees and decided to get a piece of their honeycomb on his own. At ten, he had considered himself nearly a man. Instead, he had got badly stung, but he had also got the honeycomb. He always got what he wanted.

'Curiosity. I go to great lengths to satisfy it.'

She looked stunned, her scholar's heart shocked at such an answer. 'Curiosity? Is that all this is to you?'

He shrugged, enjoying her reaction. 'I am not sure that preserving an archaeological site of Roman occupation is the best use of my land, Lady Fenwick-Clyde. The area you are exploring is excellent farming land. I believe it is also in the middle of one of my orchards.' He turned to Tatterly, who was looking at his plate, his tongue tied by the proximity of his goddess. 'Is that not so, Tatterly?'

Tatterly started. 'What? Pardon me, Sir Hugo, I was not attending.'

Hugo swallowed his laugh. There was no sense in making his steward feel even more awkward than he already did. And Hugo did not enjoy making other people uncomfortable. Teasing and provoking, yes, but Tatterly was on the thin line between heaven and hell.

'I was telling Lady Fenwick-Clyde that her Roman dig is in the middle of one of my best orchards. Is that not so?'

'Yes. Yes, it is.' Tatterly's pleasant tenor was slow and solid no matter how uncomfortable he might be.

Hugo shook his head. The poor man was besotted. 'So you see, Lady Fenwick-Clyde, I must weigh economics against the preservation of history.'

He waved his hand to one of the footmen for more wine to be served. 'Thank you, John.'

The young man smiled with pleasure, ignoring the butler's frown. Footmen were to be seen, but were to keep a bland countenance. It was hard to do so when Sir Hugo was always friendly and always remembered names.

Annabell watched the byplay with interest but said nothing. Hugo decided to gratify her obvious curiosity. And a part of him wanted to see how she would react. He wanted to see if she was the woman he was beginning to think she might be.

'Once I would have been lucky to grow up to be a footman. I never forget that. So I always remember they are human beings the same as I am, only not so lucky in their birth.'

Her attention snapped back to him but she said nothing, even though her face held an arrested look. He had truly piqued her interest. Satisfaction was a sensation he hoped to experience with her in other ways as well as this.

'Surely you jest, Sir Hugo,' Miss Pennyworth said, waving away the young man with the wine. 'A man of your position and lineage would never have been at risk of being a servant. I mean, after all...' she waved her thin, white hand to encompass the elegantly appointed room '...you have all of this and more. Why would you want to spend even a short amount of time as a footman—or worse? I mean, it is inconceivable.'

Hugo considered the woman and her words while John poured him more wine. He thought he heard Lady Fenwick-Clyde groan but she said nothing. Wise. Miss Pennyworth was not only silly and a woman who rattled on, but was insensitive to the feelings of the people who worked around her. The truth would be a rude awakening for her to the realities of life and possibly make her more considerate of others' feelings. He could hope it would curtail her nattering, but he doubted that.

He took a long drink, set the glass down and relaxed back into his chair even more than he had been. 'No, ma'am, I don't jest. Not about that. I am surprised you have not heard my story. At one time it was on the tongue of every wag in London.'

Miss Pennyworth's pale blue eyes widened like saucers, seeming to take up her entire face.

'My companion and I do not frequent London salons,' Annabell said coolly. 'We also do not follow gossip.'

Hugo slanted her a look that spoke volumes about his doubt on the last. 'You are to be commended, Lady Fenwick-Clyde. Very few people have your discretion.'

'Indeed,' she said, her tone nearly a huff.

'Back to my story.' He turned his consideration back to Miss Pennyworth. 'My father, the late Sir Rafael Fitzsimmon, was not married to my mother.' The companion's mouth dropped open before she managed to snap it shut. 'Yes, it is true. A scandal had my mother been of good birth, but she was the housekeeper. A liaison like that is not all that unheard of. Particularly when the servant is comely, as everyone assures me my mother was.'

He heard Annabell Fenwick-Clyde's sharp intake of breath. For some reason, which he did not intend to explore, her reaction disappointed him. He had hoped that with her pointed disregard for polite society she would be more accepting of his past. An emotion he could not name made him curt.

'To make a long story short, I was given a baronetcy after Waterloo. My father had already willed me the part of his fortune not entailed. My half-brother will inherit my father's title and all that goes with it when he comes of age. Until that time, his mother and I are his joint guardians and trustees.'

Miss Pennyworth's complexion went from the red of embarrassment over his origins to white with discomfort. Hugo wondered if it would modify her attitude towards servants. Possibly, but probably not. He forced away the irritation that made him want to add something more shocking to the story.

'What happened to your mother?' Annabell asked so softly he barely heard her.

He shifted to look at her. Her eyes were soft with compassion, their deep blue nearly as black as a starless night. Perhaps he had been too quick to judge her. She seemed more concerned than repelled.

His gaze dropped to her lips. He had kissed them briefly, too briefly. He regretted that lapse. She had tasted of fresh air and sweet enticement. He wanted to touch her. Hell, he wanted to do a whole lot more than just touch her.

'She died giving birth to me.'

'Oh, I am so sorry.'

He waved off her concern. 'Don't be. I never knew her to mourn her and my father adored me. I never really missed having a mother. Unlike most men of his generation, my father spent a great deal of time with me.'

'But still,' she murmured.

He watched her, amazed to see her eyes fill with unshed tears. How had she managed to survive Fenwick-Clyde when his own far-from-sad story made her melancholy? It was a miracle.

'But enough of my tale.' Hugo stood. 'Can I interest the three of you in a game of whist?'

Annabell looked at her companion.

Miss Pennyworth smiled in delight. 'I so enjoy whist, or any card game. Many's the night Annabell and I have entertained ourselves with a deck of cards while she was on one of her travels. Isn't that so? Why, I remember the time we were caught in—'

'Susan,' Lady Fenwick-Clyde interrupted firmly. 'I am sure no one is interested in our boring lives. Shall we go?' To emphasise her words and determination, she rose and started toward the door.

Hugo smiled to himself. She obviously did not like her life discussed, or perhaps just that particular incident. He would have to pursue that story. Another challenge. They kept life interesting.

Tatterly stood as well. 'I…'

'Come along, Tatterly, you used to play cards with the best of them. Why, I remember one night in London—'

'Yes, Sir Hugo,' Tatterly interrupted. 'I would like to play whist.'

Hugo laughed. 'Good.'

He moved to follow Lady Fenwick-Clyde and touched her lightly on her gloved elbow. She jerked as though he had touched her with a hot coal. He smiled.

'And how about you, Lady Fenwick-Clyde?' he said, his voice intentionally pitched seductively low. 'You have not agreed or disagreed.'

She stayed far enough away that he could not casually touch her again, but he could see the pulse beating rapidly at the base of her throat. The light scent of honeysuckle wafted from her.

'I am outvoted. So, for the time being, I would be delighted to play whist.' She did not smile and her eyes held the sardonic acceptance that some things must be done for politeness.

'Gracious of you,' Hugo murmured. He made her a short bow. 'To the—'

'Library,' she said.

He smiled. 'But of course.' He turned to Butterworth. 'Please bring tea and more brandy. I fear I drank the last of the brandy earlier today.'

'Immediately, Sir Hugo,' the old retainer said.

'After you, dear ladies,' Hugo said.

Miss Pennyworth smiled broadly and Tatterly followed her from the room. Lady Fenwick-Clyde was slower, casting him a questioning look.

'Yes?'

'You don't have to entertain us, Sir Hugo. I am sure we are not the company you are used to keeping.'

'How do you know the company I keep?'

'Rumour.'

He smiled, but it did not reach his eyes. 'Rumour is a two-headed beast. It speaks with one mouth and turns around with the other and contradicts itself.'

She took a deep breath, making her full bosom rise and fall seductively, although he doubted she was aware of that. 'I insisted on staying to be near my site, not to spend the evenings with you.'

'Blunt. How delightful.'

Sarcasm edged his last words, but he could not help it. She irritated him at the same time as she intrigued him. Pursuing her would be interesting. Bedding her would be worth every minute of time and every ounce of energy it took to accomplish.

'But I am outvoted, as I said before. So, cards it will be.'

She turned and swept from the room. Hugo watched her with pleasure. She was a tall woman and well-endowed, with hips that swayed enticingly and made him long to feel them moving beneath his.

It would be some small satisfaction to beat her at cards. A start.

The library fire roared, sending golden and orange light to the game table set in front of it. A face screen was nearby for the person next to the fire to situate to protect his or her face. Several small braziers held lit coals that added to the warmth. Expensive wax candles surrounded their playing area. A serving table held tea, brandy and an assortment of sweetmeats.

Sir Hugo enjoyed his comforts, Annabell thought.

She sat farthest from the fire and was still comfortable. Her shawl was just enough. She watched Susan sit across from Mr Tatterly, her thin frame angling unconsciously toward the fire's heat. It was a good thing her companion would not be Sir Hugo's partner. Susan enjoyed cards, but she was not a good player. She tended to talk rather than pay attention to her hand. To finish settling in, Susan adjusted the fire-screen to shield her face from the direct heat.

Mr Tatterly gave Susan a hesitant, yet warm smile. Annabell barely kept from shaking her head. The two were such opposites, yet they seemed drawn to one another. Strange.

Sir Hugo sat with his back to the fire and picked up the cards. He fanned them on the table for every one to draw to see who was high card and dealer. His fingers, long, white and impeccably groomed, drew Annabell's attention. He might be the son of a housekeeper, but every part of him was elegant and refined. His nails were short and clean, his hands smoothly muscled. In a previous age, a fine fall of lace would have covered his supple wrists.

She shivered. What was she doing, admiring his hands?

But they moved with such grace. He flipped over a card. The ace of spades.

She shook her head slightly to clear it of unwelcome thoughts about her host and picked a card. The two of hearts. Sir Hugo won the draw and picked up the cards. With a manual dexterity that, for some reason she could not fathom, was mesmerising to her, he shuffled the cards and dealt them. The game began.

Annabell considered herself a competent player. Sir Hugo was better. They won the first rubber in spite of not always having the best cards.

'Tea?' he asked, watching her with an intensity that made her uncomfortable.

'Please.'

'Miss Pennyworth?'

'Please, Sir Hugo.' She laughed, her pale blue eyes sparkling. 'I cannot remember when I have enjoyed playing whist this much.'

'Really?' Sir Hugo's voice held a hint of sardonic amusement.

Annabell gave him a sharp glance, but he met her look without expression. Even so, she sensed he was not impressed with her companion, not that it was any of his concern.

He poured the tea for both of them, adding sugar and cream without asking. 'Brandy?' he asked Tatterly. 'Since we did not stay behind the ladies and drink ourselves under the table with port, we might as well drink ourselves under the card table with brandy.'

Mr Tatterly gave his employer a censorious look, but nodded.

They changed partners. This time Annabell played with Mr Tatterly. It was a débâcle. Miss Pennyworth, more interested in conversation, bid wrong then played wrong. Mr Tatterly had not cared. Annabell noticed Sir Hugo was not made from the same cut of cloth. Sir Hugo was competitive, nor was he enamoured of the lady. Annabell and Mr Tatterly won easily, but not soon enough for her comfort.

She rose immediately. 'I believe it is time for me to leave. I hope to be at the dig very early tomorrow.'

Sir Hugo stood more slowly. 'Of course. I will walk you to your room.'

'There is no need. I am a grown woman and can find my own way.'

'You are most decidedly a woman, Lady Fenwick-Clyde.' His gaze held hers with a hint of something warmer than appropriate, which was typical for him she knew. 'And a very independent one as you have gone to great lengths to prove, but I am going that way and wish company. And…' he gave her a mocking smile '…it will save on my candle bill. We will be able to share one instead of each of us carrying our own.'

'Hah! As though you care about such small economies.' She waved a hand in a semi-circle to take in the three small braziers burning brightly and warmly nearby. Not to mention the multitude of candles lighting their play area.

'Annabell,' Susan said, her voice holding mild reproof.

Annabell sighed. Obviously Susan had not sensed Sir Hugo's growing irritation, but then Susan was always happily ensconced in her own world.

Still, the last thing Annabell wanted was his company. After the fiasco at cards, she was not sure if she was afraid of his sensuality or angry at him for his barely concealed disgust with Susan. Either way, she did not want him escorting her anywhere. But it seemed she did not have a choice.

Her acceptance was grudging. 'If you insist, Sir Hugo.'

His smile mocked her. 'Oh, I do, Lady Fenwick-Clyde.'

Rather than stay and continue to play this game of words, she pivoted on her heel and moved into the foyer and from there to the stairs. Footmen, dressed in crimson and gold, stood their ground near the banister. She nodded at them and heard Sir Hugo address each by name and wish them a good night. He was a contradiction. He baited her and barely concealed his contempt for Susan, yet treated his servants as people in their own right. Of course, as he had told them at dinner, he had nearly been one.

They climbed. She could hear his shoes on the glossy waxed steps and sense his closeness. Then he was beside her, offering her his arm.

'No, thank you,' she said, hoping her voice was reasonably polite.

'As you wish,' he murmured.

The last thing she needed was to feel that sharp, disturbing jolt his touch created in her. It was bad enough that her entire being seemed on alert. Besides, she was still upset with him over the card game.

They left the stairs and walked down the carpeted hall. Now he was closer to her, if that were possible. The hall, while wide, was not nearly as wide as the stairs had been. Annabell felt as though his hips brushed hers, although she knew that was not so. There was at least a foot between them. Cinnamon and cloves filled her senses, a very unusual combination for a man to wear. But she found she liked it.

'You are an intelligent woman.' He spoke to her for the first time since leaving the library.

'I have always thought so.' She made no attempt to modify her haughty tone.

'And not overly modest.'

She glanced sharply at him, wondering where he was headed. 'I believe in knowing one's abilities. If that is being unmodest, then so be it.'

'Very practical.'

'I think so.'

'Then why do you saddle yourself with a companion who is so obviously inferior to you?'

She bristled. 'Susan is compassionate and kind. I could not hope for a better companion and friend.'

'Possibly,' he drawled. 'But she has not a thought in her brain. Let alone interesting conversation.'

She stopped dead in her tracks. 'How dare you speak of her like that? Just because you don't seem to appreciate her finer points doesn't make her worthless.'

'True,' he murmured.

She stared at him. 'Why did you bring this up?'

'To learn more about you?'

He watched her the way a wolf very likely watched the lamb it had decided to devour. She edged closer to the wall.

'And why would you do that?'

'Because you are my uninvited guest and because you intrigue me. I have never met a woman like you.'

She edged away. His attention made her feel decidedly uncomfortable. 'Well, you must have led a more sheltered life than I had thought.'

He laughed. *'Touché.'*

She moved forward, eager to be away from this disturbing situation he had created. Even so, she felt his gaze on her back like a flame. She shivered in spite of the warmth provided by her practical dress and shawl.

He chuckled low in his throat so that the sound came out like a growl. 'I promise not to attack you out here where anyone going about their business can see.'

She glanced over her shoulder. The glitter in his eyes was unnerving.

'Just promise not to attack me at all,' she muttered, forgetting he was close enough to hear anything she said.

He laughed. 'I can't promise that. Nor would I even if I thought I could control myself.'

She paused, taken aback by his response, before forcing herself to keep walking. She picked up her pace.

'You are a self-indulgent man.'

She kept herself from looking at him to see his reaction to her censorious words. Very likely he did not like her blunt speaking—most men did not—or she had provoked him into doing or saying something outrageous. She seemed to have that effect on him.

'I am a hedonist.' He kept pace with her. 'I take my pleasures where I find them. Life is too short to deny oneself.'

She snorted. 'I believe I heard that explanation earlier.'

'Because it is true.'

Something in his voice caught her. She stopped and looked at him. He met her scrutiny without reaction.

'You truly do mean that, self-centred as the philosophy is.'

He nodded. 'If I did not, I would not have said so this afternoon, let alone just repeated it. Remember that.'

He lifted a hand to her face. She stepped back, but the wall kept her from going far enough. One long, elegantly strong finger touched the bow in her upper lip. Her reaction to him was swift and intense. Her legs weakened, and she was thankful the wall supported her back and kept her from slipping to the floor.

He closed the already too-small distance between them. 'Why should I deny myself life's physical pleasures? Particularly when they don't harm anyone else.' He paused and his eyes met hers with a hunger that made her senses whirl. 'And even give another person equal or greater pleasure?'

She swallowed hard and wondered fleetingly how she had got into this situation. Then his finger fell away from her. The hunger that had sharpened his face seconds before fell away also and was replaced by another emotion she couldn't read.

'You are leaning on my bedchamber door.'

She jumped, her eyes wide. 'Your door?'

He nodded. 'Very close to yours.'

She stood mute, chills chasing flames down her spine.

'No comment?' His voice was low and provocative, with a hint of barely concealed sardonic amusement.

She made herself shrug. 'What is there to say, Sir Hugo?

You are on the same floor as I am. That is not unusual.'
She wished her voice sounded as blasé as her words.

'True.'

He stepped back enough for her to slide away from his
door. She took a deep breath of relief, ignoring the sudden
urge to turn the handle to his room and look inside. As
decadent as he was, his rooms were likely opulent and seductive. A silly thought that had no relevance to her. Silly
it might be, but her stomach did somersaults at the thought.

She forced herself to continue down the hall to her chamber. She sensed him behind her and could swear he laughed
at her, but she could hear nothing.

She reached her door and kept herself from dashing inside to safety by squaring her shoulders and reminding herself she was a woman who met life's challenges head on.
To do otherwise was to be weak and usually at the mercy
of someone who was physically or emotionally stronger.
She had been in that position. She would never be there
again.

She turned and faced Sir Hugo. 'Thank you for walking
me here.'

He stopped, one brow lifted. 'Polite now that you are
about to get rid of me?'

She refused to let him embarrass her. 'Rudeness has not
deterred you.'

'Nothing keeps me from a goal, Lady Fenwick-Clyde.'
He studied her, his gaze travelling from her eyes to her lips
and lowered. 'Nothing.'

'Nothing?' She met the challenge of his study.

He watched her with an intensity in his green eyes that
made her jumpy. She felt breathless and hot and excited
and nervous and all manner of things that were not comfortable and yet were not uncomfortable either. He aroused
emotions in her she had never experienced. It took every
ounce of determination not to turn the handle and bolt into
her room.

He continued to watch her, his gaze lingering on her lips.
'I didn't kiss you for long enough.'

'What?' What was he talking about? What was he doing?

'I didn't kiss you for long enough earlier today.'

She felt the heat rise up her neck and stain her cheeks.
'You shouldn't have kissed me at all.'

'That's a matter of opinion. Mine happens to differ from
yours.' His voice lowered to a husky rasp. 'I should not
have stopped kissing you.'

She shook her head. 'I can't believe you are saying these
things, Sir Hugo. You are much too forward.'

He smiled, slowly and seductively. 'Then go into your
room, Lady Fenwick-Clyde. I won't follow unless you invite me.'

She gasped. But she didn't turn the handle. She wasn't
sure why not. He fascinated her, even in his aggressive
pursuit of her. She belonged in Bedlam, surely, or worse,
Bedlam in a straitjacket.

'Be assured, Sir Hugo, I won't invite you.'

His smile turned predatory. 'Not tonight.'

'Not ever.'

He reached out and she flinched, afraid of what he intended to do, but more afraid of what she would do. When
he laid a single finger on her jaw and nothing more, she
remembered to breathe.

'We shall see about that.'

It was a challenge and she rose to meet it. 'Yes, we will.'

He chuckled low in his throat. 'Spitfire. Lady Spitfire.'

He continued to look at her, his gaze going back to her
mouth. Was he going to kiss her? Here in the hall where
anyone could see? Was she going to be able to resist him?
Did she want to? This was crazy.

His finger traced up her jaw before falling away. She took
a deep breath. He chuckled again. Without another word,
he left.

Annabell stood rooted to the spot and watched him saunter down the hall and enter his room without looking back at her. She wasn't sure whether to be hurt that he'd put her from his mind so easily or glad that he'd done so. If he wasn't thinking about her then she was likely to be safe from his dangerous advances. Even if he was dangerous only because she was susceptible, it was the same danger.

She sighed and slipped into her room, no longer sure of anything. She needed a good night's sleep—with no dreams of her disturbing host.

Hugo resisted the temptation to look back. She had already tempted him too much this night.

He entered his room and went to a large, comfortable leather chair pulled in front of a roaring fire. He sank into it.

'M'lord, do you wish to prepare for bed?'

He had not seen Jamison. The valet had a knack for being unobtrusive. 'Very proper tonight, aren't we?'

He smiled as he said the words. The two of them had been through a great deal and forged a bond that went beyond employer and employee.

The valet came to stand near the fire. Jamison was a short, bandy-legged man with a bald pate and a twinkling eye. He didn't carry an ounce of extra weight and, Hugo knew very well, could handle himself in any fight.

'I'll put myself to bed, Jamison.'

'That's a shame, sir. But, for meself, there's a new barmaid at the Horse and Donkey. If you don't need me, I'll make my way there.'

Hugo laughed. 'You old reprobate.'

His valet, who had been his batman during the wars and before that had been a sergeant in Wellington's Indian army, grinned. Jamison was a farmer's son and believed in ploughing any field he encountered.

'Like I always said, sir, it takes one to know one.'

Hugo shook his head. 'It's a good thing for you I appreciate frankness.'

'That it is, sir.' For a moment only he sobered, then the look was gone as though it had never existed. 'Well, I'll be on me way then.'

'But,' Hugo said to his valet's disappearing back, 'I will be needing hot water tomorrow morning to shave. It was a little lacking this morning.'

Jamison almost looked sheepish. 'Didn't feel up to snuff after courting the lady last night. I'll be sure to do better tomorrow, sir.'

Hugo shook his head. If the water wasn't here, he'd ring and have some brought up. That's what he paid good wages for to the house servants. Jamison, he owed more than money could buy. Jamison had saved his life at Waterloo.

'Enjoy yourself, old man.'

'I'll try, sir.'

Hugo laughed. Nothing like a bout with Jamison to put everything into perspective. Miss Pennyworth might drive him to the consideration of murder, and Lady Fenwick-Clyde—Lady Spitfire—Annabell—might drive him to the point of physical pain, but both were something he could deal with. He could hand Miss Pennyworth over to Tatterly, and he could join Jamison at the pub and find a willing wench to ease the ache caused by Lady Fenwick-Clyde.

He rose and shook his head as he made his way to the bed. No, he couldn't ease this particular ache with anyone but the woman who created it. He was experienced enough to realise that about himself.

With nimble fingers, he undid his clothing and stepped out of them. From force of habit, he laid them neatly across a nearby chair. He added the nightshirt to the pile. He enjoyed his luxuries, but required that they be neatly compartmentalised. Clutter was as uncomfortable as being cold.

He snuffed the bedside candle and climbed between the satin sheets with nothing between him and them to diminish the pleasure. The smooth silky material slid along his skin. They were cool, but the warming pan had made them tolerable. Soon the hot water bottles and heated bricks would make them nearly toasty. Jamison might be rackety in some areas, but he knew to warm the bed.

Hugo rolled on to his back and stared at the ceiling of his canopied bed. Lascivious cherubs frolicked with sylphs, doing things no innocent could imagine. He imaged himself doing those things to and with Annabell Fenwick-Clyde. He was instantly, painfully aware of how much he wanted that.

Soon.

Chapter Four

Annabell woke the next day with an aching head and shoulders that felt as though she'd been carrying the weight of the world on them. She closed her eyes and wished she could go back to sleep, but that would solve nothing. Sir Hugo Fitzsimmon had figured prominently in the dreams she hadn't wanted to have.

He had done things with her and to her that made her blush to remember. Things her husband had forced her to do with him, which she had not enjoyed. With Sir Hugo— Hugo—she had revelled in the sensations. She scowled. Sir Hugo had not bound her.

To put paid to the unwelcomed thoughts, both memory and dream, she clambered out of bed. The sooner she moved about, the sooner she would be at the site and the sooner she would forget the disturbing dreams that were becoming nightly visitors.

She dropped her nightdress to the floor, planning to pick it up later. She dressed without help, a skill she had mastered in her travels. Then she went to the dresser and rummaged around the bottles and vials, looking for her brush. She knew she had left it here, but…

She found it on a table beside the chair where she normally read. A copy of Jane Austen's latest book lay beside it. She brushed her thick, silver-blonde hair quickly and secured it in a long braid, which she wrapped around the back of her head. Now it would stay out of the way while she dug.

She moved to the mirror to examine herself. She wasn't fashionable, but she was practical. That was more important.

The sound of wheels on gravel drew her to the window. She pulled back the heavy blue-velvet curtain and peered through the many-paned glass.

A post-chaise stopped in the circular carriage drive and two young children erupted from the vehicle. The boy's head glinted like a newly minted penny. The girl's shone like summer sunshine. They must be Sir Hugo's half-brother and half-sister. It had been some time since he had told her they were coming. Presumably, they had stopped someplace for the night on their way here.

Seconds later, a woman emerged, moving more sedately than her offspring, but still with a buoyancy that made Annabell think she must be a happy person. She wore a royal blue pelisse with epaulets in the military style that was all the rage since Waterloo. She was much shorter than the footman who helped her.

The woman entered the front door and passed out of Annabell's sight. She turned from the window. Likely, she would meet the three of them at dinner.

Things would be less strained with more people. Sir Hugo wouldn't watch her as carefully as he currently did. Somehow, that thought did not comfort her no matter how she told herself it should. She was not interested in him, or only a little. She couldn't help that her body desired his, she could only make sure she did not give into temptation.

Having his stepmother and two young children around them would help.

* * *

Hugo strode to greet his stepmother. 'Juliet. Welcome.'

Two whirling dervishes attacked him before Juliet could reply. He grabbed the smaller package and lifted her high.

'Hugo,' Rosalie Fitzsimmon squealed.

Hugo laughed. 'Rosalie!'

The larger of the two slowed down so he wouldn't get hit by his sister's feet as Hugo swung the girl around. 'Hugo,' Joseph said more sedately, but with the same thread of excitement his sister had exhibited. 'Put her down.'

Hugo smiled at his half-brother, catching the unspoken *and pay attention to me.* He set Rosalie down in spite of her pout.

'Joseph, I am glad to see you. It will be nice to have another man around here.' Hugo extended his hand.

Joseph took Hugo's hand and broke into a smile that nearly split his face. 'Hugo, can we go talk about Waterloo?'

Hugo glanced at Juliet, saw her frown and said, 'Perhaps later we can discuss some of it, but right now I wish to speak with your mother.'

'You *always* talk to her.'

Hugo ruffled the boy's fine hair. 'Not always. Sometimes I talk to Rosalie. You have to learn, Joseph, that women are worth talking to.' He grinned at the boy's unconcealed disbelief. 'I know it's hard to believe at your age, but trust me.'

Joseph scowled. 'I will accept what you say, but I do find it hard to believe.'

Hugo laughed at the look on Juliet's face, the mingled humour and resignation. 'You will.'

The young governess made her way through the entrance, saw them and realised it was time for the children to go to their rooms and the nursery. 'Come along,' she said, nodding her head shyly at Hugo's smile. 'We must get ready for our nap.'

'Oh…' Joseph complained.

'Don't want to,' Rosalie protested.

She herded them anyway.

'Would you like refreshments?' Hugo took Juliet's cape before the footman could reach them. He handed it to the strapping young man.

'I would die for a hot cup of tea.' Juliet undid the bow of her chip bonnet. 'In the library?'

'Where else?' Hugo smiled and waved his stepmother ahead.

She smiled back and made her way to the familiar room. She settled into her favourite chair, the one Lady Fenwick-Clyde always sat in. Hugo wondered what it was about overstuffed chintz.

He sat beside her. 'Why did you pick that chair?'

Juliet gave him a quizzical look. 'What brought that up?'

He smiled and shook his head. 'I am curious. It seems to be a favourite with the ladies.'

She took off her bonnet and set it on the table beside her seat. 'What a queer observation, Hugo. Are you sure you aren't ailing?'

He laughed. 'Not in the way you suggest.'

She sobered. 'Really?'

Tea arrived and they spent several quiet moments while Juliet prepared herself a cup. He declined any.

'I have two women here, Juliet.'

She choked, nearly spilling her tea. 'Hugo! How could you dare?'

He frowned. Even Juliet thought him an unprincipled rakehell. 'They are not my mistresses.' Honesty made him add, 'At least, not yet.'

Her expression went from relief to alarm. 'Yet?'

'That is why I am especially grateful to have you here.'

'You are?' She took a hasty sip, as though she needed it to fortify herself.

This time his smile was that of a wolf, anticipating a very good meal. 'That is what I tell myself.'

She shook her head. 'You are talking in riddles.'

'Miss Pennyworth must be rubbing off on me.'

'Hugo?'

'Lady Fenwick-Clyde and her companion, Miss Penny-worth, are staying here while Lady Fenwick-Clyde excavates a Roman ruin.'

Juliet paled, then flushed, her fair complexion coming as close to mottled as it was capable. 'Lady Fenwick-Clyde?'

Hugo watched the emotions flit across her face and wondered how she even knew Annabell Fenwick-Clyde. He had moved in the *ton*'s rarified stratosphere as a crony of Prinney's, and he had not met Lady Fenwick-Clyde until he kissed her on his property just days ago.

And what a kiss. Her lips had been soft and yielding, drawing him into an inferno he had not known existed. Now it was hell every time he saw her and couldn't kiss her. Even now, sitting in front of the roaring fire in his favourite room with his stepmother, just the thought of that kiss aroused him to the point that he was grateful to be sitting down and not standing in front of Juliet. He was many things, but he had never flouted his interests before anyone but the women who created them. Until now.

He snorted. 'Yes, Lady Fenwick-Clyde. It seems she is something of an amateur antiquarian.'

'Does she have a stepson?' Juliet's tone was innocent, but there was an intensity in her gaze that told Hugo the question meant more to her than she wanted to divulge.

'I believe so. At least I know the late Fenwick-Clyde had a son by his first wife. Don't remember the boy's name.'

Juliet's blush deepened. 'Timothy. His name is Timothy.' Her fingers twisted in her lap. 'And he isn't a boy. He is a widower. His wife and babe died in childbirth over a year ago.'

'My mistake.' Hugo watched his stepmother with great interest. 'Do you know him well?'

'No. That is, some. We met during the Season. The children like him.'

Hugo caught himself before he frowned. He did not like the sound of this. Fenwick-Clyde's son was not someone he wished his sweet stepmother to associate with. In his experience, the apple never fell far from the tree.

'Are you seeing him?'

Juliet's fair skin got fairer. Her hand stilled. 'Not exactly.'

'Do you wish to tell me what that means?'

'No, Hugo. I don't. At least, not yet.' She took a deep breath. 'But that is not why we are in here. You were going to tell me about your guests.'

'Bravo, Juliet. You have put me in my place, which is not to question you about the men you see. But I do worry.'

She smiled gently at him. 'I know you do, Hugo. But things are not that way.'

He would have believed her if she had not blushed again. But he chose not to comment.

'Back to my problem. As a bachelor, and one with a reputation to maintain,' he said, tongue-in-cheek, 'it did not seem like the best thing for everyone involved to have Lady Fenwick-Clyde staying here. Although she is a widow and has a companion, I didn't feel her good name could withstand the consequences of being here alone with me.'

Juliet's violet eyes widened. 'Since when have you cared a tuppence for that?'

This time Hugo reddened, a fact that irritated him. 'Since I am not in the habit of ruining respectable women.'

'You are in the habit of forming liaisons with widows.' Her point was pertinent and the look of disbelief she wore told him she was not sure she believed his concern.

He shrugged. 'Widows of a certain ilk. Lady Fenwick-Clyde is not in that category.'

'Really? I look forward to meeting her, for I vow, Hugo, I have yet to meet the woman who can resist you or even wants to. Most fall willy-nilly into your arms and are glad of it.' She cocked her delicate head to one side. 'There is something about you. Your father had it.'

His eyes narrowed. 'Then why didn't you succumb?'

She dropped her gaze for a long moment before looking back at him. 'Because Rafael married me for convenience. He had decided you needed a woman's hand. What he failed to realise was that you needed the hand of an older woman who could be a mother to you.' She took a deep breath. 'Still, I was wise enough to know better than to lose my heart to him. He did not want it.'

Hugo was taken aback, but hid it. She had never told him this. He had known the marriage was one of convenience, but he had not realised she had cared for his father beyond that of a dutiful wife.

He did let his sympathy show. 'I am so sorry, Juliet.' He reached across the small table separating them and took one of her hands. 'I did not realise or I would not have pried.'

She smiled. 'It is in the past, my dear. I don't dwell on it. And I have Joseph and Rosalie. I could not wish for more, yet I have it. I have your love and concern and a very generous widow's portion.' Her eyes turned mischievous. 'What more could I want?'

Hugo did not say the word that came instantly to mind. He was not even comfortable thinking it. Yet, it had sprung forward without his conscious thought. *Love.* Damn, he was getting maudlin and for no good reason.

'Well,' she said briskly, looking away from the concern in his eyes, 'I must go freshen up. I want to look my best when I meet this paragon who can resist temptation.'

Hugo stood and drew her up with him. He closed the distance between them and kissed her lightly on the top of her head that barely reached his shoulder.

'You are an angel, Juliet. Thank you for coming.'

She grinned. 'From what I've just heard, I would not miss this for the world. A woman who can resist you. Will wonders never cease?'

He watched her glide from the room. Better she think Annabell Fenwick-Clyde could resist him than she know that both he and the lady shared an awareness of each other that was like dry wood ready to burst into an inferno. Even better that she not know he intended to seduce Annabell. Juliet being here provided respectability—it did not prevent anything from happening.

Annabell stood in the salon gazing up at Sir Rafael Fitzsimmon. Sir Hugo had a look of his father. Both were tall and well formed with rich chestnut-coloured hair that fell rakishly across their broad foreheads. But where Sir Hugo's eyes were a startling grass green, his father's had been deep brown. Both men shared Sir Hugo's erotic mouth.

'He was a handsome man, even in middle age,' a light, female voice said. 'As is his son.'

Annabell jumped and turned to face the speaker she had not heard enter the room. A petite woman with masses of waving Titian-coloured hair smiled at her. Sir Hugo's stepmother was dressed in the latest fashion of pale muslin with an embroidered ruched hem. Pearls circled her wrists and throat and dripped from her tiny, shell-pink ears. She was a Pocket Venus, unless Annabell missed her mark, which she doubted. Her brothers would describe Lady Fitzsimmon as a diamond of the first water.

'Pardon me,' the lady said. 'I did not mean to startle you. I am Juliet Fitzsimmon, Hugo's stepmother.'

Annabell smiled and introduced herself. 'It is not your fault. I was engrossed in studying your husband. As you said, he was very attractive. Even his picture radiates a sense of power and charisma. I can imagine that when he spoke to someone, he gave them his complete attention.'

Lady Fitzsimmon's violet eyes, heavily fringed with pale red lashes, watched Annabell. 'You have described him perfectly. One would almost think you knew him.' She cocked her head to one side and her little Cupid's bow mouth quirked into a smile. 'But you know Hugo. It is very nearly the same.'

'Not really,' Annabell said, hoping to avoid a discussion about her host. 'That is, I don't know Sir Hugo well at all.'

She had not realised, until Lady Fitzsimmon said it, that she had attributed Sir Hugo's traits to his father. It was disconcerting, to say the least, and had been totally unconscious.

'I see you two have met,' the object of their discussion drawled, entering the room.

While Annabell and Lady Fitzsimmon had dressed formally, Sir Hugo was his usual casual self. He wore a loose bottle-green coat and black pantaloons, a style only beginning to be popular but normally never worn in the evening. They were considered casual, daytime wear. His shirt points were moderate and he wore a loosely knotted cravat. He was dressed up for himself. Still, he radiated presence and…

Annabell took a deep breath. All he had to do was enter a room and her blood warmed. What was wrong with her? She did not love the man, yet she was intensely aware of him. She shivered.

'Are you cold?' Sir Hugo asked, his voice solicitous. 'We must move closer to the fire.'

'Thank you, no.' Annabell silently berated herself for the breathiness of her voice, especially when Lady Fitzsimmon gave her a quizzical look. 'I will go get a shawl.'

'No,' Sir Hugo said. He moved past Annabell and pulled the sash to summon a servant. 'By the time you returned it would be dinner, and I don't wish to push it back.' His eyes warmed with something Annabell didn't think was caused by the thought of food. 'And I am hungry.'

Annabell closed her mouth on a retort telling him she would do as she pleased. There was no reason to be rude even if his action struck her as high-handed, even if his gaze on her made her uncomfortably aware that he was a man and she was a woman. She would not give him the satisfaction of knowing he disturbed her. She could be stubborn to a fault, but sometimes it was to her advantage.

'Hugo tells me you study antiquities,' Lady Fitzsimmon said.

Annabell studied the other woman's face for a hint of what she felt. Most females were not the least bit interested in what Annabell did. To her surprise, Lady Fitzsimmon seemed to actually care or was a very good actress.

'I like to find and preserve pieces of the past. That is why I am here. There is what appears to be a Roman villa on Sir Hugo's land—in one of his very productive orchards.' She cast him a look, daring him to say something. He kept quiet. 'But I won't know for sure until I uncover more of it.'

'Hugo mentioned something about that. However did you hear about it?'

'I was visiting the Society of Antiquaries, or rather I was there listening to one of the members give a talk about his discoveries. It turned out to be this site.'

'That explains how you found out,' Sir Hugo interrupted, his voice dry, 'but not why you are the one here instead of a man.'

'Hugo.' Lady Fitzsimmon's voice was low.

He glanced at his stepmother before turning his attention back to Annabell. Annabell took a deep breath, telling herself not to explode. This was his house, his Roman villa and his money was funding the dig. He could tell her to leave, now, this instant, and very nearly had already.

She took a deep breath. 'I was the only one present who was not already committed elsewhere. Besides—' she met his gaze defiantly '—I am as well qualified as anyone else—male or female.'

As though realising Annabell was a power keg just waiting for the right spark, Lady Fitzsimmon intervened. 'How long do you expect your work to take?'

It took Annabell a second to appreciate that Lady Fitz-simmon was trying to direct their conversation away from a volatile area. Only the lady did not know that this was equally risky. Annabell wanted to say not long at all, but honesty forbade her. She knew Sir Hugo wanted her gone quickly and feared if he knew how long she really thought the excavation would take he would order her out of his house immediately. That would be very inconvenient for her. He had made it abundantly clear he did not want her under his roof for long, and her digging was going to be longer than he would like. When his stepmother left, which she anticipated would be before she was finished, she would have to relocate. And that would be the least evil.

'Many months.' She sighed. 'Or possibly even years. It is very hard to gauge.'

'That is a long time. You did not tell me that.'

Sir Hugo's deep voice startled her. She had been thinking so hard about her dilemma she had not realised Sir Hugo had come up beside her.

Annabell shrugged, trying doggedly to ignore the jump in her pulse. Cinnamon and cloves engulfed her. He smelled good enough to eat. The image that provoked made her face flame.

When she spoke her voice was rough. 'I...I didn't think it mattered. And, as I said, I could not give you a definite time. It just depends on what we find. And how thoroughly we excavate, and a host of other things I can't begin to see at this stage.'

'Mama!' a light-pitched voice yelled.

'Hugo!'

All three adults turned simultaneously. Relief flooded Annabell. For the moment she would be off the hot seat.

She watched with pleasure as two whirlwinds swept into the room and launched themselves at Lady Fitzsimmon and Sir Hugo. Naturally, the girl went for Sir Hugo. Annabell could understand perfectly.

'Easy, or you will knock me down.' He caught the bundle of white muslin skirts and guinea-gold hair and swung the girl into the air. 'You just saw me this afternoon, Rosalie. Why all this excitement?'

The girl giggled. 'Because I missed you. You were gone to the Continent for ever so long.'

Sir Hugo set her gently on her feet. 'Yes, I was. Too long. I missed you and Joseph, but the Duke of Wellington needed my help.'

He said it so solemnly that it took Annabell a minute to realise he was teasing about his importance to Wellington. Although from the way he continued to hold the child's hand, she knew he meant what he said about missing her.

The boy's eyes turned wide as saucers, and he wiggled out of his mother's hug and rushed to Sir Hugo. 'Jolly well done, Hugo. To be important to Wellington.'

Sir Hugo smiled and put his arm around the boy's shoulders. 'Actually he had plenty of help. I left early. Many are still with him.'

'Ah, you were teasing us,' the girl said.

The boy frowned. 'I thought you were serious, Hugo. I am quite old enough that you should not tease me about important things like Wellington and Waterloo. I know we defeated Napoleon and kept him from conquering the world.'

Sir Hugo's face turned solemn, even the gleam disappeared from his eyes. 'You are right, Joseph. I should not talk down to you. I won't in the future.'

'Thank you, Hugo.'

Joseph's smile lit his face and accentuated the trail of freckles that started at the outer corner of one cheek and marched across his snubbed nose to the corner of the other cheek. He had the former Baronet Fitzsimmon's dark brown eyes and enticing mouth. Otherwise, his colouring was his momma's.

The girl, on the other hand, had the deeper olive skin

tones of Sir Hugo and his father. Her eyes were the clear
violet of her mother's, and her mouth was a sweet Cupid's
bow. She would be arresting when she was older, her snub
nose and light dusting of freckles only adding to her appeal.

'Joseph, Rosalie, you need to meet Hugo's guest.' Both
children immediately quietened and turned to face Annabell. 'Rosalie, Joseph, this is Lady Fenwick-Clyde.'

The girl curtsied and the young man bowed. Both looked
serious and curious all at once.

'How do you do?' Joseph said, obviously hoping she
would treat him as the adult he considered himself to be.

Annabell smiled. 'I am pleased to meet both of you.'

She saw some of the tension leave the boy's shoulders
at her formal reply. The girl cocked her head to one side
and smiled widely.

'You are very tall,' Rosalie said.

'Rosalie!' Lady Fitzsimmon groaned in gentle exasperation. 'Children. No matter how you try to drum manners
into them, they will leave them behind.'

Annabell chuckled. 'No matter, Lady Fitzsimmon. I was
much worse at their ages.'

'Really?'

'Somehow I find that not surprising,' Sir Hugo drawled
in a dry tone.

She shot him a minatory look before focusing back on
the children. 'I was the despair of my poor mother. But I
believe all children are that way, usually through no fault
of their own.'

'How interesting,' Sir Hugo said, ruffling Rosalie's fine
hair so that wisps escaped out from its braid. 'I dare say
most parents are not so sanguine.'

Annabell laughed. 'Neither were mine. I spent plenty of
time in the nursery with no dinner. But then, so did my
brothers, so it was not at all bad.' She winked at the children. 'The nursery maid would sneak us up food.'

'Well, enough of this before they decide to emulate you,'

Lady Fitzsimmon said, a laugh in her voice. 'Miss Childs is come to take them up to supper and bed.'

The governess moved shyly into the room. She was of medium height with a pleasing figure and dressed demurely in grey wool. Her hair was light brown with gold highlights, and her nose was a trifle long. But her eyes were striking. They were grey with long straight lashes that made them appear to droop at the outer corners, giving her an exotic, sultry look. But she did not move like a siren, she moved like a young woman out of her depth.

Annabell smiled at the governess and noticed Sir Hugo did the same. Instantly, to her shame, jealousy tightened her stomach. This was awful, this envy of a woman she didn't even know simply because Sir Hugo Fitzsimmon smiled at her. This was not like her, nor did she like this reaction. She made her smile wider in an effort to compensate for her thoughts.

'You must come back and join us for dinner,' Sir Hugo said.

'Yes, Melissa,' Lady Fitzsimmon added. 'We would enjoy having you.' She smiled. 'And I am sure the sound of adult conversation would be welcomed.'

'Mama,' protested Joseph.

His mother smiled down at him. 'Joseph, I know you are maturing, but you are not a man yet. Just as Rosalie is still a young girl. Melissa should mingle with adults, if for no other reason than to have a reprieve from your demands.'

Before the children could protest again or Melissa accept the invitation, Miss Pennyworth arrived with Mr Tatterly in tow. Both smiled and were introduced to the governess and children.

'Remember,' Lady Fitzsimmon said to the governess, 'I expect you back shortly.'

Hugo smiled. 'We will hold dinner until you return.'

Miss Childs blushed, but looked pleased with the invitation and the attention. 'Yes, my lady,' she murmured before shooing the children from the room.

'What a delightful young woman,' Susan Pennyworth said. 'She must be wonderful with your children, Lady Fitzsimmon. Why, I remember when I was a governess in India. Hot, nasty climate, but I enjoyed the children.' She caught Annabell's raised brow. 'All but the last. She was the devil in child's form. Fortunately for me, Annabell rescued me and I have never looked back.'

Everyone politely listened, but Annabell noticed a sardonic curve to Sir Hugo's mouth. She frowned at him. Even when Susan made perfect sense, he chose to see her as frivolous.

Thankfully for her increasing temper, Miss Childs returned quickly and Lady Fitzsimmon led them into dinner. Now, if only they would eat as quickly and she could retire.

Chapter Five

Annabell watched Sir Hugo dance around the music-room floor with the governess, Miss Melissa Childs, and wondered why she was not enjoying herself. Probably because she had wished to escape to her room after dinner, but had been put to the blush when she had suggested it. Now she was here against her will, but a guest often did things she did not wish.

She knew for a surety that her discomfort was not caused by Sir Hugo smiling at something Miss Childs was saying. In order to reaffirm her conviction, she looked at the other people in the room.

Lady Fitzsimmon sat at the pianoforte, playing a lively country tune. Susan blushed and tittered as Mr Tatterly carefully swung her around, mindful not to step on her feet. The servants had rolled back the Aubusson rug so that the highly polished oak planks provided more than enough room.

There! She knew she did not have to watch Sir Hugo. She was perfectly happy watching everyone else.

The music came to a rousing finish and Annabell clapped, glad of another diversion. 'You play very well, Lady Fitzsimmon.'

Lady Fitzsimmon laughed. 'Please, call me Juliet. If we

are to spend the next couple of weeks—or more—together, let us not stand on formality.'

Annabell smiled and wondered why this quick affinity between them seemed so right. 'Only if you will call me Annabell.'

'Most certainly.' Juliet cast a conspiratorial glance at Annabell. 'Shall I play a waltz? It is all the craze.'

Annabell shrugged. 'If you wish. You are, after all, the musician. The rest of us are at your mercy.'

'Fie,' Susan said, coming to a breathless stop by the two women. 'Do not be so ungracious, Annabell.'

There were times when she wondered why she tolerated Susan. Immediately she regretted the spurt of irritation. She tolerated her companion because she loved her. They had been together a long time and had gone through a lot of things together. And she had been churlish. The thought of Sir Hugo waltzing with Miss Melissa Childs had not been a pleasant one, no matter how she had tried to mislead herself. Which only made her feelings that much more unacceptable.

'You are right, Susan.' She smiled down at Juliet. 'Please, give us the pleasure of a waltz.'

Juliet smiled back. 'Do you waltz?'

Before she could reply, Susan answered for her. 'She will not learn it. I have implored her to do so, for it is vastly entertaining. Like flying free. But she refuses.'

'Perhaps I can persuade her,' Sir Hugo's deep, honey-rich voice said from too close to Annabell's back.

She willed herself to calmness and pivoted to face him. 'Better men and...' she cast a glance at Susan '...women than you have tried, Sir Hugo.'

'A challenge?' He raised one mahogany brow.

'No, a refusal. Nothing more.' She forced herself to laugh lightly. 'But I am sure you can find a willing partner, even from so limited a supply.'

He made her a mocking bow. 'I would ask Juliet, but she must play the tune—unless you also play the pianoforte.'

'Unfortunately, Sir Hugo, that is not one of my accomplishments.'

Only after the words were out did she realise how defensive she had sounded. He seemed to bring out the worst in her.

He gave her a knowing look before turning to the governess. 'I fear you must do me the honour once more, Miss Childs.'

She smiled timidly at him before her gaze dropped. 'I should look in on the children, sir.'

'No, no, Melissa,' Juliet Fitzsimmon said. 'You deserve to have some fun. Dance with Hugo, for I swear he is very graceful.'

Miss Childs blushed to the roots of her ash-brown hair. 'I don't know how to waltz.'

'Is that all?' Sir Hugo held out his hand. 'I will teach you.'

'Oh, dear. I could not.'

He smiled. 'Yes, you can. You are light on your feet and have a good sense of rhythm. You will learn quickly. Juliet, if you will.'

Juliet turned back to the keyboard, flexed her fingers like a maestro and began with a flourish. Music filled the room.

Mr Tatterly bowed to Miss Pennyworth, who laughed delightedly as she moved into the stiff and very proper circle of his arms. They waltzed away.

Annabell watched from the side and told herself it did not matter if Sir Hugo's arm was around another woman's waist. It did not matter at all. Absolutely not.

But she knew better.

He moved with consummate skill, leading his faltering partner with grace. One would never know he had suffered a war injury in his left leg. He bent down to say something to Miss Childs, who smiled and blushed wildly. He was charming the girl.

Annabell gritted her teeth against the urge to offer herself for the next waltz, if there was one. Better judgement said the less she had to do with her host, the better off she would be. Still, she was sorely tempted.

To distract herself, she watched Susan and Mr Tatterly. They made a very disparate couple. She was tall and lean while he was just barely her height and solid, although not fat. Yet, each wore a look on their face that spoke of wonder, as though neither had thought they would ever find someone to care for and who would care for them in return.

Annabell smiled wistfully. Her oldest brother had found that happiness with Felicia. There were times she envied him, but, for the most part, she was content going on as she was.

The music stopped with a flourish, drawing her back to the picture of Miss Childs in Sir Hugo's arms. He escorted her back to the pianoforte, his attention on her heart-shaped, upturned face. The young woman was besotted. Annabell found herself feeling sorry for the governess. Sir Hugo would break the girl's heart and not even realise it.

'Perhaps,' Juliet said, a worried look on her face, 'you would do me a favour, Annabell, and dance with Hugo next. While I know he has no designs on my governess, I do not wish to see the chit hurt.'

'I agree, Juliet. That would not be fair to her.' Annabell sighed. 'Perhaps we should stop for the night?'

'Never say so,' Susan said, hurrying over and pulling Mr Tatterly with her. 'We are having so much fun, aren't we, Mr Tatterly?' She turned adoring eyes on her escort, who reddened with pleasure.

He returned her look. 'I do not generally enjoy dancing, Miss Pennyworth, but tonight is an exception.' He smiled, a tiny thing, but one that lit his brown eyes. 'I would be sorry to have it end so soon.'

Annabell shifted so she did not look at the couple. If she left, the gathering would likely break up. If she stayed, she had to save Miss Childs from Sir Hugo's unconscious charm, which would end with the chit sitting or standing by herself, and her in Sir Hugo's arms. Neither was ideal. Nor was the flush of heated anticipation that seared her senses from just the thought of having Sir Hugo holding her. She was behaving like a ninnyhammer, instead of the independent woman she had worked so hard to become.

Sir Hugo and his partner reached them. The warmth that had plagued Annabell just seconds before intensified. She scowled at her nemesis, wondering what it was about him that aroused her so. He flashed a rakish smile that showed strong white teeth and hinted of things done in the dark. Her pulse jumped, and she knew this was still another thing about him that appealed to her. He was a rebel who went his own way. His path was hedonistic pleasure. Hers was independence, but neither of them played by society's rules.

'Changed your mind?' His voice, so deep and enticing, made her decision easier than she would have liked.

'Yes, Sir Hugo, I have.' She looked at Miss Childs. 'If you don't mind, I would like to learn to waltz as you are doing. You seemed to enjoy doing it and to have learned rapidly. I find myself curious to experience it.'

The girl blushed so her face mottled. 'I am not very good.' She cast a surreptitious glance at her partner. 'And I stepped on Sir Hugo's feet more times than the floor, but I enjoyed it immensely. It is…' she paused, searching for the right word '…it is exhilarating.'

Sir Hugo made Miss Childs an elegant leg. 'For your first time, you did very well. It was my pleasure to teach you, and I will be delighted to do so again.'

Annabell watched with sardonic amusement as the young woman's blush deepened to a shade closely resembling the flames in the nearby fireplace. She was more susceptible to Sir Hugo's charms than a puppy to a kind word.

'Well, Juliet,' Annabell said firmly, 'I am ready when you are.' Juliet gave her a startled look, and Annabell realised she had sounded like a martyr going to the stake. 'I am truly not a good dancer,' she added in an effort to lighten her words.

Juliet gave her one last considering look before starting. Sir Hugo stepped toward her and smiled his predatory smile that did nothing to ease the butterflies beginning to flutter in Annabell's stomach. Dimly she was aware of Mr Tatterly asking Miss Childs to dance and Susan sitting in the chair beside the pianoforte. But only vaguely did she notice what the others were doing because Sir Hugo chose that moment to encircle her waist with his arm.

Her mouth was suddenly dry.

'It is customary for the woman to put her left hand on the man's shoulder,' he murmured with just a hint of amusement.

'Yes.'

She did as he instructed and nearly recoiled. Even through the fine kid of her gloves and the weave of his jacket she felt his muscles. There was a casual dissoluteness about him that had misled her into thinking he was soft. She had been vastly wrong.

He took her right hand in his left. 'By the time we are through positioning our hands and arms, the music will be over.'

He was needling her, but he was right. She was behaving strangely, even to herself. And why? He had already kissed her and invited her to his bedchamber. She should be immune to his nearness. But she was not. The waltz would be much longer than the kiss. They would be farther apart, but he would still be touching her.

She took a deep breath and he whirled her away.

She did her best to follow his lead, but she was so focused on his closeness that she found it hard to concentrate on her steps. He radiated heat and the scent of cinnamon and male muskiness. The muscles under her left hand flexed with a strength she found exciting.

'You must relax in order to waltz well.' His deep voice penetrated to her core.

Instead of answering, she concentrated on ignoring her reaction to him. *This is just a dance,* she told herself. *He is not going to kiss you. He is not going to seduce you. He is merely holding you at arm's length and twirling you around the floor. Nothing more. This means nothing.*

She swallowed a groan at her inability to discipline herself. She might as well be inebriated on the brandy he drank so liberally for all the good her will-power was doing.

He swung and dipped her in one smooth motion. Annabell gasped and would have stumbled if not for the iron band of his arm around her waist. He steadied her.

'You did that on purpose.'

His dangerous smile was firmly in place. 'If you would relax, you would enjoy it when I do that to you.'

She grimaced. 'I am sure I would enjoy any number of things better if I relaxed. Unfortunately, it is not in me.'

He moved back, drawing her with him. 'Take a deep breath and let it out slowly. If you concentrate on that, you won't be so aware of dancing.'

She laughed a short burst of sarcasm. 'I doubt that. It is very difficult to ignore your arm around my waist and your hand at the small of my back.'

He raised one brow. 'Really?'

She bit her lip. Why had she said that? It was true, for his hand felt like a hot brand that seared through clothing, skin and bone and into a part of her she had never known existed before now.

When he inched her slightly closer, she went. She told herself she did so because resisting him would make it even more difficult to learn the dance. In truth, she did it because his warmth, his masculinity, called to that part of her that was uniquely female.

He bent his head down to whisper in her ear, 'You smell of honeysuckle and mystery.'

Her short, abrupt laugh, meant to cover her embarrassment at his unexpected compliment, failed. She felt breathless and titillated, as though she balanced precariously on the edge of a precipice and to fall would be the end of everything she had worked so hard to achieve. Her susceptibility to the man was frightening.

He twirled her around, his face intense as though he put his entire being into this dance. Somehow she managed to follow him. He was very skilled at this, just as Juliet had said.

He pulled her still closer. She went.

Her breasts grazed his chest and lightning shot through her. She looked up to see if she was alone in this storm. She was not.

His eyes were like twin green flames. They caught her gaze and threatened to burn her to ashes in his passion. He no longer smiled. His beautiful mouth was the only soft thing in his face. His cheeks and jaw were razor slashes.

'I want you,' he said softly.

She stared, not sure she had heard correctly, or that he had even spoken, for she could not imagine him saying what she thought he had. Even for him the words were brazen. He had implied as much when he invited her to his room, but she had been able to tell herself the offer was something easily ignored. This blatant statement was so much more.

'I want to do things to you in the dark.'

She gulped hard. 'You should not be saying things like that to me.'

'I know, but if I don't, how will you know I desire you?'

She forced herself not to look away from his green eyes. They were filled with a hunger that quickened her pulse. But she would not succumb to temptation.

'If you don't stop talking such nonsense this instant, I

will be forced by your rudeness to stop right now, calling attention to us that neither of us wishes.'

If only she hadn't sounded so much like Susan, she would have been proud of her defiance. He did that to her intelligence. He banished it beneath a desire so hot and thick it threatened to smother her.

'For the moment, but only for the moment,' he murmured, a satisfied look on his face.

He swung her into a circle that took her breath away and she was glad for it. She closed her eyes to the invitation he made no effort to hide and focused on her steps. Only then was she able to ease some of the tension from her shoulders and—other areas. For the moment.

To her chagrin, Annabell did not hear the music end. She had been too caught up in the spell Sir Hugo had wrapped around them. When he stopped, she staggered.

His arm tightened until she rested against his chest, their mouths inches from each other. Her pulse beat painfully at the base of her throat. She fought to take in air.

He stared down at her. 'If I kiss you, will you slap me?'

Her eyes widened. 'I don't know.'

'Come to my room.' The words were low and spoken in a husky whisper no one else could hear.

Unable to answer for fear she would accept without realising it, Annabell shook her head.

He released her and stepped back.

She swayed, but managed not to wobble. Nothing like this had ever happened to her. She felt vulnerable and raw.

'Hugo,' Juliet Fitzsimmon's voice intruded. 'Stop flirting with poor Annabell and bring her over here. We are taking a vote to see if we continue or if we stop for the evening.'

Annabell flinched. She had completely forgotten there were other people in the room. Somehow she managed to walk to the pianoforte, although she didn't remember doing so. She was too conscious of Sir Hugo moving at her side.

'I say we stop,' she said, angry at herself because her

voice was breathy and weak. 'I need to get up early to finish uncovering a mosaic. The longer I dally, the longer I will be obliged to impose on Sir Hugo's hospitality.'

'Come, Annabell,' Susan said. 'Just one more.'

Annabell looked at her companion. Susan's cheeks glowed with happiness and her eyes sparkled. She had rarely seen her friend like this. But she had to leave. Another dance with Sir Hugo would put her very being in jeopardy. The man called to her like a siren called to unwary sailors. He was everything she did not need or want in her life.

'No, Susan, I am sorry, but I must get some sleep.' She pasted a smile on her face and looked around at everyone, skimming over Sir Hugo. 'Surely the rest of you can continue without me. After all, you will be two couples to dance and Juliet to play the music.'

There was grudging acceptance. Miss Childs had a wishful look on her face, and Annabell realised the young woman wanted very much to dance again with Sir Hugo. For a moment jealousy raised its ugly head once more, but she would not let that awful emotion keep her from escaping. She just hoped Sir Hugo didn't break the girl's heart.

Susan said, 'I will be up early to go with you. I imagine you will want the mosaic sketched as you uncover it.'

Annabell smiled. 'That would be perfect. I will see you then.' She looked at everyone else. 'And thank you, Juliet. I enjoyed myself very much.'

'I am glad to hear that, Annabell. For a moment, when you first stood up with Hugo, I thought you were going to change your mind.'

Annabell kept the smile on her face. 'I am made of stronger stuff than that, Juliet.'

Juliet laughed. 'Go to bed.'

Annabell did not wait any longer. The way her goodnights were going, she would be here for ever if she didn't leave. To her chagrin, she sensed Sir Hugo close behind her.

She reached the door and paused. 'I am perfectly capable of going to my room alone.'

'Fleeing?' Sir Hugo's tone was sardonic in the extreme.

'You?' She lifted her chin. 'I think not.'

'The waltz. You found it to be much more intoxicating than you had anticipated.'

She glared at him. 'Only a prude would not enjoy the dance, Sir Hugo. I am many things, but I am not a prude.'

He smiled, but it was not amusement that shone in his eyes. 'I imagine you aren't.'

She caught her breath, conscious of the other people who still grouped around Juliet and the pianoforte some distance away. 'If you will leave me alone, I am going to bed.'

His eyes narrowed, his jaw sharpened, but he said nothing. Instead, he made her a mocking half-bow.

She snapped her mouth shut, heard her teeth click in irritation, and whirled around. She could not get to her room any second too soon. She was fit to explode from irritation and something she refused to name.

Instead of going directly to bed, she paced the spacious room, her speed increasing until she fairly whirled around. When she finally burnt off some of her energy, she started undressing. She left the clothes where they landed. Tomorrow would be soon enough to put them away.

She fell into bed and an unrestful sleep, where her host twirled her around a massive ballroom that looked suspiciously like an inferno. No doubt, she had succumbed to him and they were in Hades.

The next morning, Annabell walked to the excavation. She needed the fresh, cold air to clear her head. She was becoming strange and unfamiliar to herself. It was all because of Sir Hugo. She kicked at a rock, her harem pants billowing out around her legs.

Birds twittered and she caught a glimpse of a russet tail. The foxes were coming out of hibernation. Then there were the wild flowers poking up from the ground and the pale green shoots of new grass. She stopped and gazed at the beauty. This was a rich, verdant land, something the Romans had known or they would not have settled here.

She resumed walking and reached the site quickly, only to find Molly, Sir Hugo's mare, munching on the tender spring grass. Sir Hugo had to be nearby. Annabell frowned as she searched the area for him. Movement caught her eye and she angled to watch him saunter toward her.

He moved with athletic grace, only a slight hitch betraying his bad left leg and then not with every motion. Funny, she had not even noticed it last night when he danced. He was very adept at concealing any hardship the wound might cause.

'I forgot you were wounded.' The words were out before she realised she had said them. Awkward even for her bluntness. 'You move so gracefully.'

He waved his arm as though pushing away her comment, but his eyes darkened as though he remembered a past pain. 'It was nothing. Many others were hurt worse.'

'Many were killed,' she said softly, 'but that does not make less of what happened to you.'

She was nearly as surprised at her gentle words as she had been at her blunt ones. He made her erratic. Not a good thing for someone who prided herself on her sensibility.

He looked carefully at her, as though seeing something that had not been there before. Perhaps he did. She had not felt compassion for him until this instant and, even so, it was quickly gone. He might have been hurt, but he was still dangerous. To her.

'Tell me exactly what you do here.' He closed the distance between them.

She studied him for long minutes, trying to decide if he really wanted to know. He wasn't laughing.

'I am carefully, and consequently quite slowly, uncovering this villa.' She edged away from him and glanced around the area. 'I believe I told you that much before.'

He nodded. 'I am more interested in how you are doing it and how it was discovered and how Tatterly chose you. Antiquities are not his area of interest, and his letter explaining everything was brief to the point of uninformative.'

'One of your tenant farmers found it after ploughing up the field that runs with your orchard and hitting a large stone, which turned out to be a water basin in one of the rooms. As I said last night, I heard about it quite by accident.'

She walked to where a cloth lay over a large expanse of ground. She lifted the corner and pulled the cover to one side. 'I contacted Mr Tatterly.' She paused, even now discomfited by how she had misled the man. 'I wrote to him through my man of business, offering a specialist in antiquities free of charge to excavate the newly discovered site. I told him I came highly recommended by the Society of Antiquaries.' She glanced up to see what he was thinking, but his face was noncommittal. 'I believe Tatterly was relieved to have the matter so easily resolved.'

'I believe he was. His letter to me on the solution was briefer than the first.' His words were as dry as the Egyptian desert.

She knelt down, took a nearby brush and began to carefully sweep away dirt from the mosaic that lay beneath. 'It was not his fault. By the time he knew I was a female, I had already arrived.'

'He should have sent you packing.'

She paused in her cleaning to look up at him. 'As you would have?'

He nodded curtly.

'He has not your determination and coldness.' She brushed back a strand that had come loose from her braid and slipped out of her bonnet. 'Besides, I gave him no choice. Just as I gave Susan none when she would have left, particularly after she learned whose house we would be staying in.'

'She was not happy? That doesn't surprise me.'

'No respectable woman would be happy.'

'Except you.'

'I have an overriding purpose for being here.'

'Ah, your calling.'

'Sarcasm will not deter me, Sir Hugo.'

'I believe that.' He ran his fingers through the thick locks that fell over his forehead. 'Shall we change the subject, Lady Fenwick-Clyde? This is getting us nowhere and keeping you from your work.'

It was her turn to nod curtly. The man always distracted her from her goal. No matter that they were discussing how she came to be here. If he didn't distract her with his masculinity, he distracted her with his questions that implied doubt of her abilities.

'Why don't you hire someone to help you?' He squatted down beside her.

She blinked. 'I intend to do so, but I thought we were changing the subject.'

'This is. We are talking about the present, something we have the power to change, not the past, which is done.'

'A hedonist and a pragmatist.' She angled her head to study him. His mouth was still sensually mobile and his clothing comfortably loose. He had not changed, yet… 'Somehow I had never put the two together in one person.

'I am eminently pragmatic, as you will see.'

His eyes spoke of actions that were far from practical for her to be doing with him. She ignored them.

'Back to your question, Sir Hugo. I did not want to spend your money freely, and I wanted to get a better idea of what is here. Now that I'm nearly positive it's a Roman villa, and probably belonged to a very prosperous farmer, I will have a better idea how to tell a crew to go on. I also intend to pay the workers myself.'

'This means a lot to you, doesn't it?'

She paused in the act of carefully scraping mud from what appeared to be a woman's face. 'Is there anything wrong with that? Just because I am a woman doesn't mean I don't have a brain or that I don't find the past interesting and worth preserving.'

He shook his head. 'I never said it did. You are very sensitive.'

She bit her bottom lip. 'I am very independent.'

'That too. But I will pay for the workers. This is my property and…my villa.'

She scowled. 'Yes, it is your…villa. And the more help I have the sooner I will be gone. You are right. You will pay for the workers.'

'Of course.' There was an underlying rumble to his voice, as though he laughed at her to himself. 'And what if I get tired of all this and decide you must stop? After all, this Roman antiquity is on my property. I might not like all the activity.'

She set the brush carefully down and twisted to face him. 'If you meant to do that, I believe you would have already done so.' She quirked one brow. 'Do I misjudge you?'

'Probably not, but it is still on my property. Doesn't it bother you to spend time and a great deal of effort digging on someone else's land? Particularly when I might not preserve it as you would wish.'

She twisted into a cross-legged position, which she always found comfortable, for this conversation seemed to be expanding. 'Of course that bothers me. But what can I do about it? Not excavate it at all, or let someone else do it?'

'Some people would likely do that.'

She snorted. 'Well, I cannot. No, I will do whatever it takes to uncover and preserve the thing and then I will leave it to you and hope you will take care of it.'

'Aren't you afraid I might not?'

She looked into the blue sky and let go some of her tension before replying. 'You cannot be all play and no responsibility. After all, you rode out to inform your tenants you were home the very first day you arrived. Not many men of my acquaintance would have been that diligent. So, I have to hope you will feel the same about this when I am done and you see what a beautiful thing it is.'

She gave him a sly look. 'And besides, you could earn quite a bit of money from this, you know.'

'Really?' He smiled as though he did not believe her.

'Really. I have seen it done not far from here. The owner is still excavating, but he has already opened it to the public for a small entrance fee. He seems to be doing very well.'

Sir Hugo laughed. 'Very good, Lady Fenwick-Clyde. An antiquarian and a business woman. What else have you dipped your interesting head into?'

She was not sure whether to feel complimented or insulted. He implied she was intelligent and interesting, but he had also laughed as though he found the entire situation amusing and not very serious. This was not funny to her.

'My affairs are none of your concern, Sir Hugo. I merely mentioned a way you might turn this to a profit when all is said and done.'

He stopped laughing. 'So you did. But I've an aversion to strangers tramping my land, and you already said this will take months or years. Just the thought of people mucking all about leaves me unenthused.'

She sighed. 'Very likely. But I don't intend to be involved that long. I find there is never a shortage of gentlemen willing to come in and finish a project or share the work involved.'

He looked intrigued. 'You have done this before?'

She smiled in remembered pleasure. 'I didn't start it. I was one of the latecomers who helped finish the project. It was in Egypt. The pyramids. Totally fascinating. A strange land with a stranger past. Imagine, embalming your dead royalty.'

'I imagine Prinny would not be adverse to that. He has already built himself a temple. That monstrosity at Brighton. The only thing it lacks is a gold and jewel-encrusted sarcophagus for his mummified body.'

The image his words conjured was too much for Annabell's sobriety. She started laughing. 'How naughty of you to suggest such a thing. And rumour says you are an intimate of the Prince Regent.'

He laughed with her. 'I am, but that does not mean I am blind to his faults. He can be generosity itself, and he may single-handedly preserve the finest of English arts and crafts, but he is also vain and prone to spend money he doesn't have.'

She nodded. 'So true. His minuses are as big as his pluses.'

'But enough of him.' Sir Hugo stood. 'What can I do to help you? After all, I stand to profit from all of this, so the sooner it is finished the better for me.'

She shook her head at his levity, but rose with him. 'I imagine you have plenty of other things to occupy you, Sir Hugo. You don't need to help me, and I will even be glad to see you get the entrance fees.'

'I want to help.'

She looked away from him. He was too intense in spite of the half-smile curving his tantalising lips up at one corner. She did not want him here. He muddled her thoughts, made her think of things that had nothing remotely to do with the excavation.

She arranged her refusal carefully, determined not to say something he could interpret as encouragement. 'I appreciate your offer, Sir Hugo. But at this point, as I said before, it is much easier for me to work by myself. I know exactly what I need to do and can do it quicker if I don't have to direct someone else.'

'Really?' He brushed at a speck on his loose-fitting country coat. 'You can do all the work here by yourself? Surely you are overly optimistic about your time.'

He had her there. She fully intended to hire people from the nearby village, and they would not constantly disturb her peace of mind and make her wish for things she had determined not to wish for. But she was not about to tell him that.

'You are not dressed to be grubbing in the dirt. Your buff pantaloons, while the height of fashion, would be ruined after less than an hour here. Surely you don't want to destroy them when you don't have to.'

He shrugged. 'It doesn't matter to me, and I doubt Jamison would care either. He's a better soldier than a valet.'

She angled away so he wouldn't see her mounting frustration. She had work to do and he was a distraction.

He closed the distance between them and touched her arm to make her look back at him. 'Surely I can do something you don't need to supervise.'

The contact made her jump. Her entire body felt suddenly, gloriously alive. This was exactly why she didn't want him here.

She scowled. 'There is nothing you can do that I don't have to keep an eye on while you do it. Is that clear enough?'

His eyes widened slightly before narrowing. 'Are you sure the fact of the matter isn't that you just don't want me here? If that is so, then at least be honest about it.'

'Right. That is exactly it.' She pulled her arm away and stepped back.

He watched her move, but did not follow. 'Honesty will get you a lot further with me than polite subterfuge.'

'I don't want to get far with you. I want to be left alone by you.'

His face took on a dangerous sharpness. 'Really? I don't

thing so, Lady Fenwick-Clyde—Annabell. I think you are afraid of the way I make you feel.'

'Nonsense.' But the breathiness of her voice ruined her denial, and she inched further away.

'I think you want me to touch you. I think you want me to be around you.' His voice was low and raspy, the melody normally in it gone.

'You are absurd.' She jerked her head to one side. 'Absolutely delusional.'

Good, she told herself. She sounded definite. Her voice had been firm, and she had not edged away. She had hit just the right note of dismissal. So what if her heart pounded and her palms were moist? She was merely uncomfortable because of his confrontation.

'No,' he murmured. 'I am honest.'

She watched him carefully, wondering if he was really as dangerous as he looked this instant. He reminded her of a stalking lion she had seen at the Tower some months back. He watched her with the same predatory gleam the lion had directed at its dinner. Sir Hugo was many things, but she doubted that he intended to eat her.

'So am I,' she said in her haughtiest tone.

He laughed, but it was not an amused sound. It was more of a challenge. 'No, you are lying to me…and to yourself.'

She shook her head.

'Yes,' he said softly. 'Your body was alive and tingling last night when I held you in my arms. You even moved closer when we danced.'

'I did not.' She was affronted by his forward words and assumption that she was that type of woman.

'Yes,' he murmured. 'Your face was soft and your lips were swollen. You swayed in my arms as though you belonged in them.'

She shook her head again. 'No.' But her rejection was barely a whisper.

'Prove it to me,' he said, closing the distance between

them. 'Resist me when I take you back into my arms and kiss you and…' He trailed off, leaving the rest to her imagination.

She shivered and stepped back more from instinct than any intentional decision to avoid him. Her foot hit a rock and her ankle twisted. She gasped. Her arms windmilled, and he caught her around the waist.

Before she could regain her breath, she found herself pressed to his chest. She stared into his eyes and wondered where this would lead, how far he would go and how far she would let him.

'Annabell.' Susan Pennyworth's voice penetrated the haze of desire that enveloped Annabell. 'I know you're here. I've come to finish my drawing of the Zeus mosaic.'

Annabell pushed hard on Sir Hugo's chest. He released her with a sardonic twist of his lips. She stepped away, feeling dizzy and lost. Something she had wanted very badly had just been taken away from her.

In a voice she barely recognised, Annabell called, 'I am over here, Susan. Behind the bush near the geometric mosaic.'

'There you are,' Susan said, rounding the barrier. 'Oh, Sir Hugo. I didn't know you were here.'

He made her an abbreviated bow. 'I am just leaving.'

'Oh, dear,' Susan said, 'don't leave on my account. I am sure you are interested in what we are doing. I don't mean to chase you away. I am merely here to draw the mosaic. Nothing more.'

A pained expression moved over Sir Hugo's face. 'Rest easy, Miss Pennyworth. I am leaving.'

Annabell watched him with relief and regret as he made true his words. Susan had come just in time—or had she?

Chapter Six

Annabell peeked into the library. The last thing she wanted was an encounter with her host. Their interlude at the site was enough to last the rest of her life, or so she told herself. She shivered and wondered why she felt suddenly cold. It was as though something had been taken away from her. She shook her shoulders, told herself not to be fanciful and entered the room.

Even with summer nearly upon them, there was a fire in the grate to keep the chill and damp from the air in this old house. Several lit candles cast a golden glow. The room was always ready for Sir Hugo. For a man of his licentious reputation, he was very bookish. She could not fault him for that trait.

'Come in,' his deep voice said from behind a large, leather wing-back chair pulled close to the fireplace.

She started briefly. 'I should have known you were here by the half-full glass of brandy on the table.' And she should have. He seemed to have a particular taste for the drink.

He looked around the chair. 'Had you been more observant, you would have.'

'You are right, but a gentleman would not be so blunt about the fact.'

He laughed. 'But I am not a gentleman. I thought we had settled that.'

'True.'

She entered the room, pulling her paisley shawl tight around her shoulders. The fire might be roaring, but there was a cold snap, as though winter wanted one last fling.

'Come sit here.' He indicated a large, fat-cushioned chair near him. 'The warmth will reach you.'

She hesitated. 'I did not come here to socialise.'

He raised one brow. 'Really. Did you come for a book?'

She nodded. But the shabby, chintz-covered chair was inviting, as was the roaring fire. They were cosy, a word she would not have associated with Sir Hugo Fitzsimmon, the scourge of London's fairer sex—and the man who had nearly seduced her this afternoon.

She cast a glance at him. He appeared perfectly at his ease, as though he had never invited her to his bed.

He beckoned her. 'Come, Lady Fenwick-Clyde, I won't bite.' His lips curved wickedly. 'Not unless you ask.'

She shook her head at him. 'Innuendoes, Sir Hugo?'

'Always.' He took a drink of brandy. 'Particularly when I have sampled something I long to know better.'

A faint blush mounted her features. 'You are being deliberately provocative.'

He took another sip and eyed her speculatively over the rim of his glass. 'Not nearly as much as I would like to be.'

A *frisson* ran her spine and she stopped. Danger lurked here. 'Perhaps I should leave.'

Unfortunately, her voice was breathy, which ruined the effect she had tried for of haughty coldness. But it was hard to be cool when your blood was starting to heat. He always had this effect on her. It was unnatural as well as unseemly.

'No,' he said. 'I will mind my manners—unless you invite me to do otherwise.'

She took a step back.

'No, I meant it. Sit, and I will pour you a glass of brandy.'

'I don't drink. I watched my brothers consume whisky the way you swig brandy. Inebriation doesn't appeal to me.'

She recognized the disgust in her voice that she always felt when her younger brother, Dominic, had come home, barely able to move. He was much like Sir Hugo—a womaniser, a drinker, and a charmer no member of the opposite sex seemed able to resist. She should leave now before her attraction to her host allowed him to lead them into deeper waters.

Instead of moving to the door like her mind directed, she moved toward the chair. She was like a moth drawn to the flame of his masculinity. He burned with an energy that never failed to excite her in ways she had previously never experienced. He was very dangerous indeed.

'You drink sherry,' he said, a curl to his mouth. 'This is much better.' When she sank into the opposite chair without accepting his offer, he added, 'Trust me.'

She laughed. 'Trust you? I don't think so, Sir Hugo. And I never drink more than a small glass of sherry.'

He smiled. 'Well, at least try the brandy. A sip. If you don't like it, you needn't finish it. Here,' he said, holding out his glass, 'I will even let you drink from mine. That way you won't feel as though I am pressing a great amount on you.'

She eyed his outstretched hand holding the goblet of liquor in the way she might eye a dangerous cobra poised to strike. On one level, his offer seemed perfectly innocuous. But on a deeper level, he was asking her to put her lips where his had already been. When thought of like that, his offer was temptation in the extreme.

She appreciated that he was flirting with her. It was oddly appealing. But then, so was the mesmerising sway of an aroused cobra.

'Perhaps a little.' When a slow, sensual smile intensified

the harsh angle of his jaw, she added, 'Just to make you hush about it. I am sure I won't like it.'

She stared at him for a long moment, wondering how far he intended to take this, and then wondering how far she wanted him to take it. He said nothing, but his gaze was intense, as though he found her fascinating. In its own way, that look was more seductive than anything else he could have done. Even more so than the anticipation of putting her lips to the glass he held out to her—his glass. Annabell found herself wishing he would reach across the table and touch her. Anywhere. Just touch her so she could feel his flesh against hers.

She settled for touching his fingers with her own when she took the brandy. Her reaction to him was swift and strong. Her stomach clenched in pleasure and her fingers trembled. He held on to the glass even though she also held it. He leaned forward so she could put the rim to her lips. Somehow she knew he meant for her to sip from the very spot he had just drank from. She shivered in anticipation.

She took a sip of the brandy and fire welled up her throat. Fortunately, he still held the goblet. She barely managed to swallow before a coughing fit took her. She gasped.

He knelt in front of her before she realised he had moved. 'Easy, Lady Fenwick-Clyde—Bell,' he murmured, using her family's pet name for her. He set the glass on the nearby table.

'Oh,' she gasped. 'I didn't conceive it could be so strong.'

'It isn't. You gulped it. That will make anything seem overpowering.'

She hadn't noticed that he had moved again until his knee nudged hers. She shivered and tried to shift so they didn't touch. He shifted so they did.

Her eyes watered, blurred his image. His hand cupped the side of her face, his touch warmer than the fire. With his thumb, he wiped away the tear trailing down her cheek.

It was a gentle gesture, yet her body reacted as though he had crushed her to him. There wasn't enough air for her to inhale. Her mouth opened.

He leaned into her and his lips touched hers.

He did not hold her or in any way confine her. She could pull away, and she knew it. But she didn't. She was caught, like a butterfly pinned to a board. Only she didn't want to escape.

Her eyes drifted shut, and she sank into his caress.

His mouth drank from hers. She tasted brandy on his lips and tongue. It was sweet and strong and intoxicating. He sucked at her, nipped at her and made her want him with nothing more than his kiss. He barely touched her.

When he finally broke the contact, she sighed in regret. She opened her eyes slowly to see him watching her carefully.

'Will you come to my room, Bell? You want me as much as I want you.' His voice was low and raspy, his hands clenched on his thighs. He still crouched so their knees met.

She swallowed her need. 'No, Sir Hugo. I… That is not what I want from life.'

He rocked back so they no longer touched, his face blank. 'What do you want?'

She had to look away from him in order to think straight since, seeing him so close, all she wanted was him, but in her saner moments she knew she wanted more. She wanted freedom to do what she wanted when she wanted to do it. Marriage to Fenwick-Clyde had taught her well that a wife has no freedom. She was subject to her husband's every whim.

'Independence,' she whispered and wondered why it hurt to say that.

'You can have that and still come with me,' he said, his offer sweet and beguiling.

She shook her head. 'No. What if I became pregnant? What then?'

He frowned, his beautiful mouth turning down at the corners. 'I am not some callow youth with no experience, Bell. I would protect you.'

She tilted her head to the side and studied him. He was not classically handsome. Her brothers were more attractive. But there was a magnetism about him. And his body was firm, broad in the shoulders and lean in the hips. He had an athlete's body, a body that belonged on a Greek marble.

And he intrigued her.

'How would you protect me? I don't believe there is any such thing for the woman when she and a man make love.'

'Of course there is,' he said gently, still not touching her. 'Your husband was a cad or he would have shown you.'

Her eyes widened slightly. 'You malign someone who can't defend himself.'

He held her gaze without flinching at her criticism. 'Could he defend himself? I don't think so.' His voice hardened. 'What I find hard to believe is that your parents gave you to him.'

She was instantly defensive. 'They did not know.' He raised one brow in doubt. 'They didn't. They did not go about in society. He came from a good family. Besides…' she sniffed '…it was a marriage of convenience. They had made one and found they fell in love. They thought the same would happen to me.'

He snorted. 'They were fools.'

She felt her shoulders begin to bunch. They were skirting uncomfortable memories. She wanted to be angry with him for bringing this up, but instead she found she wanted to discuss Fenwick-Clyde. She wanted to find out what another man thought of her husband. She had never been brave enough to discuss her husband with either of her brothers. She had sensed that his actions would have infuriated her brothers to the point where they might have done something everyone would regret.

'Who are you to say that?' The question was as close as she could come to asking him what he thought of Fenwick-Clyde.

'Do you really want to know?'

She clenched her hands and wondered if she really did. How could she even contemplate discussing what Fenwick-Clyde had done, and to someone she barely knew? Yet, she sensed she could discuss this with him. Strange. She even trusted him, at least in this.

'Yes,' she finally said.

He settled himself more comfortably on his knees as though sensing this conversation would be long. 'I knew your husband.' When she started in surprise, he held up his hand. 'Not well, but we often ran into each other during the course of a night. We frequented many of the same places.'

She bit down hard on the urge to make some scathing comment. She had not asked him to talk to her so that she could denigrate him or accuse him.

As though he sensed her disapproval, he said, 'I am not going to ask you to understand. I am a man and I do as I please. And what I please is to enjoy my life as I see fit. For me that is often women, gambling and drink.'

She nodded, trying desperately not to show him how his words hurt. She was being silly and knew it. What he wanted from her was sex, not love. She knew from watching her brothers that for a man the two were often mutually exclusive.

'Your husband obviously felt the same.' His face hardened. 'The only difference between us is that I believe in making my encounters enjoyable for everyone involved. Fenwick-Clyde did not.'

She jerked. Her nails dug into her palms, but she said nothing. He was absolutely right.

'There were rumours about him. Unsavoury ones. After

a while, many of the women refused to service him. From what I heard, I didn't blame them.'

The memories rose inside her, memories she had tried so hard to bury so deeply they would never surface again in her life. She stared, not seeing the present. Her breathing increased.

'Annabell!'

Sir Hugo's firm voice called to her, but the memories would not stop. Once Fenwick-Clyde had tied her, spread-eagled, to the bed. He had done things to her she had never imagined possible. That had been their wedding night.

'Annabell, stop!'

This time Sir Hugo's voice penetrated her misery. She blinked and focused on him. Her breathing eased.

'I'm sorry. I didn't mean to do that.'

He laid a hand over one of hers. 'I wish he had not misused you.'

She blanched and started to pull her hand away from his, then hesitated. He was warm and strong, and his touch made her feel safe. She stared at his concerned face and realised she cared for him. Cared for him a great deal.

'It is in the past,' she finally said, wondering how she was going to deal with the man kneeling in front of her now that she appreciated the fact that he meant more to her than he should or than she wanted him to. 'He is gone and cannot touch me ever again.'

'Nor can any other man because of what he did to you.' His tone was bitter. Not at all like him.

'You have certainly touched me,' she said with more irony than necessary.

He studied her. 'I kissed you. That is only the beginning. But you keep who you are locked away.'

He was much more perceptive than she would have thought. It must come from his experience with women.

'Why do you care?' she asked without thinking and instantly regretted it. 'I'm sorry. It is none of my business. Please ignore that question.'

He held her gaze with his. His tone was rueful. 'Because I find myself intrigued by you. I want to know more about you and at the same time my body aches for you.' When she gasped, he added, 'Is that sufficient reason?'

Shocked, she nodded.

His smile was wry. 'Surely, I've told you enough times how I feel for you that you should not be surprised.'

'Well…' She noticed that he still held her hand. She pulled free. 'Yes, you have been very forward in regard to your physical wants, but this is the first time you've indicated an interest in anything else.'

He leaned back, as though deciding that more distance between them would help prove his attraction was more than skin deep. 'In all honesty, this is the first time I realise that I want more from you than physical pleasure.'

He stood and moved back to the chair he had vacated what seemed eons ago. He sprawled with his slippered feet nearly touching the fireplace grate. He was relaxed and enticing all at once. A heady combination.

'Are you serious?'

He turned to her. 'Regretfully, yes.'

'Regretfully?' She was not sure if she was offended or amused.

'Yes, Annabell, regretfully.' He picked up the glass of brandy and drained it. 'I don't normally become interested in the workings of my lover's mind. Usually I am more than satisfied to understand how her body responds to mine.'

The image conjured by his last words sent tingles through her spine. He was being prosaic, and she was finding him seductive. No wonder she found him nearly impossible to resist when he set out to entice her. She wanted him to make love to her, and she went cold with the realisation.

She licked suddenly dry lips and tried desperately to find

a subject to scintillate him with and take her thoughts from the image that seemed lodged in her mind. Nothing came to mind.

'I can't image what you find interesting,' she finally said. 'All I can think about is y—' She stopped herself, her fingers shaking at her near admission. 'All I can think about is antiquities. I can't image that interesting a man like you.'

He watched her from the corner of his eye. 'Why?'

'Because you are a rake,' she blurted out.

'Rakes have more than one interest,' he answered, his voice sardonic.

'Gambling?'

'More than two.' He turned to face her full on. 'Are you flirting with me?'

'I...' She had not intended to. He was making her lose control of herself. This was unacceptable. 'No.'

He laughed, a short bark that wasn't really amused. 'I didn't think so. More's the pity.'

'It is time I left.'

She stood, no longer able to withstand him this close. One minute he was trying to seduce her, the next he told her he admired her brain, and now he was being charming. He was as multifaceted as she was confused.

He got to his feet. 'Wait a minute. I have something you might want to take to bed with you.'

She paused, wondering if he had meant to be provocative. The blade-sharp angle of his jaw told her he had.

He went to one of the shelves and pulled two books down. Handling them carefully, he came to her. 'You probably already have these, but, if not, they will make for interesting reading.'

She looked at the top book. 'William Camden's *Brittania*.' She looked up at him. 'This is considered the first book to give topographical descriptions of monuments in Britain. It was written in 1585.'

'I know. This copy is from the early 1700s.' He lifted

that one and put it underneath the second book, which was actually a bound manuscript. 'This is part of John Aubrey's *Monumenta Britannica*.'

She gaped. 'That is extremely rare.'

'I know. But I also know you will handle it as though it was a relic.'

She glanced sharply at him. Was he being sarcastic? She couldn't tell from the neutral expression he wore.

'I will certainly treat it with the respect it deserves,' she said more tartly than he deserved. 'But where did you get this?'

'One of my ancestors must have been friends with the man. Who knows?'

'Spoken like a man who isn't interested in the contents.'

'Take them and enjoy them. I read them a long time ago.'

She took them with reverential care. 'I am sorry for implying that you hadn't read them.'

He shrugged. 'It has been a long time. I studied antiquities at Oxford and read them then. I have forgotten most of what I learned.'

She doubted that. She was fast learning that Sir Hugo was a very intelligent man with a superb memory.

'I imagine you remember everything you intend to remember,' she said drily.

'Perhaps.' He stepped back. 'Goodnight.'

She gave him a hesitant smile, wondering if he was going to add an invitation to his bed as he had already done several times. When he said nothing further, she turned and left.

Sir Hugo watched her leave the room. She was tall and elegant and intelligent, all attributes he valued and admired. He would have a difficult time leaving her when the affair he intended to have with her ended.

Which reminded him that there was still Elizabeth. She must have reached London by now and would be expecting to hear from him. A task he was no longer looking forward to fulfilling.

He returned to the chair and sank down. He poured another full glass of brandy and lifted it to his lips. For a fleeting moment, he remembered Annabell putting the glass to her mouth. He shifted the glass to where he imagined she had sipped from it and downed the contents. The liquor burned all the way down.

The hairs on Annabell's nape tingled as though someone watched her. She looked up to see Sir Hugo in the morning-room entrance. He didn't look much different from last night in the library. And he still aroused feelings in her that she didn't want to experience.

She felt a fleeting sense of embarrassment caused by the memory of their talk last night. She also found herself glad to see him, something she did not want to be happening. But it was.

'I see you have invaded my breakfast room as well as my library and my orchard with my Roman villa.' He sauntered toward her. 'I am curious to discover what other areas of my property you intend to inhabit.'

She thought instantly of his bed and blushed a bright pink. The idea had been unbidden and unexpected. He always took her by surprise.

'Good morning to you too.' She ignored his leading statements. Some things were better left unaddressed. 'You are up early.'

He came closer. 'I see you are going to ignore my comment. Never mind. You will show me sooner or later. I am a patient man.' Before she could think of a retort, he gave her a mock frown. 'And you seem to have a jaundiced opinion of me. I am often up this early.'

'Really?' She put all her doubt into that one word. Still, she would rather this conversation than his original one. She felt mildly safe discussing this. 'I thought you drank

and gambled the nights away. It has been my experience
with my brothers, particularly my younger one, that when
a man does such, he doesn't get up early the next day.'

He reached the dainty desk she sat at. 'I didn't drink and
gamble the night away.' His voice deepened to a rasp. 'Nor
did I entertain anyone in my rooms.'

Instantly what safety she had felt evaporated. Leave it to
him to turn any conversation in a dangerously erotic direction.

She had thought at her advanced age and previous marital
status that she was beyond blushing at implied improprie-
ties, but she was not. Her fingers froze in the act of shifting
a paper.

'You are very bold for so early in the day.'

'True.'

He spoke as nonchalantly as he was dressed. He had no
coat on and no cravat or belcher tie either. His shirt was
open at the neck to reveal curling brown hairs, and his buff
breeches were like a second skin. Even his less than perfectly polished Hessians called to her. Annabell suddenly
found herself trying desperately to ignore a heightened
awareness of him, which wasn't helped by his cinnamon-
and-musk scent. This was unacceptable.

'What can I do for you?' she asked with more asperity
than he deserved. But she was battling for her sanity, and
the sooner he left the sooner she would return to normal.

His eyelids drooped suggestively. 'Now that you ask…'

His deep voice trailed off, and she found her irritation
mounting with her growing arousal. 'You are behaving beyond the pale. Stop it this instant or I shall leave.'

He shrugged and his voice returned to its normal melodic
baritone. 'You bring out the worst in me, I'm afraid.'

She looked at him in surprise. 'I do? I thought you behaved like this as a matter of course.'

'Not with every woman I meet.' He gave her a rakish
grin that told her was completely unrepentant.

He grabbed a nearby ladderback chair and pulled it close to the desk. He straddled it and crossed his arms over the back of the chair, much like her younger brother always did. She found herself softening toward him because he reminded her so much of Dominic.

'You are so much like my brother.'

'Should I be offended or flattered?'

'It depends on whether you want to be known as a libertine or an upstanding man.' She eyed him. 'Which will it be?'

'Libertine, I think.'

'Then you should be flattered.' Her tone was acerbic with disappointment.

Although they were teasing each other, there was a seriousness about his demeanour that told her he meant every word he spoke. The knowledge saddened her. Libertines were not the type of men she wished to become better acquainted with. Her brother was enough.

'What are you studying?' All trace of seduction had left his voice.

She blinked. 'One minute we are talking about your unsavoury proclivities and the next you are quizzing me on my work. You are a conundrum.'

'I try. It keeps the ladies on their mettle.'

She shook her head. 'Now we are back to that. Well…' She pushed the top sheet closer to him. 'I am studying these drawings taken from the excavation and labelling them as I go.'

He studied the finely drawn pencil illustrations. 'These are excellent.' He looked up at her, his eyes alight with renewed interest. 'Did you draw these?'

She laughed in an effort to chase away the thrill caused by his piqued interest and the following disappointment at realising the look would fade from his eyes when she told him the truth.

'No. Susan did. She is a superb artist.'

His mouth opened as though he wanted to speak but was speechless. He looked back down at the drawing, then back up at her. 'Surely you jest.'

She shook her head, a tiny spurt of irritation forming at his obvious disdain for her friend and companion. 'She is good enough to illustrate for any antiquarian. Not many people have that talent.'

'But she has not a coherent thought in her head,' he muttered. 'She speaks one inanity after another ad nauseum.'

'Shame on you for thinking so uncharitably of her.' She pulled back the picture as though by taking it from him she was protecting Susan from his criticism.

'I'm only calling a spade a spade.' His lip curled sardonically. 'Just as I am doing when I call her artwork some of the best I have ever seen. The woman is a contradiction.'

'Well…' Annabell huffed in spite of her effort to let go the irritation his denigration had caused '…I believe artistic talent does not have to be accompanied by perfect sense. *I* always understand Susan perfectly.'

A small twinge of conscience caught her. She might always understand her companion, but that did not mean Susan's sometimes empty chattering didn't upset her or make her impatient with the other woman. But she was not about to admit that to Sir Hugo with his smug face.

'I am sure you do.' He stood. 'But I'd also wager you sometimes wish she would stop chattering so that you can hear yourself think.'

She dropped her gaze from his penetrating study and gathered the sheets of paper and carefully straightened them into a single pile with all the edges lined up. She glanced up at him from the corner of her eye. He stood patiently waiting for her reply.

She let out a huff of air. 'All right. You are correct.' She hastened to add, 'But not often.'

'I thought so.'

She picked up the papers and stood abruptly. 'If you will

excuse me, I need to put these back in their portfolio and get out to the site.'

'By all means.' But he didn't move to let her go around him.

She frowned. There was only one way to go. The other end of the desk abutted the wall. 'Will you move?'

His mocking smile returned accompanied by a half-bow. 'Of course.'

He stepped aside, but it was slow and infuriatingly provocative. She gathered the papers close to her chest as though they were a shield and edged by him, ignoring the slow grin he gave her as though he knew exactly what he was doing to her.

She scowled at him. 'You are the most difficult man, Sir Hugo.'

His smiled widened. 'I aim to please, Lady Fenwick-Clyde.'

Her heart skipped a beat, and she hugged the papers closer. In spite of the unease he created in her, she managed to keep her voice cool. 'I imagine you do.'

He laughed outright. 'I've been told I do.'

'Insufferable,' she muttered, making her escape to the door and into the hall.

He could be so irritating. He even used the same word to describe Susan's incessant talking: chattering. She shook her head. He was beginning to have altogether too many similarities to her. It was uncomfortable for her peace of mind.

Chapter Seven

Annabell stood, hands on hips, and surveyed her handiwork. A large, nearly intact mosaic stood out. It was geometric, with all the colours of the surrounding rocks from which the small tiles had been made. But it was unprotected and a storm threatened. Hopefully the men from the nearby village would arrive with the poles and large awning she had commissioned last week.

She heard a horse's hooves and turned, anxious to get the cover up. 'Oh, it is you.'

Sir Hugo sat astride Molly just where the road passed by the clearing Annabell stood in. His hair was wind blown, accentuating its unfashionable length. It was suddenly difficult to breathe. And she had seen him only several hours before in the breakfast room.

Eyes narrowed, he said, 'I'm sorry to disappoint you, Lady Fenwick-Clyde. You were expecting someone else?'

'I was expecting the men from the village with the cover.'

'Ah.'

He dismounted with only a small hitch in his fluidity to show that his healed wound pained him. Funny, she had not noticed him limp earlier today. Probably because, honest with herself for once where he was concerned, she had been more interested in the way his shirt had been open at the neck and his breeches had hugged his muscles. Ladies were not supposed to notice those things about a man, or, if they did, they simply said he had a fine figure.

She watched him from the corner of her eye. She did not trust him—or herself. Not any more. The more she learned about him, the more she liked him in spite of herself. With a start, she realised she had been looking at the lean musculature of his hips and thighs—again. She bit her lip and turned away. It was better not to watch him at all than to ogle him. This was so unlike her. But everything since he came into her life was so unlike the way she normally was.

'Is something wrong?' There was a glint in his eyes that told her he knew exactly what was wrong.

Her entire body flushed, making it nearly impossible for her to answer him with even a modicum of nonchalance. She tried anyway. 'No. Nothing.'

'Of course,' he murmured.

He spoke in such a way that she knew he knew she was having difficulty continuing to resist him. She supposed a man of his experience sensed when women were near to succumbing. That was what would make him so successful a rake—and rumour said he was very successful indeed.

He moved past her with only a cursory glance that took in her flushed face and loose hair. His gaze slid down her body to her harem pants. 'You look wicked and enticing in those. But I suppose you know that.'

She hadn't thought it possible to feel more uncomfortable, but he had made her so. 'I don't choose my clothes to look any way. I wear what is practical for clambering over rocks and working in dirt.'

He gave her the smile she was becoming too familiar with. It said he believed her but it was time for her to learn about reality. She glared back at him.

He stopped just short of where the mosaic started. 'You have the mosaic completely uncovered. Very impressive.'

She took a moment to digest the fact that he had changed the subject. Then she nodded, before realising he couldn't see her with his back to her. 'Yes.'

He looked over his shoulder. 'You truly enjoy this.'

She felt like shaking her head. His habit of flitting from one subject to another was disconcerting.

'Yes, yes, I do,' she finally managed, her pleasure warming her voice. 'I have always been intrigued by the ancients. This gives me a chance to see how they actually lived, perhaps even tells me a little about how they thought. Much more satisfying than reading about them.'

'Tell me about it.'

She met his eyes with hers. 'Do you really want to know?'

He laughed, his rich baritone sending shivers down her spine. 'I believe you have asked me that before. The answer hasn't changed. Yes, I am interested. I may be a debauched rake, but before travelling down this dissolute road, I studied antiquities at Oxford, as I told you last night. I just never pursued my interest as you have yours.'

She digested his words. 'Still another side to you.'

He shrugged. 'Most people have many facets.'

'I suppose they do.'

She moved closer to him, still careful to leave a safe distance. Last night and the intimacy of shared experiences was too fresh. He was becoming more than a one-dimensional rake. He was becoming an interesting human being.

He laughed. 'You say that as though you wish it weren't so.'

One corner of her mouth inched up in a rueful smile. 'Sometimes it is easier to deal with people on a more simplistic level.'

He sobered. 'Are you talking about us?'

She nodded, wondering how he always seemed to know

what she was thinking. It was unsettling and appealing and made resisting him all that much harder.

To change to a safer topic, she waved at the mosaic and adopted her most prosy voice. 'What you are looking at was the floor of the triclinium or dining room. It was not heated, so probably was only used in warm weather. I imagine if there is more here, which I suspect there is, we will find other rooms where the floors were heated by lead pipes laid beneath through which hot water circulated. The Romans were very sophisticated.'

'In many ways, more than we are today.'

'True,' she said.

In moments like this, her affinity with him was frightening. He could seduce her with his mind as easily as with his body. She shivered.

'You are cold. Your harem pants are not as warm as skirts and petticoats.'

'They are perfectly warm. I should have worn a pelisse.'

She had left Rosemont in a hurry, eager to be away before he accosted her again. And here she was with him in spite of her effort.

He shrugged out of his greatcoat, and before she could protest, threw it over her shoulders. Warmth and his scent engulfed her, a dizzying combination that made her sway. He was at her side immediately, his arm around her waist, his face inches from her own.

'I am fine,' she managed to say in spite of the dryness that made her tongue feel thick. 'Nor do I need your coat.'

He did not release her. 'You shall keep my coat and I shall keep my arm around you.'

She licked her lips. 'Please, Sir Hugo—Hugo, don't do this.'

'Do what?' His voice was a challenge. 'Make you desire me?'

She turned away from the twin green flames that were his eyes. His musky scent combined with the fresh smell of a fine winter day permeated her senses. His arm around her was security and threat. A small breathy laugh escaped her.

'What?' His gloved fingers caught her chin and gently forced her face up. 'What is funny?'

She took a deep gulp of air and turned her gaze back to him only to be caught by the passion in his face. His lips were curved, their well-defined outline begging to be traced by her finger…by her tongue.

'Funny?' he reminded her.

'You. Me. The feelings you create in me.' The words tumbled from her mouth, making no sense. 'Both safe and yet scared.'

'As though this is completely new?'

She nodded. Was he going to kiss her? Would he stop with just a kiss? Did she want him to? She no longer knew what she wanted.

'I am going to kiss you, Annabell. If you don't want that, then tell me now.' His voice was low and urgent.

Her eyes fluttered shut. Fool that she was, she wanted his kiss, his touch. 'Please.'

He scattered gossamer kisses across her cheeks. 'How do you feel now?'

Her breath caught as his lips paused to caress the curve of her jaw. 'Safe in your strength. Scared of my reaction to you.'

'Scared?' He lifted his face from hers and one thick brow quirked up.

She nodded. 'You are so thoroughly comfortable with who you are and your appetites. It can be frightening.'

'No more frightening than the need you create in me, Bell.'

He had used her family nickname last night too. Then, as now, it created a sense of homecoming in her. As though he had a right to use it, although she knew intellectually that he did not.

He lowered his face until his lips skimmed her cheek. He barely touched her, and she felt as though she would erupt into molten desire. Nothing in her life had prepared her for this response. Nothing.

She sucked in tiny gulps of air. 'Don't, Hugo.' She turned her face away and closed her eyes as though doing so would close out his warmth and nearness. 'I've changed my mind. I don't want this.'

'Liar.' But he let her go.

She felt bereft, silly, weak creature that she was. The warmth that had engulfed her seconds before was gone as though it never existed. Suddenly she was more aware of the sharp wind and chill in the air than she had been all morning. She stuffed her hands into the pockets of her pants.

She wanted to continue lying to him and tell him he was wrong. She did not want to become his lover, but the same innate honesty that had always made her confess to any infraction of the rules—even if it meant a night with no dinner while her brothers made faces at her and had their fill of every sweet—forbade her from compounding her untruths.

She faced him and spoke some of the most difficult words she had ever had to utter, simply because she did not want to want him. But she did.

'You are right…I am a liar.' Her hands clenched. 'I do want you. I want you to kiss me… I want you to do more…but that would be the worst thing for me.'

He ran his finger along her jaw, but made no move to take her back into his arms. 'Why? You are a grown woman, an independent woman who fully understands what we would be embarking upon.'

She caught his hand to stop the caress. 'And I do not want any of it.' She sighed and moved his hand from her face. 'That is not true, and yet it is. I don't want to be your lover because of all the complications and ramifications.

Yet, at the same time, I want you to make love to me.' Her brows knitted in frustration. 'Can you understand that?'

He raised her hand for his kiss. She would swear she felt the soft firmness and heat of his mouth even through her glove.

'Yes. Would you feel any better if I told you I feel the same?'

She laughed, a weak disbelieving sound. 'You? You have done this more times than you can probably remember. I have never done this.'

His grip tightened painfully. 'No matter how many times I have done this with other women, Bell, I have never made love to you.'

'True.'

His hold loosened and he chuckled ruefully. 'Until I tell you why you are different, you will think I am splitting hairs.'

She nodded. More than anything she wanted him to tell her she was special, different from the others. A vain wish, she knew, but still hope twisted her stomach. She did not want to be just the latest in a string of mistresses.

He sat on one of the nearby recently uncovered stones and pulled her down on to a second one so they were eye level. 'You are different from the others.'

'I'm sure,' she said sarcastically, unable to help herself. She felt so vulnerable.

He scowled. 'See. You want me to tell you why making love to you won't be as simple for me as you think it will, but when I try you immediately belittle what I say.'

She notched her chin up. 'I find it hard to comprehend that you are willing to talk to me about this. It has been my experience that men don't talk about their feelings. They talk about horse flesh or their sporting pursuits and even politics—but never their emotions. So, why now?'

'Because if I don't, you will never believe that I find you different from the rest. You won't understand that you are special to me.' He shrugged. 'Women like to talk about their feelings. I am trying.'

'Another skill in your arsenal?'

Anger tinged his words. 'You are very cynical for a woman who wants reassurance.'

She sighed. 'I can't help it, Hugo. I am new to this and you are an old hand. I can't help but think you have more practice. It makes for an uneasy melding.'

He nodded. 'But not impossible.' She tried to pull her hand from his, but he held tighter. 'No, don't break this contact. If you do, the next thing you will do is stand and then you will walk away. You will escape this conversation and avoid me.'

'You know me too well,' she murmured, conscious that he was not going to let her ignore what was between them. 'You are determined to bring our response to each other out into the open.'

'I will do whatever it takes to get you into my bed.'

His simple statement took her breath away. Somehow, she managed to say, 'You are moving too fast.'

'Not fast enough.'

She yanked her hand free and jumped up. 'Too fast for me. I don't care how much you talk about your feelings, I need time to adjust to what you are telling me. I am…' she took a deep breath '…I am not used to this openness with a man.'

He rose slowly. 'I have always considered myself a patient man when it comes to getting what I want, but with you my patience is fraying.'

She eyed him askance. 'You make the assumption we will become lovers. Assumptions frequently do not become reality.'

He caught her and pulled her to him even as she splayed her hands on his chest to stop him. 'This one will.'

This time his kiss was hard and demanding. His lips forced hers to part and his tongue invaded her mouth. She gasped, but her body responded immediately. A soft warmth started in her abdomen and spread outward. Her hands crept up his chest and wrapped around his neck.

All thought of escape fled as she sank into the inferno he created in her. Her inhibitions disappeared. Her body wanted what he was doing to her. She angled her mouth to give him better access.

His hands roved up and down her back, pressing her closer to him so her breasts were crushed against his chest. Her nipples tingled with tight awareness. She wanted him to caress them.

As though he had heard her thoughts, one of his hands slid to the front and cupped her aching flesh. He kneaded and massaged her bosom until she thought she would scream if he did not do something, but what? She didn't know what she wanted from him, just that she wanted more than this.

She clung to him and drank in the taste, feel and smell of him. He intoxicated her.

His free hand skimmed down the length of her hip and thigh, slid back up, the fabric of her harem pants caught in his fist. He splayed his fingers and slid around to cup her derriere. He drew her against him so her breasts flattened against his chest.

'Feel what you do to me?' His voice was low, nearly guttural, yet…

He pressed against her abdomen. He was hard and long and enticing. Desire, hot and aching, welled in her, just as it had last night. Just as it did every night since she met him. She wanted him inside her, moving with her. The realisation that she was a breath away from giving herself to him shocked her. She shook her head, more at her reaction than what he was doing.

He increased the pressure until he pushed into her. 'Don't deny this, Bell.'

She shook her head again. 'This is not like me. I'm not like this. Passion doesn't rule me. Never.' Only now it did.

His eyes deepened. 'Don't challenge me.' His lips curled into a smile that would have been cruel if it had not been so seductive. 'It only makes me more determined, and I am already convinced I must have you.'

She stared up at him, her stomach doing funny things. Her entire body felt strange, lethargic, while at the same time she felt edgy, as though something was just beyond her reach.

His mouth lowered…

The sound of wagon wheels intruded. He released her and Annabell jumped back, her pulse skyrocketing.

'The awning,' she said, unsure whether she was relieved or regretful. Much as she knew it would only create problems, she was drawn to him in ways she could not explain.

He stepped away, leaving his caped greatcoat around her shoulders. She reached up with shaking fingers and fumbled with the button.

'No,' he said, his voice harsh. 'Keep it for now. You will be here for some time while they set the contraption up and it is only going to get colder.'

'I can't. What about you?'

'I am going home. To a warm fire and a stiff shot of brandy.' His voice turned rueful. 'I have things to get under control.'

She flushed, knowing he meant his body's reaction to her. For that matter, her stomach was still a knot of desire and her legs felt weaker than normal.

Without answering, she watched him mount Molly, noting, as always, the slight hitch in his otherwise graceful movement as his wound caught. It was as though he forgot about it until it reminded him that it was always there, always a reminder of Waterloo.

She forced her attention from him to the lumbering wagon, driven by a labourer with his hat pulled low to protect him from the wind. She had been so caught up in what was happening between her and Sir Hugo that she had failed to notice the storm was nearly upon them. She would be thankful for his coat before she got back to his house.

'We must move quickly,' she said to the driver.

A second man jumped down and secured the mules pulling the wagon. Then the two set to work erecting the awning and tying down the poles to withstand the oncoming storm.

Annabell entered the hall late that afternoon. She was tired, her back ached and the last person she wanted to see was Hugo. So, of course, he was the first person she saw.

'Ah, Lady Fenwick-Clyde,' he drawled, closing the distance between them.

His hair was mussed and his shirt was open. She was beginning to expect that of him. Her heart skipped a beat. She was beginning to expect that of herself when she saw him.

'Sir Hugo,' she replied, trying her hardest to sound as though it didn't matter a jot to her that he was here, that they might have made love if the workers hadn't arrived when they did.

He smiled. 'You were gone a long time today.'

She nodded. 'The men took longer than either they or I had expected. And the women were late.'

'Women?'

She eyed him narrowly, wondering if his voice held censure or if she was over-sensitive, a fault she sometimes displayed. 'Yes, women. I hired a number of females from the village.'

'How very independent of you.'

She would swear he was trying to needle her, and he was succeeding. 'As I have told you repeatedly, I am nothing if not independent. And women can uncover the villa as well as any man. Many times better. They tend to be more patient, which I attribute to sewing, knitting and weaving, all of which require concentration and agile fingers.'

His smiled widened. 'I imagine you are right.'

It was on the tip of her tongue to say something scathing.

'Hugo,' a young voice shrilled. 'Watch me.'

Annabell looked up and Hugo whirled around. Rosalie sat perched precariously on the edge of the ornately carved wood banister. Her hair rippled unbound down her back, and her skirts were hitched high enough so she could comfortably slide down sideways. Coming around the upstairs hall corner was the governess, Miss Childs, but she would be too late.

'Rosalie, don't!' Hugo said in a tone that brooked no nonsense.

'Oh, my goodness!' Annabell took a step forward just as the child launched herself downward.

Hugo lunged for the stairs. The child teetered precariously on the banister, nearly falling backwards. Hugo altered his course. Annabell saw him lurch and pain lanced across his features, then he was beneath Rosalie, who lost her balance and plunged over the edge. He caught her, going to his knees from the force of her impact.

'Oh, Hugo, Hugo,' Rosalie sobbed, fear making her childish voice higher than normal. Tears streamed down her face.

Annabell reached them as Hugo stroked the wild hair from the girl's face. 'Are you all right?' she asked, more concerned for him than she wanted to be.

He glanced at her, his green eyes dark with pain. 'Fine.' Turning his attention back to the child, he crooned, 'It's all right, Rosalie. I have you. You aren't hurt, are you?'

She shook her head, but the sobs continued.

Miss Childs rushed down the stairs, her eyes wide with shock. 'Rosalie, dear, let me see you.'

The girl shook her head. 'Stay with…hiccup…Hugo.' She burrowed into his arms.

Annabell understood perfectly. Hugo was a man who would keep a child—or a woman—safe.

Still holding Rosalie, he stood up, wincing as he shifted so that his weight was on his good leg. 'Hush, now, Rosalie. The more you cry, the worse you will make yourself feel. You are scared, not hurt.'

She nodded and hiccupped.

Juliet rushed into the hall from outside. 'I heard a scream.' She saw her daughter. 'Rosalie!' She hurried to the group and held out her arms for her child. Hugo handed Rosalie to her mother. 'Are you hurt, Rosalie?' After the girl shook her head, Juliet looked at Hugo. 'Thank you so much, Hugo. She slid down the banister, didn't she?'

'It is tempting,' he said with a grimace.

'You are hurt,' Annabell said to him, finally having seen enough. 'You should take care of yourself.'

He gave her an inscrutable look. 'A little. Nothing that won't heal.' But when he tried to walk, he winced again and stopped. 'Perhaps a little more than I thought.'

Butterfield, who had been hovering in the background, stepped forward. 'I have sent for Jamison, sir.'

'Thank you,' Hugo said, standing perfectly still. 'Why don't you take Rosalie upstairs, Juliet?'

Juliet frowned at her daughter, who still snuggled in her arms. 'I think Rosalie needs a lesson.' The child looked up, apprehension clear in her violet eyes. 'Yes, a lesson. I have told you repeatedly not to slide down that banister, haven't I?'

Rosalie nodded.

'But you did it anyway.'

'Yes,' the child said in a tiny voice.

'You could have been hurt very badly.'

Rosalie hung her head.

'I think you can spend the afternoon inside today and think about what you have done.'

There was no protest from Rosalie as Juliet carried her

up the stairs to the nursery. Annabell watched them go and sighed.

'I suppose you slid down the banister,' Sir Hugo said drily.

Annabell looked at him ruefully. 'Many times.'

'But you did not fall backwards.'

'No.'

'Sir Hugo,' Jamison said, interrupting them, 'what have you done this time?'

Hugo grimaced. 'I think I pulled the muscle the ball went into.'

Jamison clicked his tongue. 'Let's hope that's all you did. The last time you attempted some fool stunt, you were laid up for a month. Wounds like them don't ever completely heal back to normal.'

'Don't I know that,' Sir Hugo said.

'You've done this before?' Annabell asked, impressed that he had moved so quickly to save his half-sister despite knowing what it would do.

Jamison gave her a sour look. 'More times than he should have, my lady.'

'I do what I must,' Sir Hugo said in a flat voice that brooked no argument.

'That you do, sir,' Jamison said, putting an arm around his employer's shoulders. 'Lean on me and we'll get you into the library. I think a poultice is called for.'

Sir Hugo's fine mouth was a thin line by the time Jamison had his shoulder under Sir Hugo's arm. It thinned even more when they began moving. 'If you will excuse us?'

Annabell nearly laughed at his drollness, but sympathy quickly kept her from doing so. He was so obviously in a great deal of pain. 'Of course.'

She watched Hugo hobble away, supported by his valet. The man never ceased to amaze her and intrigue her. She had thought him too self-centred to jeopardise himself like he just had. And he had done it without a thought for himself. He would not have caught Rosalie if he had hesitated.

Her liking for him and attraction to him took on a deeper dimension. She admired him. This was not good. Not good at all unless she left here soon. Otherwise she feared she would weaken and do something about her feelings for him.

But what? Make love to him as he had already suggested so many times? Her stomach did somersaults at the idea and her heart pounded painfully against her ribs.

Perhaps?

Dinner was a desultory event. Hugo was in the library with a tray and Juliet, feeling badly that she had had to discipline Rosalie, had chosen to eat in her rooms. Susan and Mr Tatterly carried on a lively conversation, but Annabell didn't bother to follow it. Her thoughts were on her host.

As soon as dessert was served, she rose. 'Please excuse me. I want to look in on Sir Hugo and see how he is feeling.'

'He is in some pain, but I believe he said the poultice Jamison applied is helping,' Mr Tatterly said, standing while Annabell made her way to the door.

'Oh, dear,' Susan murmured. 'He was such a hero, saving poor little Rosalie, it is too bad he hurt himself.'

'True,' Mr Tatterly said, 'but that is the way he is. That wasn't the first time he's risked himself for someone else.'

Annabell paused, arrested by Mr Tatterly's words. 'Really?'

He nodded. 'Oh, yes, Lady Fenwick-Clyde. That is how he got the wound in the first place. He won't tell you.'

'But you will, surely,' she prompted.

He turned a dull red in embarrassment. 'Probably shouldn't. He doesn't like the story told, but—' he gave her a speculative look '—I will.'

She moved back to the table and took her seat so he could sit. 'Please do.'

'Oh, yes,' Susan added her encouragement.

'Right.' Mr Tatterly took a deep breath. 'It was at Waterloo. You know he was shot there.' Both women nodded. 'Well, he was shot by a Frenchie while he, Sir Hugo, stood guard over Jamison. Jamison had been knocked unconscious by the concussion of a cannon blast and Sir Hugo had been determined not to leave him and several other men. But Sir Hugo was alone, his horse having thrown him and bolted because of the same blast, and he couldn't carry all three men to safety. So he stayed until help arrived. He ran out of ammunition and a Frenchman shot him in the leg. Fortunately for us, the Frenchman came in for the kill and Sir Hugo is more than handy with a sword. Ran the man through and took his ammunition.'

Annabell's mouth rounded in admiration and awe. 'That is incredible.'

'Oh, my. Oh, my,' Susan said. 'I would have never thought it of him.' She realised what she'd said and blushed. 'That is, I believe him capable, but he is such a hedonist that one doesn't think of him putting himself in danger for someone else. That isn't very comfortable.'

'No,' Mr Tatterly said. 'It isn't comfortable, but that is Sir Hugo. He likes his creature comforts all right, but he also has courage. Don't ever try to mistreat someone when he is around. He will put you down with a word or with his fists. He believes in standing up for what he believes in.'

Annabell realised her chest felt tight and her eyes burned. There was so much more to Sir Hugo—Hugo—than she had seen or even imagined. She rose slowly.

'Thank you for telling us, Mr Tatterly. It was very enlightening.'

He gave her a grim smile. 'I hoped it would be, my lady.'

Something in his tone made her look closely at him. If

she didn't know better, she would think he had done it on purpose to show her another facet of Sir Hugo. The expression on his solid face implied that he had done it for that reason.

She smiled at him. 'I am even more interested now in seeing how Sir Hugo is doing.'

'Give him our regards,' Susan said. 'We will be in there shortly. He would probably like a good game of whist to occupy his time, don't you think, Mr Tatterly?'

Annabell didn't hear what Mr Tatterly replied, but she picked up her step. She would warn Sir Hugo of the treat in store for him.

Chapter Eight

Annabell entered the library expecting to see Hugo in his favourite chair. She was not surprised. The only difference was that his bad leg was propped on an ottoman.

'How are you feeling?' she asked, moving toward him.

He eyed her. 'About what I expected.'

She reached him and choked. 'What is that awful smell?'

He grimaced. 'That is the poultice Jamison put on me.'

'What is in it?'

'The same thing one would use for a horse's sprain.'

'Certainly you jest?' She dug her handkerchief from inside the small puff sleeve of her dress and held it to her nose. 'That is barbarous.'

He smiled wryly. 'Perhaps. But Jamison's philosophy is that if the medicine is good enough for the horse then it is good enough for me.'

'I find that hard to believe.'

He shrugged. 'Have it your way, but it is true nonetheless.'

She gave him a lopsided grin. 'It definitely does not do anything for your appeal.'

His face took on an arrested look. 'Do I take that to mean you find me appealing?'

She felt heat creep up her neck. The urge to evade his

question was strong, but that was not what she really wanted. She had come in here to tell him how much she admired his earlier actions. She was not going to let her nerve fail her.

She licked her dry lips. 'I… Yes, that is what it meant. What you did earlier was remarkable.'

'And until then I was just a rake?'

There was an edge to his voice that told her he was not all that happy to hear the reason for her reversal of opinion about him. She tilted her head and studied him.

'I suppose that was rather arrogant of me to assume you would be happy to know my opinion of you is improving.' She paused before adding, 'Or that it took such a painful action on your part to bring it about.'

He shifted as though his leg irritated him. 'I had hoped you were interested in me before this afternoon. I am not any different than I was yesterday or the day before.'

'No, you aren't.' He was not making this easy. It was almost as though he resented her thinking better of him because he had saved Rosalie. 'But yesterday and the days before, I didn't know this side of your personality.'

'I believe we have had a similar discussion before,' he said drily. 'You seem to continually find it amazing that I am more than a drunken wastrel.'

She sighed, beginning to take affront at his belligerence. 'Perhaps you are in great discomfort and that is why you are behaving like a boor.'

He snorted. 'No more pain than earlier today. I am merely curious that you can change your opinion of me so readily.'

She stood. 'Well, so am I. Still, I am willing to admit that I might have misjudged you. You could at least give me credit for that.'

His eyes softened. 'You are right. I have not portrayed myself in the best light. Suffice that I wanted you to know the worst.'

'Before…'

But she could not finish the sentence. She could barely finish the thought. *Before we become lovers.*

She shivered in the heated room. Just the thought of making love with him scared her at the same time that it excited her.

How had she come to this? Just because she had seen him put another before himself?

She stood abruptly. 'I am tired, Hugo—Sir Hugo. I will see you in the morning.'

She fled the room before he could follow up on her unfinished statement. She was not ready to deal with the progression of their relationship. Not yet.

Hugo watched her escape the room and smiled. He knew what she had left unspoken, and he knew that soon they would be lovers. He only wished the idea did not cause the breath to catch painfully in his throat.

Annabell reached her bedroom, locked the door behind herself and wished she could as easily lock away her burgeoning feelings for Sir Hugo Fitzsimmon. She tossed the key on to a table in passing and paced to the end of the room before turning and retracing her steps.

Tension ate at her spine. She wanted to make love to the man. She was half in love with the man. She froze.

Surely not. Desire and love were not the same thing… only for her they seemed irrevocably intertwined.

What was she thinking? She was crazy, a Bedlamite to have even intimated they would become lovers—to even be considering it. Where was her vaunted freedom from involvement with the opposite sex? Where was her sense of self-preservation?

Gone up in the flames Hugo always ignited in her body. And her mind must have gone with it.

She threw herself on to a chair and stared at the wall.

Her emotions were raw and on the surface. Her need for

what Hugo offered was to the point where she knew if she walked away from him, she would always wonder what she had let go. A silly, stupid idea, but there it was.

She wanted to make love with Hugo Fitzsimmon. She wanted to have the memory of him touching her, loving her. More than anything, she wanted him to erase the memory of Fenwick-Clyde, something she knew he could do.

She jumped to her feet, determined to seek him out before she changed her mind and lost her courage. It was now or never. Or wait until the next time he tried to seduce her. But she did not want to wait.

Annabell took a deep breath that did nothing to calm her trepidation. What if he sent her away? How mortifying. Even worse, it would mean he didn't want her. Not only mortifying, but so painful that the possibility of his rejection did not bear thinking upon.

Funny, that a woman with her independent streak could contemplate giving her body to him even as she tried to keep her soul free. She was not sure she could give one without the other. Yet, she did not want to love Sir Hugo, to have him mean more to her than her freedom.

She only wanted to share his bed. Just once.

She had given Fenwick-Clyde her body because she had had no choice. They had been married and she had been under law to provide him whatever he wanted of her physically. Nothing in the world would have induced her to give her dead husband that which she contemplated giving Hugo... Her heart?

Her heart.

The enormity of what she was about to do swamped her. She stopped. She shook. Her pulse thundered in her ears.

How could she think she was giving Sir Hugo her heart? She was only giving him her body. She did not love him. Could not love him. Could she? Did she dare?

Her shaking increased. Her chest rose and fell in rapid, shallow breaths. Surely not.

Enough. He wanted her. She wanted him. That was all that mattered.

She went to her door, opened it and slipped outside. The hall was cold and dimly lit. Everyone must have gone to bed. She had spent more time pacing and agonising than she had realised. She moved forwards.

Minutes later, she stood motionless in front of his door where anyone passing by would see her. She smoothed her moist palms down the fine satin of her evening gown and told herself to stop overreacting. Everyone had gone to bed. She raised her clenched hand to knock and paused. What if someone heard? Did she dare enter without announcing herself? Did she dare risk someone else knowing what was happening? Neither choice was good.

And if he answered? Would that be any better? All her doubts and fears swept over her like a tidal wave crashing to shore. She swayed in indecision.

'Hello?' Hugo's voice came from the other side of the thick oak door.

His words were like being doused with a jug of ice water. She heard the discomfort he now took no effort to hide. He was in no condition for what she contemplated, even if what she had come here for was something they should be doing. And he was not alone. And she was a fool.

As though awakening from a dream where she had seen paradise and then had it taken away, she turned away. She had been right earlier. She belonged in Bedlam, not Sir Hugo's bed.

She was a widow and he was a rake. They had no future together. She had never engaged in a relationship just for the pleasure. She had never slept with any man but her husband.

This was too huge a step for her to take.

She retraced her footsteps. She locked her door once more, and this time she put the key to her room on the very top of the wardrobe. Perhaps if she had to make an effort to let herself out, she would stop and think more clearly. She could only hope.

But he was a great temptation, and she was learning just how weak she was.

Annabell woke with the sun the next day. She had barely slept, tossing and turning, until she dozed. Now she felt exhausted and had a headache that she knew would be with her all day. She dragged herself from bed. The maid would be here with hot chocolate soon. The way she felt, a tot of Sir Hugo's ever-present brandy would be welcome.

She ran her fingers through the tangle of her hair, having forgotten to braid it the night before, and told herself that succumbing to Sir Hugo's brandy was nearly as bad as succumbing to the man himself. The maid chose that moment to knock.

Thankful for the interruption to her disturbing thoughts, Annabell called, 'Come in.'

The doorknob twisted, and only then did Annabell remember she had locked herself in and put the key on top of the wardrobe. She pulled the chair to the piece of furniture, climbed on top of the cushions and found the key. Before letting the maid in, she put the chair back in its spot. No sense the entire household knowing where she had hidden the key. Coupled with her locking the door in the first place, that would precipitate more talk about her eccentricity than there already was.

Unlocking the door, Annabell said, 'Thank you, Sally.'

The young maid bobbed a curtsy as she entered. She cast a look around. 'Here, my lady. I'll just pick up your gown, if you please.'

The gown was the mauve silk she had worn last night and left lying on the floor after coming back from Hugo's room. She had never been neat except in her antiquities work. She sighed. 'Thank you, Sally.'

The girl smiled. 'Shall I help you dress, my lady?' She

flushed at her temerity. 'I ain't a fancy French lady's maid, but—'

'You will do just fine. I've never had any use for a lady's maid to begin with. If you will just help hook the dress in the middle of my back where I have difficulty reaching, that will be more than enough.'

'Yes, my lady.' Sally bobbed another curtsy.

After the girl was gone, Annabelle quickly twisted her silvery blonde hair into braids and secured them on her head before studying herself. Her dress was serviceable. Grey kerseymere cut loosely. She had not put on her harem pants because… She frowned at herself. Why had she not put them on? She had not made a conscious decision not to, she just hadn't thought to. Was this another example of her indecision about Hugo, not being able to dress in her normal working attire?

She twisted away from her reflection. She was totally confused about what she wanted.

She stalked to the door and threw it open just in time to see her nemesis leaving his room. He turned to look at her, his gaze catching her attention and holding her captive.

'What a fetching gown.'

His murmured voice seemed to caress her even though the upward curve of his sensual lips told her he did not think the dress was fetching at all. Yet his eyes told her he didn't care what she wore.

She frowned, as irritated with him as she was with herself. 'I dare say you tell all the women that, regardless of how they look.'

He shrugged. 'Why not? Anything else only hurts their sensibilities.'

'Honesty.'

He raised one dark brow. 'Sometimes it is better to compliment than to denigrate.'

She moved toward him. 'You are the one always harping about honesty.'

He watched her. 'In emotions and intent. I never lie about what I plan to do or how I feel about something.'

She stopped near enough to him that she could see the fine lines of dissipation that radiated from his eyes and the slight tension around his mouth. Suddenly their bickering was not worth the energy and ill will.

'Are you still in pain?'

He laughed. 'Changing the subject?'

She shrugged, but returned his smile with a small one of her own. 'I suppose I am. It just suddenly seemed so trivial to be arguing about a compliment when you are likely still in pain from yesterday.'

'We are back to my heroism, I see.'

'Is that so bad?'

'No.'

He spoke so softly she only knew what he said by the movement of his lips, lips that could move so expertly over her own. Her eyes widened even as his narrowed.

'Did you come to my door last night?' His words were barely a whisper, meant only for her.

Shock erased her arousal of seconds before. 'Of course not.'

'No?' That eyebrow rose again. 'I thought I heard a sound outside my room. It was too late for a servant and Jamison was with me.' He continued to watch her.

She felt a flush rise from her neck to her cheeks. 'I am not so craven as to come that far and then retreat.'

'Aren't you?'

The collar of her gown was suddenly too tight, and she could no longer meet his eyes. 'Oh, very well,' she said ungraciously. 'I did come to your door. I meant to see how you were doing.'

'But you had seen that just hours before in the library.'

She studied him and wondered how long she could skirt his questions, or if she even wanted to. Just as she wondered how long she could continue to deny her own attraction to him. She was in uncharted territory and didn't know what to do.

His eyes darkened. 'You came to my room for a different reason, didn't you?'

She continued to look at him, knowing she should say something, but not able to. This was all so much more complicated than she had ever imagined. She did not plan the words that tumbled from her mouth.

'Yes. I wanted… I wanted…' She twisted away so she would not have to see his face. 'I don't know what I wanted.'

His hands touched her shoulders, his fingers warm and firm through the kerseymere dress. He did not try to turn her, only spoke gently to her. 'You want me to make love to you, Annabell. You want to know what it is like between a man and woman who desire each other and want to give each other pleasure.'

She took a deep shuddering breath, aware on a bone-deep level that she felt as though a great burden had been lifted. His words, so blunt and truthful, spoke directly to the core of who she was. He understood her.

She nodded, still unable to turn back to him. 'Yes. More than I ever imagined possible.'

The sound of a heel on the carpet came from behind them. They jumped apart and Annabell whirled around. Desire still etched furrows in Sir Hugo's cheeks. Annabell felt like a small child caught doing something unspeakable. Her breath wheezed through a painfully tight throat.

Juliet Fitzsimmon rounded the corner from the stairs and stopped. 'Good morning, Annabell. Hugo.' She looked searchingly at her stepson and then her guest. 'It seems I came along at an inopportune time, but that will happen when private matters are discussed in public places.'

'So true.' Hugo's voice was dry, his gaze on Annabell.

Mortified at how close they had come to being discovered, Annabell spoke hastily. 'I must be on my way.' She paused. 'I am sorry for having put you in the position of having to find us this way.'

Juliet looked at her. 'Sometimes the heart is stronger than our sense of caution, Annabell. I am glad I was the one to come around the corner.'

'You are a true friend,' Annabell murmured as she left.

Hugo watched Annabell walk away before turning to Juliet. 'It seems we are becoming indiscreet. My apologies.'

Juliet put her slender white fingers on Hugo's arm. 'Do not break her heart, Hugo. She does not deserve it.'

He scowled down at his stepmother. 'I have no intentions of doing so.'

'Then your intentions are honourable?'

His scowl deepened. 'Lady Fenwick-Clyde is a widow and knows what she is about, Juliet. Just as you are.'

His stepmother's pale complexion pinkened. 'You always know exactly what to say, Hugo, to stop someone from prying when it is none of their business to begin with. I hope you know what you are about this time.' She walked away without waiting for his reply.

Hugo watched Juliet disappear down the hall that suddenly seemed to lead to everyone's bedchamber. Much as he did not like to agree with what she had said, Juliet had spoken truly. He just was not going to let her words influence him. This was between him and Annabell and to hell with everyone else.

Annabell reached the front hall, feeling as though she had just escaped from mortal danger. Emotional danger. Her mouth twisted. She had never considered herself fanciful, but the things Hugo made her feel were frightening to someone who never wanted to be controlled by another person.

'My lady,' Butterfield intoned. 'A letter.'

Annabell jumped, not having seen him approach because she was too engrossed in her worries. 'Oh, thank you.'

She managed to smile and take the letter, thankful Hugo had not witnessed the incident. He would know her preoccupation was because of what had just occurred between them. She glanced down at the letter, the delicate writing and franking telling her it was from her new sister-in-law, Felicia, Viscountess Chillings.

Eager for news about her family, Annabell moved instinctively to the library where she could read in comfort and privacy. Sitting in her favourite chintz chair, she peeled off the wax seal and unfolded the single sheet of thick vellum.

Dearest Bell,

I would not write this, but I need to share my thoughts with someone and I do not think Guy could easily deal with my worries. He was too afraid of losing me and the babe from the beginning.

The breath caught in Annabell's throat. Something horrible must have happened for the normally calm Felicia to write this. And the next words were blurred by what had been tears.

Adam is sick. The physician says it is merely croup, but my baby coughs day and night and is not eating well. I know I am being silly, but seeing him this way makes me worry that something will happen to him. Absolutely silly. Absolutely. But…

The rest of the letter was about other family matters, the disreputable Damien and what a wonderful husband Guy was. Annabell smiled. Felicia understood so much about the two brothers. Her sister-in-law ended with love and a request for a reply.

Annabell set the paper down and gazed at nothing. Croup was not unusual in babies, and the physician they called would be the best. Probably Prinny's own, and what was good enough for the Prince of Wales should be good enough for the future Viscount Chillings. And Felicia and Guy would give their son all the love and attention a baby needed. Likely, Adam was perfectly fine by now since Felicia had written the letter two days ago.

Still, Felicia's worry made Annabell's heart hurt. Felicia had lost her two children from her first marriage because of an ice skating accident several years ago. Although Felicia had had amnesia when she first came into their lives and had not remembered who she was or the children she had lost, she had been consciously aware of a deep hurt. Annabell understood how something, anything might make Felicia worry about this child. And she had been right in saying Guy would have difficulty if his wife openly worried because it had been constant torture for Guy during the delivery, having lost his first wife and heir in childbirth. Life was so fragile, and sometimes too short.

Annabell took a deep breath, surprised at her last thought, and felt unexpected tears well up. She wiped them away, appalled at her maudlin reaction. Her emotions were all twisted up. She had not consciously thought about how long life was or wasn't since her parents' untimely death in a boating accident.

But life was short.

The library door opened and closed, and, without looking, she knew Hugo had come in. There was a sense of electricity in the air—and his scent of cinnamon.

She folded the paper and made herself smile as she stood to face him. 'I was just leaving.'

He studied her, not moving from the door so that she could exit. 'What is wrong?'

Her gaze skipped away. He was too perceptive. Would he understand her upset when she didn't really understand it herself? She sighed and looked back at him.

'I have a letter from Felicia—my new sister-in-law.

The…' She stopped to clear the catch in her throat. 'It seems baby Adam has the croup and Felicia is worried. Not that there is really anything to worry about,' she added hastily. 'Croup is so much a part of being a baby. I dare say Felicia isn't getting enough sleep and the tiredness is making her more emotional about the situation.'

Instead of the cynical curve of lips she expected, Hugo crossed the room to her. 'And you are worried too.'

He was so close that cinnamon seemed to surround her, and she could feel the heat from his body. She wished he hadn't got near enough that a step—just a tiny little step— would put her in his arms. He did not want to comfort her in his embrace, as she wanted right now, he wanted to seduce her. Two totally different goals.

'Yes. Silly as it seems, her letter made me think how short life can be.' Her voice became little more than a whisper. 'She lost her two children by her first husband in an accident. Felicia will never forget.'

'No mother would.' Hugo's voice was as quiet as hers, and his arms gathered her in.

She went, knowing it was a mistake, but no longer wanting to resist. He was gentle, his hands cradling her back. He made no move to kiss her, only held her.

She revelled in the feel of him and the security his solid chest gave her. For a brief moment, she let herself sink into his warmth before pushing away.

'And I am not even a mother, just a silly woman who has let her emotions get the better of her. Adam is not even in danger. I am merely reacting to Felicia's worry.'

He let her go, but did not step away from her. He made her do that. 'You are the furthest from silly that I have ever encountered in a woman. You let your head rule your emotions nearly all the time. You must be tired.'

Her eyes narrowed, wondering if he was jesting with her or serious. 'Why would I be tired?'

He shrugged. 'I don't know, Annabell. I only know I've never seen you distraught over anything.'

She moved, realising she had not put any real distance between them. 'It is past time for me to be getting to work. I have much to do and the sooner I do it, the sooner I will be out of your way.'

He stepped aside for her with an ironic bow that made him grimace. 'As you say.'

Concern lined the space between her brows. 'You are in no condition to be making bows yet.' She sniffed. 'And where is that nasty-smelling poultice Jamison made to help you heal faster?'

A smile hovered over his full lips. 'He is making me a fresh one.'

'A more potent one.' She shuddered. 'Do not come near me when you are wearing it, please.'

He laughed outright. 'Obviously, Jamison's ministrations do nothing for my appeal.'

She shook her had. 'Absolutely nothing.'

He sobered instantly. 'That is unfortunate.'

Her eyes widened as she realised his mood had changed instantly, like a storm that had hovered in the distance and finally blew in without warning. No longer comforting, he was now flirting.

'I must be leaving.'

This time, she did not wait or hesitate at the pinching around his mouth created by his movement as she skirted past him. He was too dangerous to her sensibilities. First he seduced her with desire, then he seduced her with concern for her feelings. He was too skilled for her.

Hugo watched her escape, for that was what she did, and smiled. She was much more susceptible to him than she wanted to admit, and it was making her emotions raw. Like her, he knew croup was likely not dangerous to the baby, and he believed that normally she would not have been so upset. But he also knew she was undecided about what to do about him and the sensations he created in her.

He limped over to his favourite chair and sank gratefully into the cushion. He lifted his injured leg with a sigh, wondering briefly if he would be up to making love to Annabell when she finally decided their joining was inevitable.

He only wished she would realise soon that they were meant to be together. Or did he? He grimaced as his old wound knotted. Kneading the muscle, he knew he hoped it would be soon and be damned to his injury.

Chapter Nine

Late that night, exhausted by an intentionally long day digging, Annabell took refuge in her room from the activity still going on in the drawing room. Susan and Mr Tatterly had got Lady Fitzsimmon and Sir Hugo to play cards. The last thing Annabell felt like doing was watching Hugo try to control his exasperation with Susan, who was blithely unaware that she constantly irritated the man.

Annabell dug her portable writing desk from the trunk where she had packed it when it had seemed she was to relocate to the inn. It seemed eons ago, but was only days. Sinking into the nearest chair, she settled the desk on her lap and took a thick sheet of paper from under the hinged top and dipped her quill in ink.

She wasn't sure what to say to Felicia. Her first inclination was to make light of Adam's problem and tell Felicia not to worry, but she knew that would not help her sister-in-law. Felicia had written because she had needed someone to share her fears with, not someone to tell her they were unfounded. The woman had already lost two children—any threat, serious or not, to Adam would be enough to cause near panic. And Guy would be no better than his wife if Felicia tried to confide her fears to him because of his previous loss.

Annabell sighed and laid her quill down. Who was she to say Felicia was overreacting? Life could be too short. She had seen that often enough. Her parents. And even Hugo. He might have died at Waterloo instead of becoming a hero and knighted for his bravery. Many men had died during that battle.

Hugo. What if something happened to him? Not that anything would, but what if? What if he were thrown by a horse? That wasn't uncommon, and his thigh often caused him to hesitate just as his leg went over his mount's back. It might also cause him to land badly.

Her heart clenched painfully. *Stop it!* She closed her eyes, trying to close her mind to the possibilities.

The mantel clock struck the half-hour. Annabell opened her eyes and stared at the timepiece. Hugo would be in his chambers by now. He would have escaped the cards as soon as possible.

She wanted him. She wanted what only he could give her.

As though walking in a dream, her actions already planned, she set the writing desk on the floor and stood. She took a deep breath and ran her damp palms down the sides of her dress. She would go to him. It was what she wanted to do, what she had nearly done last night.

She moved to the door and inched it open, belatedly worrying about someone being in the hallway. Life might be too short to deny herself and Hugo the pleasure of loving one another, but it could be all too long if her reputation were ruined.

Not seeing anyone, she slipped into the hall. The sconces were still lit, throwing her shadow against the wall. She moved swiftly and quietly.

She stopped at Hugo's door. Breathing deeply, wondering if she was going to faint from nervousness, she raised her hand and tapped lightly with her knuckles. Her heart pounded so loudly, a herd of horses could have come down the hall and she would not have heard them. When there was no answer, she gripped the door handle, telling herself he had invited her to his room so many times he would not mind her letting herself in.

She slid inside and shut the door behind herself, her chest rising and falling like a bellows. Her gaze darted around the room until she located the bed. It was empty. She scanned the room slowly this time. It was empty. He wasn't here.

She slumped against the solid wood of the door at her back. The butterflies that had rioted through her blood disappeared as though they had never been. Disappointment was a rock in her stomach.

She sighed. All her trepidation, all her strength of purpose needed to come here, and he was still playing cards. She giggled at the release of tension and to keep herself from crying. Until now, feeling this keen disappointment, she had not realised just how much she truly wanted to make love with Hugo. She had known she wanted to, but this bone-aching, heart-wrenching need seemed too big for her body to contain.

She took a deep shuddering breath and pushed away from the door, intending to leave. She stopped and turned back around. She could wait for him. There was no place else for him to go at this time of night. He would be here eventually.

So would his valet. She did not want the servant, or anyone else, to know she was here. She shook her head sadly. No, she couldn't wait for him. If he had already been here and the valet dismissed, that would have been different. She could have left before daylight and no one would have been the wiser. She had to go.

She took one last look around his room, as though a part of her thought Hugo might be hiding somewhere. The walls were golden, the furniture finely carved and heavy. The carpet under her feet was thick and well cushioned. The fire roared in the grate and a small brazier stood by the bed to heat that area. Everything was neatly in its spot or folded. She knew from her own experience that not even the best servant could keep a room this immaculate if the person who lived here wasn't fastidious.

A smile lifted one corner of her mouth. She was such an untidy person, who left things lying where they fell or where she last put them. She looked once more around his room, noting his dressing robe folded neatly over the back of the chair nearest the fire so it would be warm when he put it on. Several books lay on a table near the same chair. Each spine was centred on the one below it. In some ways, Hugo was her exact opposite.

A gilt Louis XIV clock chimed the hour, its high tinkle disconcerting in the quiet room. Annabell started. She had been here too long.

Still bemused by her discoveries, of herself and Hugo, she cracked open his door, made sure no one was about and slid into the hall. She ran to her own room, heart pounding, and slipped inside.

She collapsed onto the chair she had climbed on just the night before to hide her bedchamber key atop the wardrobe. Her hands shook. Her chest rose and fell as she dragged in air, more winded by her emotions than her exertion. She was also exhilarated.

She realised with no real surprise that she was going to go back to Hugo's room. She was going to make love with him. She was going to take this chance to be happy, to be a woman experiencing one of life's greatest pleasures. Life was too short not to. But he wasn't there yet. She would reply to Felicia's letter while she waited.

Once more she gathered her writing desk and set it on her lap. She took a deep breath to calm herself and dipped a quill in ink and started.

Dearest Felicia,

I hope this finds Adam much better. I will not make light of your fears. I know how you love him and worry about him, as does Guy. I also know you will not leave him alone and that he will receive the best care possible and your love will surround him, giving him strength. My thoughts are with you. If you need me, I can be there in a day.

Love, Bell

She had written from the heart. She sanded the paper and quickly folded it and sealed it. She would ask the butler to see that it was posted. She set her desk on the floor and stared at the fire.

Annabell thought about what she had written. She had written about love and its power to make even the toughest situation somehow bearable. We give love to others no matter what the risk to ourselves. She had loved her parents and lost them. She loved Guy and Damien and now Felicia and Adam. She would risk anything for them.

But why was she risking her reputation to go to Hugo? Because she desired him? Because he made her blood course hotly through her body until she thought she would burst into flames for the want of him?

Because as she got to know him better, she found she liked him better? She sighed. She even admired him. He was a rake and a womaniser, but he was not callous about it. Nor did he lie. And he risked himself for those he loved, as he had demonstrated with Rosalie. And even more amply when he had stood guard over his valet at Waterloo.

If she denied herself this opportunity for happiness with Hugo, she feared the chance would never come again.

The mantel clock that had chimed hours ago chimed again. It was one in the morning. Surely Hugo was in his room by now—and alone?

Suddenly calm for the first time in days, Annabell rose. This time she would not turn back. With a determined tread, she went to her door and into the now-unlit hall. The candles in the wall sconces had been snuffed. Even the servants were abed.

She made her way as quietly as possible across the small distance that separated her room from Hugo's. Her breathing was the loudest noise in her ears. She grimaced. Though she had made this journey twice already, she was still scared.

He had asked her to his room and to be his lover often enough that she should feel confident. But she did not. She had never had a lover. And she was the one making the final move.

She stopped, but only for an instant. She wanted this. Either she went to him tonight or she waited for him to ask her again. She did not want to wait. She covered the rest of the distance to his room.

Annabell took another shuddering breath and reached for the doorknob. Her fingers shook as she twisted the brass lever. Her entire body trembled as she slipped into Hugo's bedchamber.

The fire still simmered in the grate, giving the room a warmth that normally was not present during this time of year. Hugo pampered himself.

The curtains at the window were open and the full moon spilled through the tiny diamond glass panes in a river of silver prisms to the floor. Light fell across the bed where Hugo lay, raised on one elbow watching her. His eyes met hers.

She shifted her gaze, unable to meet the intensity of his. Half his face was in shadow, the other was outlined in harsh angles of cheek, jaw and enticing mouth. His shoulders and chest rose from the bed in firm delineation against the dusky sheets beneath him.

The linens draped dangerously low on his hips. His lean, muscular hips. She swallowed.

'Annabell?'

His voice was deep and raspy and made her insides turn to lava. Then he threw aside the sheet and rose. He was naked. Somehow, she was not surprised.

Annabell reached for the back of a nearby chair to support her suddenly weak legs. He was everything she had ever imagined a man could be. More.

The fire turned his right side to burnished copper. The moon silvered his left. His muscles rippled with each movement. He was magnificent.

Dark hair fell over his forehead in waves of reckless abandon. His shoulders swayed just a little, just enough to draw attention to how broad and well formed they were. His torso tapered into narrow hips, leading to strong, muscular thighs and calves that needed no padding for their shape.

'Annabell?' he said again, moving inexorably toward her.

'Hugo,' she managed to say around the constriction in her throat.

She collapsed into the chair she had recently used for support. What was she doing here? She belonged in Bedlam. And yet…

He reached her and squatted down in front of her. His face level with hers, his bare knees brushing hers through the fabric of her dress, she saw him wince. His wound.

'Oh, Hugo,' she said, her voice a hoarse whisper, 'I should not be here. You are still hurting.'

His firm lips formed a seductive, wry smile. 'Only a little, Annabell.'

'Are you sure?' She barely got the words out, her throat was so tight. He smelled of cinnamon and brandy and desire.

She glanced to the inside of his thigh, where the wound was, and her hand reached instinctively to touch the scar. But it was too close to another part of his body, a part that was more than ready for her visit. She felt a rush of hot blood.

'What are you doing here?' He had seen her glance, and now his voice was hoarse.

There was a look of hunger in his eyes as they met hers without wavering. His mouth, that temptation that haunted her dreams, quirked up at one corner. She reached out without conscious thought and lightly, oh, so lightly, touched the left corner of his lips with her right index finger. This was much safer than touching that other part of him, no matter how she longed to do so. Carefully, she traced the outline of his mouth. He let her, the only evidence that he felt her touch being the sudden stiffness of his jaw. The need in his gaze intensified.

He caught her hand and held it away from his face. 'Annabell, don't start something you have no intention of seeing through to the finish.'

She let him keep her hand in his. 'I know what I'm doing, Hugo.'

'Are you sure?'

'If you are sure the pain from your wound will not be too much.'

She did not want him to hurt when he made love to her. She wanted him to enjoy it as much as she knew she would.

His mouth twisted. 'Look at me, Annabell, where you did before.'

Aghast at his bluntness, she hesitated. But only for a second. She wanted to do more than look at him there, she wanted to touch him there. She licked her dry lips.

'And?' she managed to ask.

'Do I look like a man who cares about anything other than you being here?'

A small laugh of sheer surprise and something else escaped her. 'No, you don't.'

Instead of answering her, he rose, pulling her with him. His gaze never left her face as he bent and lifted her into his arms.

'Your leg.'

He shook his head. 'To hell with my leg, Annabell.' He carried her to the bed and laid her down.

She watched him, nearly paralysed by what she was doing, what they were about to do. She had wanted this for weeks, since the first time he kissed her. Yet, the enormity of what she was about to do nearly overwhelmed her.

He laid on his side beside her, propped up on his left arm, his bare flesh gleaming in the pale light from the window. She turned to face him, still fully clothed.

'We'll go slowly.' His voice was thick with desire and his eyes were nearly black with his arousal.

'Not too slowly.' She did not think she could bear to have what they were about to do take forever. She had been anticipating it too long already.

He smiled. 'Eager?'

She couldn't smile. 'Yes.'

He traced the line of her chin to her jaw and up to her ear with one finger. Shivers chased down her spine. No man had ever touched her so gently, so erotically. Then his hand slipped into her hair and she felt him pull the pins out one by one and saw him toss them to the floor.

'You have beautiful hair,' he murmured. 'I want to bury myself in it.' He dug his fingers into her curls and spread her hair out on the pillow behind her head. 'Lovely.'

Unable to lay passively, Annabell followed his lead. She took hold of his waving hair and combed her fingers through the thick satin.

He grinned at her. 'Shall we play follow the leader?'

'Yes,' she whispered.

He laughed outright, the sound joyous and sexy and incredibly arousing. 'Who is the leader?'

'You,' she said without hesitation.

'My pleasure.' His eyes turned slumberous. 'This time.'

His hand left her hair and travelled down her neck to the edge of her bodice. The fine linen of her nightdress was nearly transparent and cut just below where her breasts began to swell. He traced the line of fine fabric with his finger, followed with his tongue, then with his lips. She felt alternately hot and cold as his mouth caressed her sensitive skin. Her fingers flexed in the thickness of his hair, holding him to her.

He moved to a nipple and nipped it through the thin material of the bodice. She gasped as lightning jolted to her loins. As though he sensed her reaction, he took the sensitive nub into his mouth and sucked long and strong until she thought he pulled a string that directly connected her breast to her womb.

He looked up at her, a knowing gleam in his eyes. 'This is just the beginning,' he promised.

'Just the beginning,' she said so softly she barely heard herself.

Her fingers fluttered along the smooth expanse of his shoulders. She wanted to dig her nails into his muscles and urge him closer, but she knew he intended to take this slowly. Agonisingly slow. She closed her eyes with a sigh.

His hand cupped her left breast, his mouth still caressing the other one. The fine wool of her robe and finer linen of her chemise were all that separated his flesh from hers. She could feel his heat like a brand. Or maybe that was her skin that burned because of his touch. His thumb found her nipple and flicked across it, creating a friction that made her want him to do other things to her. Deeper, more penetrating things. He squeezed and rubbed until she felt as though the centre of her being was intimately connected to her bosom and that what he did to one would be instantly, crashingly felt by the other.

He moved on. She felt as though paradise had been instantly taken away.

'Oh,' she breathed, 'don't stop.'

He chuckled low in his throat. 'That was only the beginning. I have much more to show you.'

She released a shuddering breath and came back to hover

on the edge of sanity. Vaguely she knew it was her turn. She was to do to him whatever he did to her, but his hand was smoothing down her hip, kneading and caressing as it went, leaving fire in its wake down her outer thigh. His fingers caught at the thin material of her gown and pulled it inexorably up until she felt the warm air of the room on her bare skin.

She licked suddenly dry lips and opened her eyes. He stared at her, his gaze intense and questioning. Without his saying so, she knew he was giving her one last chance to flee, to stop this madness they were embarked on.

She lifted her face to his and caught his head with her hands and pulled him to her. His kiss was fire and ice and heat and passion and everything she had ever imagined it would be, everything it had always been and more. But it was not gentle. The gentleness was gone now that need rode them like a demon.

She met his demand with everything in her. Her tongue darted out to meet and dance with his. Her lips slanted to give him better access to her moist warmth. She revelled when he accepted everything she offered and gave her back more in return.

She could feel his heart beating hard and fast against hers. She felt his chest rise and fall with each ragged breath he took. His fingers clenched against the skin of her outer thigh.

'Help me,' she muttered. 'Too many clothes.'

He chuckled and his fingers were everywhere. Before she could appreciate how skilled he was, her robe was on the floor with her nightdress beside it.

He rose above her before easing himself down so his chest crushed her breasts. His skin was hot and rough against the tender flesh of her bosom. Looking down at her, his eyes slumberous with passion, he began to rub against her. The wiry hairs that spread across his chest scraped and tickled her nipples, making the buds harden in exquisite delight.

When she was hot and needy and thinking she could take no more, he lowered his mouth to hers and hungrily took her lips and her moans. She wanted him to never stop. His hands spread her legs apart and she wanted him to sink completely into her.

'Please, now, Hugo. Now.'

She wanted this more than she had ever wanted anything. She lifted her legs to give him access. She shifted her hands to his hips and pulled him to her.

He deepened the kiss and slid into her. She gasped and he swallowed the sound. He moved slowly and he swallowed her moan of desire. He lodged fully inside her until it felt as though he touched her very soul.

He released her mouth and rose up on his hands to look where their bodies joined. She felt him spasm.

'Ah,' he murmured, 'I have wanted to see this for so long and to feel it for longer still.'

He turned his attention to her face and began to move slowly again. He teased her with mounting pleasure, never taking his gaze from her face.

She watched him with equal avidity. The angles of his jaw were razor sharp. His beautiful mouth was pulled back against his teeth as though he was in great pain, but she knew differently. His pupils dilated until the clear green of his irises was nearly gone. And still he moved slowly, yet each thrust was full and penetrated to the point where she gasped from tiny bursts of delight.

With each steady, slow entry he moved his hips so her pleasure increased. She thought she would explode.

She gasped and let out a low scream of release. He stayed motionless inside her until she relaxed. Then he slid out and reached for something on the nearby table.

'What?' For a second apprehension held her. For the first time in her life she had enjoyed making love, but Hugo had stopped. She remembered her husband had used many toys in his bedroom games, none of them to please her.

In the act of picking up whatever it was he wanted, Hugo glanced at her. He left the object.

'What is wrong, Bell?'

'Nothing.' Her throat was suddenly dry, all her previous delight gone as though it had never happened.

'Don't lie to me.' He rolled off her, but did not take his hands from her. 'That is not how we are to deal with each other. Ever.'

She realised he was upset with her. But she did not want to tell him the truth. What had happened to her before was the past. Still, she had been the one to flinch.

'What were you reaching for?' She couldn't keep the apprehension from her voice.

He frowned. 'Protection.'

'Protection?' What was he talking about?

'Yes,' he said patiently, 'protection. To keep you from conceiving my child.'

She blushed. How incongruent. He had just made very thorough love to her, exploring her body with an intimacy that had held her enthralled and she had not been embarrassed. But the talk of carrying his child made her feel vulnerable as nothing before had.

'I…I did not know there was such a thing. I thought…' how very, very uncomfortable to talk of these things '…I thought you would just withdraw or I would use something afterwards.'

He gave her a rueful grin. 'I would like to think I have the control to withdraw in time, but I am not sure. This is safer. Safer than you douching afterwards.'

Her blush deepened at his frank talk.

'But that is not why you were scared when I reached for the condom, Bell.' His voice held a firm determination she had not heard before. 'Tell me what frightened you.'

She rubbed her eyes, feeling suddenly tired. 'Fenwick-

Clyde used to stop, but he did so in order to find his latest toy.' She sighed. 'I had hoped loving you would erase that memory.'

Compassion darkened his eyes and a bone-deep anger clenched his jaw. 'I promise to do everything in my power to make you forget that man. I promise, Bell.'

She looked at him and knew he meant what he said. 'Thank you, Hugo.'

He came back to her and made good his word.

Chapter Ten

Hugo took the proffered billet-doux from the silver tray Butterfield held and strolled to the library. The paper smelled strongly of tuberose, Elizabeth Mainwaring's favourite scent. He scowled and ran his fingers through the unruly wave of hair that always wanted to spill down his forehead. He should have been expecting this, but he had completely forgotten his arrangement to meet her in London.

He sat down in the chair near the desk so that the morning light fell on his former mistress's handwriting. *I am in London. Come immediately, my dear. E.* Sweet and brief, not at all like Elizabeth. Normally her words overflowed the page. Something was wrong, or she thought something was. Very likely the fact that he had not been in London to welcome her. He had meant to be.

Things had changed drastically since he last saw Elizabeth.

Hugo wadded up the expensive paper and held it in his fist, staring out at the grounds. The last of the daffodils formed yellow carpets across the garden. Soon the roses would begin to bloom and their scent would perfume the air. But not yet. It had snowed lightly last night.

He had made love to Annabell last night, their passion

keeping them warm in spite of the cold outside. He still smelled of her, honeysuckle with a hint of woman. He wondered if his scent remained with her. She had taken one of his shirts back to her room with her, saying she wanted the smell of him near her. When she had explained why she wanted the piece of clothing, he had responded instantly. They had made love until it was nearly too late for her to get back to her room without meeting a servant doing early morning tasks.

And now this.

'Damnation!'

He rose and went to the grate where a fire roared. He tossed the note into the flames and watched it burn, the smell of tuberose mingling with the acrid bite of smoke.

He had not ended his liaison with Elizabeth, even though he had known she was seeing another man as well. He had even known who her other lover was. St. Cyrus, another one of Wellington's aides. It had not mattered to him that Elizabeth was sharing her favours. He had enjoyed her company and revelled in the lushness of her body, but that had been all. He had not loved her.

He would have to go to Elizabeth. His honour dictated that he end their connection face to face. And, she would like an expensive bauble to ease her disappointment at receiving no more—from him.

He returned to the desk chair and swivelled it around so he could gaze once more at the grounds. The bright sun had already started melting the dusting of snow. The roads would be a quagmire.

He had to tell Annabell.

He didn't think she would appreciate him leaving her to visit his former mistress, no matter what his reasons. His hands clenched in white-knuckled fists. And, damn it, he could finally understand why. All these years he had been doing whatever took his fancy, loving women with no thought for the future. And now there was Annabell.

She was so independent. What if she left him over this? Surely not. He had not proposed marriage to her, wasn't sure he would. Nor did he think she would accept if he did. But he didn't want to lose her. Not yet.

He was a selfish bastard.

A knock on the door broke his reverie. 'Come in.'

'Hugo,' his stepmother's high, sweet voice said, 'I need to speak with you.'

He turned to face her and stood up. 'Come in, Juliet, and have a seat.'

She glided into the room and sat down in the chair he had indicated. Her strawberry-blonde hair curled around her heart-shaped face, but her complexion was so pale that the faint dusting of peach freckles stood out in stark relief. Something bothered her.

He smiled and put aside his own problem. 'Come, Juliet. What has upset you so?'

She returned his smile, but it was forced and didn't reach her sherry-coloured eyes. 'Oh, Hugo. I have a request, but it is an awkward one at best.'

'Why?'

She sighed and wrung her fingers. 'I don't wish to inconvenience you and I would return to London, but then you would have no chaperon for Annabell. I don't want her reputation ruined. But I fear what I am about to ask will make her very uncomfortable here.'

Hugo quirked one brow. 'How so?'

Juliet's gaze skittered away from him, only to return with a resolute look. 'I wish to invite Lord Fenwick-Clyde to visit. Or rather, wish you to invite him.'

'What?' Hugo wondered if he had misheard. But, no, the look on his stepmother's face told him he had not. 'Isn't he Lady Fenwick-Clyde's stepson?'

Juliet nodded. She looked miserable, yet hopeful. Telling her 'no' would be like kicking a puppy, something Hugo would level another man for doing. Yet, if he told her it was acceptable, Annabell might leave. Devil take it, she might leave when he told her why he was going to London tomorrow. Not that any of that would keep him from doing what was right. Some things had to be done. Going to London to see Elizabeth and asking Fenwick-Clyde to visit for Juliet were two of them. Life was a series of risks, something he had learned very well during the Battle of Waterloo.

'This is your home, Juliet. If you wish me to invite the man, then I will.'

Relief flooded her expressive features, but she continued to wring her hands. 'I don't want to offend Annabell.'

'Neither do I, but this is your home. And, as you said before, if you leave then there is no chaperon. I imagine she can tolerate the chap for a couple of days.'

Juliet's pale face flamed. Hugo's eyes narrowed. 'It is for more than a few days.'

She nodded. 'I had hoped to invite him for several weeks.'

'I see.'

And he did. His stepmother was interested in Annabell's stepson. Could things get worse? He doubted it, but wouldn't bet on it.

'Now you understand,' she said, relief easing the wrinkle between her eyes. For the first time since she entered the room, her fingers stopped twisting.

Hugo found his fingers drumming on the top of his desk. He stopped them. 'When do you wish to invite him?'

'I would like the invitation to go tomorrow asking him for a week from that day. If you have time to do it that quickly?'

Her eyes held such a look of hope that Hugo was glad he had not refused her. Not that he would. This was her home as much or more than it was his.

'Is he in London?'

She nodded.

'I will deliver the message in person.'

She looked surprised. 'You are going to London?'

'Yes. I have some unfinished business.'

Her puzzled look intensified. 'I… That is, I don't mean to be intrusive, but I thought you and Annabell were doing very well together.' Her pale cheeks turned pink.

Hugo considered her. He and Annabell must not have kept their interest as circumspect as he had thought. Juliet would never pry like this if they had.

He considered his words carefully and kept his voice neutral. 'We enjoy each other's company, but we are not in one another's pocket.'

'Yes, yes, of course,' she murmured. 'I had rather thought it was more, but I must have been mistaken.'

Rather than lie to her, he said, 'Is there anything else you wish of me, Juliet?'

'No, nothing, and thank you, Hugo. I know this may be inconve-nient for you and Annabell.'

Hugo stood. 'That is not the issue, Juliet. But would you mind telling me where you met the man and how long you have known him?'

She stood as well, her head barely topping his shoulder. She was what the London beaus called a Pocket Venus. And she was a wealthy widow. Fenwick-Clyde had done well. Hugo stopped the cynical thought. Fenwick-Clyde was no fortune hunter by any stretch of the definition.

Juliet smiled and her face took on a contented glow. 'Last summer. After he returned from Waterloo. His wife had died in April and he had joined Wellington in an effort to forget. He is so sensitive.'

She looked besotted. Hugo swallowed a groan. 'You care for him, don't you?'

'Yes.'

Her hands fluttered, something he was not used to seeing in her. All the time he had known her he had never seen her lose her composure to this extent. He hoped things would work out.

'Does he return your regard?'

'Oh, yes,' she breathed, her voice full of wonder.

'Then I wish you the best of it.' He meant every word.

She gave him a beatific smile. 'Thank you, Hugo. You have always been so understanding and accommodating. I have been fortunate in my stepson.'

He smiled down at her. 'We are nearly of an age, Juliet. It is not my place to tell you what you can and cannot do.'

'Thank you anyway. You could have made this harder and you have not.'

'Only if I thought the connection would harm you, and then I would explain my concerns to you.'

'I know.'

She left the room, leaving Hugo to ponder the wisdom of what she had asked him to do. Her marriage to his father had been one of convenience. She had been barely seventeen and just out of the school room when she had married the late Sir Rafael Fitzsimmon. Their marriage had been happy, but far from ecstatic. Hugo was glad to see her finally find a man who made her glow. He just wished the man wasn't Annabell's stepson. Fortunately he had not heard any rumours that the son had his father's unsavoury proclivities. If he had, he would have refused to allow Juliet to extend the invitation. He hoped he was not making a mistake. Better to have the man under his roof for a period of time so he could watch him. He would also ask Annabell if she knew anything.

He sat back down and rang for Butterfield. This was one hell of a morning, and he still had the hardest part ahead of him. He had to tell Annabell about Elizabeth and his forthcoming trip.

Annabell groaned and forced her protesting muscles to lift her from the ground where she had been painstakingly clearing the dirt from what was definitely a mosaic floor in the Roman villa. She had left Hugo's bedchamber nearly lethargic from physical satiation, but had forced herself to dress and come to the site instead of going back to bed. She was determined not to let her liaison with Hugo interfere with her reason for being here. Her excavation had to come first.

She was a widow of independent means, and she fully intended to stay that way. Ten years of marriage to Fenwick-Clyde had taught her the downfalls of being legally attached to a man. The man owned his wife, and he could do *anything* to her that he chose.

She would not readily put herself in another man's power. Not even Hugo—should he ever ask. So far, neither one of them had mentioned wanting anything more than what they shared right now. She did not think he wanted commitment and marriage anymore than she did.

For a moment the sun seemed to dim, then everything was normal. Surely she was not upset because Hugo did not want more from their liaison. She had no reason to be so since she did not want more—or, at least, knew she should not want more.

'Annabell,' Susan Pennyworth's breathy, light voice intruded. 'What are you doing here by yourself?'

Annabell nearly groaned. She had not heard Susan arrive. She had been too focused on her thoughts of Hugo.

'I am excavating.'

Annabell kept her tone reasonable, even though she felt a spurt of irritation. It was barely nine in the morning. She had arranged for the men to arrive at ten to begin helping, and she wanted to get as much done as possible before they got here and she had to stop and direct them. Susan would remember that if she stopped to think about it. Ordinarily, she did not let Susan's inanity irritate her, but right now she wanted to be left alone.

Still, she kept her voice pleasant. She and Susan shared

a long history and, unless Mr Tatterly got his courage up, they would continue on together for a long time.

She tried again. 'I wanted to come here and get some work done before the men get here. Sometimes too many people make it hard to protect this precious mosaic. People tend to forget to watch where they step. After all...' she smiled as she warmed to her topic '...these are country folk. They are not used to valuing this type of discovery. They normally plough up a find like this and think nothing of it because to them the farm land is more valuable.'

Susan sniffed. 'Of course. Nothing like Mr Tatterly with his sensibilities. Why, just yesterday, he asked me how your work was going, and he was truly interested in what I had to tell him.'

Annabell smothered her laugh. Susan was several years older than she, but the other woman was as naïve as a school miss.

When she was sure she would not burst into laughter, Annabell said gently, 'I believe Mr Tatterly is interested in you, Susan.'

Susan flushed scarlet, her normally pale, nearly pasty complexion mottling. 'Oh, no, Annabell. You refine too much on his consideration. Mr Tatterly is university educated and very interested in anything having to do with science or history or the such.'

Annabell turned away to hide her smile, which she feared was closer to a smirk. 'As you wish, Susan.'

She was not going to argue with her companion. Susan would either see Mr Tatterly's interest or she wouldn't. Annabell knew from experience that there was nothing she could do to open her friend's eyes or change her friend's opinion.

'Do you have time to help, Susan?' she asked instead of continuing the previous conversation.

'Most certainly. I intend to stay here while you go back to the house. Sir Hugo has requested your presence.' Her voice lowered to a conspiratorial whisper. 'I believe he is going to tell us to leave. I heard the servants saying that Lady Fitzsimmon wants to invite other guests.'

Annabell stopped. More people would increase the risk of her and Hugo being discovered. Great as the damage would be if they were found out, she was not sure that even the increased danger to her reputation could keep her away from him now. He had penetrated her defences.

To cover her unease, she spoke more sharply than she had intended. 'Surely not, Susan. Rosemont is more than large enough for Lady Fitzsimmon to invite a dozen other people and still not require our rooms.'

She heard Susan sniff and realised too late that her tone had been curt. She had been reacting to her own fears about her relationship with Hugo and had hurt her friend. Susan talked too much and often did not make sense, but she was one of the most sensitive and easily hurt people Annabell had ever met. The slightest inflection of disdain or look of superiority and Susan was immediately cowed.

Annabell whirled around, instantly contrite. 'Susan…' She put her arms around the other. 'I did not mean to sound so short with you. I…I was thinking of something else that worried me and took that fear out on you. Please forgive me.'

Susan sniffed. 'No, no, Annabell, it is not your doing. I am too easily hurt. I must get a thicker skin, as you so often tell me. I know you did not mean anything by it. I can be irritating with my chattering. I know that.'

'No, you are who you are, Susan, and that is the way I like you.'

Susan smiled, her pale blue eyes lighting with affection. 'You are always so kind and ready to defend me.' She took a deep, steadying breath. 'But you must be on your way. Sir Hugo looked very upset. I shudder to think what must be wrong.'

Annabell nodded, her stomach clenching in worry. Hugo

never sent for her. It was an understanding they had reached. He knew how independent she was, and it did not look good to be seen together more than was necessary now they were lovers.

She sighed. This—relationship—was so complicated.

Annabell headed toward Rosemont, thankful for the modified pants she wore. They enabled her to move easily over the site without the worry of catching her skirts on a shard or upturned rock.

She reached the road and started walking, having decided against riding so that she could enjoy the crisp morning air without having it overwhelm her as it sometimes did when one travelled quickly on horseback. A brisk pace would put her at Rosemont in thirty minutes or so.

She heard a noise and saw a horse and rider coming toward her. She recognised Hugo's easy sway and comfort in the saddle. He must be very anxious to speak with her. She smiled and waved.

He stopped Molly several feet away and dismounted. The pale sunlight lit his chestnut hair, creating a sharp contrast with his grass-green eyes. He wore a casual jacket over a shirt that wasn't buttoned to the top. A handkerchief knotted around his strong neck gave him the aura of a sporting man. She knew he enjoyed sports, but realised with a start that she did not know which ones he participated in. It was unsettling to note that for all they had shared, she still knew so little about him.

She smiled as he closed the distance between them. 'Hello.'

'Thought I'd find you're here.'

Her smile widened. 'You know me too well.'

He strode to her. His thigh muscles rippled beneath the fine buckskin of his breeches. The hitch in his walk caused by his wound was only slightly more noticeable than usual. The poultice had healed the sprain better than she had thought possible. His Hessian boots sparkled from the champagne and blacking his valet used to polish them. He was, as always to her, magnificent.

'Admiring my manly attributes,' he said, his eyes sparking with an awareness she was very familiar with.

Her laugh was embarrassed because she had been so obvious in her perusal, but she retorted, 'Your boots are better polished than usual. Jamison must have had time on his hands.'

'That and the tavern wench.'

'Shame on you, Hugo.'

He shrugged. 'It is only the truth.'

'But I did not need to know that.'

'And why is that?'

'It is none of my business what your valet does.'

He stopped close enough that if she reached out she could touch him. Somehow, she resisted the urge to do so. But it was hard. She knew how his skin felt beneath her fingers; the sparks that flew between them when she touched him; the hunger that drove them to take risks they should not take.

'It can wait,' he murmured, closing the distance between them with one predatory movement.

She was in his arms and her fingers were undoing the knotted handkerchief before she quite realised what they were doing. Her hunger rose like a ravening beast as his mouth bent to hers. It was always thus, before his lips met hers and all conscious thought stopped.

He kissed her, the soft, moist sound of their joining exciting her. His hands slipped inside her pelisse and rubbed up and down her back, going lower with each stroke until they cupped her to him, nearly lifting her off her feet.

'It has been too long.' His voice was a hot breath against the side of her neck.

She arched into him. 'Only a couple of hours.'

'Too long.'

He rubbed his hips against hers to emphasise his meaning. She laughed softly and met his mouth once again with her own.

The kiss was long and wet and charged with need. She melted against him, his arms the only things holding her up. As though sensing her need for his support, he swung her into his arms and carried her to a patch of grass and dead leaves well away from the road. Bushes and trees screened them from any passers-by. He laid her gently down and followed her to the ground.

The scent of earth and growing things filled her nostrils. The sky behind his lowering head filled her eyes. She rose up to meet him.

With hands made deft from practice, he undid the buttons on her waistband and inched her loose-fitting pants down her hips until only her undergarments covered her. He unerringly found the place where her fine muslin opened. He skimmed a finger along her before slipping deep inside her.

He lifted his head, his eyes filled with wonder. 'You are ready.'

She nodded. 'For you.' Her fingers, not as skilled as his, fumbled with the buttons that held his breeches together. 'I fear I haven't your expertise,' she murmured against his lips.

'But you have something more important.'

Through the haze of desire that only he could create in her, she looked at him. 'More important than skill?'

He nipped at her mouth, tiny kisses that were as intoxicating as a deep penetration. 'Yes. You have a passion to match mine. That is a greater aphrodisiac than any skill.'

His fingers delved deeper, and she forgot what they were saying as her body reacted to his ministrations. Her hips matched his rhythm. Her heart beat erratically, and her breath came in sharp gulps.

His mouth suckled hers as his fingers brought her to climax. He swallowed the sharp cry of release she could not hold back.

She looked up at him and saw his eyes were now a deep green, his pupils nearly consuming the irises. 'Hugo…'

'Hush,' he said, pausing to put on his protection before slipping between her thighs. 'Now it is my turn.'

His breeches were open so that he spilled forth. She caught her breath, then caught him and guided him to her. He slid in and she gasped.

'Always,' she murmured. 'Always it is like this.'

His eyes barely focused, he smiled at her. 'Like nothing I have ever experienced before.'

Then he started moving and all else fled.

An eternity later, a second later, she lay beside him, both of them striving to get back their breath. She still tingled where minutes before he had caressed her, and she also felt a contentment she had never known before him.

He stroked the hair back from her face and gently helped her back into her harem pants. Only then did he pull her into the crook of his arm.

He kissed her on the forehead. 'Thank you, Bell, for the gift of yourself.'

She smiled at him. 'I receive more than I give, Hugo.'

He shook his head. 'Never.'

She put one finger against his lips. 'Let's not argue about who receives more.'

He laughed against her finger before catching it and kissing the tip. 'Let's not argue about anything.' He kissed her again, his lips lingering long enough for hunger to build once more in his eyes. 'Ever.'

Her stomach clenched with fresh desire. He had that power over her.

'Never,' she murmured, letting him keep her hand which he tucked against his chest.

They lay there while their hearts slowed. Drowsiness drifted over her, and Annabell knew she needed to get up or she would accomplish nothing this afternoon. She pulled her hand free and sat up, thinking to stand. He wrapped his arm around her waist.

'Bell, wait. I have something to tell you.'

He sounded so grave, nearly apprehensive, that she gave him a quizzical look. 'Susan said you wanted to see me.' She blushed. 'I thought we just finished doing what you wanted to see me about. Obviously I was mistaken.'

He continued to hold her hand. 'I couldn't help what we just did, Bell. I want you every waking moment.' He laughed wryly. 'And most of my sleeping moments as well.' His face sobered. 'But that is not why I sent Susan after you.'

She tried one last time to pull her hand free; when that failed, she tried to relax. But it was not easy. 'Talk to me while I work. I haven't all the time in the world to uncover this villa.'

He sat up beside her. 'Yes, you have. You have as long as you wish. I won't chase you off. I promise.'

Was his promise for time only, or did he mean something more? She stilled, the breath catching in her throat. She looked at him, searching for a meaning beyond the words. He gazed at her, but she could read nothing on his face.

Finally she spoke. 'I thought you wanted me gone from here as soon as possible.'

'How can you think that when I can't keep my hands off you every time I see you?' He shook his head. 'But it would be best for your reputation if you left. Still, selfish bastard that I am, I don't want you to go.'

He slid his palm up her ribs until his hand cupped one of her breasts. His thumb flicked the nipple that had hardened before he even touched it. She closed her eyes and sighed. It took so little for him to make her want him. So very little.

He pushed her gently back to the ground and she went willingly, so very, very willingly. Her body started to hum.

'Bell,' he said softly, tracing one of her black eyebrows, 'I need to go to London for a while.'

'London?'

He nodded.

She looked up at him, feeling the bed of leaves they lay on. The rich, earthy smell of decay filled her nostrils. Overhead the sun peeked from behind scudding clouds. It was a glorious day.

Yet, suddenly, a cloud seemed to move across the perfection of her world. She chided herself. He was likely going because of business. A small voice told her he was a man who had many mistresses. She was being unreasonable. They had made no promises.

She was not sure she could bear not to be with him at night. She told herself that loneliness was the source of the dread building in her. She had reached the point where she couldn't wait for night to fall and the house to quiet so she could sneak to Hugo's bed. And now he was leaving. But she could not stop him from doing as he wished, no matter how it might hurt for him to resume his old habits.

'For how long?' she finally asked, wondering if he was going back to gamble and womanise, and knowing it did her no good to think about it.

He rubbed her cheek with his thumb, sending a wealth of sensation coursing through her system. She wanted him to never stop touching her. But she knew he would. It was inevitable. Even now, he was preparing to leave her.

'A couple of days. No longer.'

Relief filled her, easing some of the pain and uncertainly of only seconds before. Surely he was not going to see someone else if he was only going to be gone so short a time? She knew if he came to visit her after a long absence, she would not let him leave in just a couple days. She would beg him to stay forever.

She would do what?

She stopped herself short. She was thinking like a woman

in love, not a woman who valued her freedom. She stiffened in his arms and drew slightly away.

'Don't pull away, Bell.'

His voice was deep and husky. His arm tightened around her, holding her so close she could feel the thud of his heart. She made herself relax. They had not promised fidelity to one another, or even love. He could do as he pleased. Still...

'Will you tell me why you are going?'

The words were out before she realised she was going to ask them. From the very beginning she had told herself this was a liaison only for her time here. When she was finished here, so were they. Now she was acting as though their affair meant more than that. She was crazy.

'Forget I asked that. It is not my place.'

'I came here to tell you, Bell.'

She turned on her side so she could see his reactions. 'You don't owe me anything, Hugo.'

'I know.' He met her gaze without wavering. 'But I want you to know. I want you to hear it from me and not some gossip-monger.'

Her stomach clenched in dread. 'You make it sound as though someone would enjoy telling me.'

'Some might...if they found out about us.'

In a voice smaller and tighter than she wanted, she said flatly, 'You are going to see another woman.'

He nodded. 'Elizabeth Mainwaring.'

Annabell went still in the circle of his arms where only minutes before she had felt safe from all harm. She had not counted on him being the one to hurt her. Not yet.

She had heard of Lady Elizabeth Mainwaring, the widow of Viscount Mainwaring. The woman was a fixture in the *ton,* although some wags said she was a fixture in the bedrooms of the wealthy gentlemen of the *ton.*

She looked away from him. She did not think she could

bear to see what he thought when she asked, 'Is she your mistress?'

The words were hard to say, but she had to know. Lady Mainwaring was only linked to men whose beds she shared.

'Was.' He held Annabell tighter. 'Not since I returned here. Never again now that I've met you.'

She wanted to believe him, but… 'You cannot be sure until you see her again.'

'Annabell,' he ordered, 'look at me.'

The last thing she wanted to do now was look at him. He had the power to break her heart, something no one else had ever had. Power she had not realised he had until this very instant. It was a frightening realisation. Her hands turned cold.

He caught her chin in his fingers and forced her to look up. 'I meant every word I've ever said to you.'

She tried to look away, but he wouldn't let her. She settled for saying nothing. She was afraid of what she might say. She was still emotionally reeling from two blows: his departure and her realisation that he had the power to hurt her.

His fingers tightened and his voice lowered ominously. 'Don't you believe me?'

The anger in his eyes seared her. She had to say something, but she did not want to beg him not to go. Nor did she want to lose what little pride she still had where he was concerned.

She had to speak carefully. 'I don't know what to believe, Hugo.' And she didn't. 'I…' She licked her lips. 'My marriage taught me not to trust men. Except my brothers,' she added, unable to malign them even in such a small way.

His eyes narrowed into green flames. His voice filled with disgust. 'I am not Fenwick-Clyde. Nor have I ever been.'

She made herself look at him. His jaw was clenched. She could feel the tenseness in his arm that still held her close.

'I know. I just…' She took a deep breath. 'It's hard to get beyond the past.'

'You let me touch you.'

'Yes. I don't know why, but from the beginning I not only let you touch me, I longed for you to do so. But to trust…' She sighed. 'That is the hard part.'

She didn't add that his reputation made it even harder to believe he would not rekindle his affair. The last thing they needed now was recriminations over their pasts.

'I am not going to see Elizabeth to restart our affair, Bell. I am going to end it. You have to believe me.' His voice held such sincerity.

'I want to, Hugo. Truly I do.'

'Then do, Bell. Put your past behind you. Fenwick-Clyde had no honour. Not where women were concerned or men. He cheated at cards just as he cheated at everything else.'

She had heard rumours of her late husband's activities, but no one had ever told them to her face. She did not doubt Hugo's word. Then why did she doubt him about his own behaviour?

She looked into his eyes and saw sincerity and frustration. If they were going to continue their relationship, she would have to take the risk of trusting, and part of trusting was believing him.

She took a deep breath. 'Make love to me, Hugo. Now and tonight and tomorrow. Don't let me go until you leave.'

Tenderness softened the harsh angles of his jaw and muted the sharp glint in his eyes. He smiled down at her as his arm pillowed her against his chest, against the steady beat of his heart.

'Ah, never, Bell.'

Chapter Eleven

Hugo waited to be announced by Elizabeth Mainwaring's butler, periodically slapping his ebony cane against the side of his Hessians. As recently as two months ago, he would have entered her salon without thought. Now he did not. He intended his relationship with her to change.

'Sir Hugo Fitzsimmon,' her butler said in sonorous tones.

'Hugo,' Elizabeth purred, rising and coming to him, hands stretched out. 'You know better than to be so formal. It has been many months since last you were announced.' She slanted a seductive look at him. 'Before we became more than friends.'

Hugo made himself smile at her. It was not her fault he no longer wished to see her. She was everything a man could want in a woman. From the immaculately coiffed gold curls crowning her elegant head to the tips of her feet with their painted nails, she was perfect. Large periwinkle-blue eyes, tilted at the corners, thick lashes that were the pale brown of her true colour, to the full red lips that could drive a man crazy, she was Venus rising from the crumpled sheets of a well-used bed. Even in this cool room in the middle of the afternoon.

She did not have to stand on tiptoe to press her mouth to his. 'I knew you would come immediately.'

Her voice, husky as only a satiated woman's could be, caressed each word she murmured. It was a trick she had that titillated even though she was fully clothed and had not been pleasured recently. She used it well.

Just months ago, he would have been achingly hard and ready to take her here on the carpet. Now he felt nothing. The mind was a powerful thing, he mused.

He stepped away and released her fingers. 'What do you want, Elizabeth?'

She frowned at him. 'I wanted to see you, Hugo. It has been over two long months since you left me in Paris. I have missed you.'

'Have you?'

He moved to a chair and sat. He crossed one ankle over his other knee and looked at her. She was ravishing, and dressed to be ravished. It was the middle of the day, but she wore muslin as thin as netting. The rich red of her nipples showed large and engorged through the material of her bodice. The skirt clung to her full hips and dipped into the area between her legs. She was temptation personified.

After Annabell's artlessness, Elizabeth's calculated display left him not only cold, but mildly repulsed.

Hugo took a deep breath, glad to know he could be faithful to one woman. He had never been so before, and in spite of his assurances to Annabell there had been that tiny seed of doubt. He was, after all, a connoisseur of women and had always indulged himself regardless of the circumstances. Until now.

'Why do you really want to see me, Elizabeth?'

His voice was colder than he had intended, but there was no reason to let her think he felt something he did not. Honesty had always stood him in good stead. He didn't think it would fail him now.

She shrugged and moved to stand in front of him so the weak sunlight coming in the window limned her long legs.

'I want you to make love to me, Hugo. What else have I ever wanted from you?'

Tuberoses engulfed him.

'Money? Jewellery?'

'Sarcasm isn't one of them,' she said tartly, stepping back, her full mouth a pout. 'What has happened, Hugo? You were never like this before.'

He eyed her dispassionately. 'I had never before decided to end our involvement.'

She gasped, her eyes narrowing. 'You are seeing someone else.'

It was a flat statement that brooked no argument. It was spoken as though she knew without a doubt. It was his turn to narrow his eyes.

'And if I am?'

'She will not satisfy you for long.' She ran one long-fingered hand over her ample hip. 'You are insatiable. Most women are incapable of your stamina.'

He ignored her comment. The last thing he intended to do was drag Annabell's name into this. 'I am prepared to be more than generous with you, Elizabeth.' His voice dropped. 'More so than St. Cyrus will be.'

She blanched. 'Whatever do you mean? The Earl and I are acquaintances. I am known to most members of the *ton*.'

He let her comment go. There was no sense in being hurtful or disparaging or reiterating a fact she was prepared to deny. However, her willingness or need to lie to him did her no favour in his opinion. He should have ended this connection long ago. He had been lazy and not wanted to do without his comforts, and Elizabeth was very creative. Now he was paying the piper for that attitude.

'I have been to my solicitor and have drawn up papers leaving you sufficient funds to maintain your lifestyle without the need to present your favours where you do not wish.'

Without warning, she leaned forward and slapped him. Hard.

'How dare you, Hugo. I am not a whore, no matter what you seem to think.'

'No,' he said dispassionately, 'you are a well-born courtesan. If we lived during Charles II's time, you would be having one of his royal bastards. It is not an insult, Elizabeth, it is a statement of fact. A compliment, if you will.'

She stepped away, scowling. 'I do not need your money, Hugo. Mainwaring left me well provided for.'

'I know, but more never hurts. It will buy you the trinkets you enjoy.'

She turned and stalked to the fireplace. Turned and stalked back to him. 'I don't need your settlement, Hugo. I need you.'

Her voice was suddenly all business. His nerves started twitching, a signal he had learned to trust. The reaction had saved his life at Waterloo when he had felt an itching between his shoulder blades, and turned in time to see a French soldier he had taken for dead aiming a pistol at his back.

Carefully, he asked, 'What do you need me for, Elizabeth?'

She licked her lips until they glistened like ripe cherries. Normally he would have said she did so to be provocative, but there was no responding gleam in her eyes. A glance told him her nipples had lost their hardness. Sex was not on her mind.

'I am with child, Hugo.' Her voice dropped until he could barely hear it. 'Yours.'

He stared at her. If he had been standing, he would have sat down. 'You are carrying my child?'

'Yes.'

He frowned. 'I find that hard to believe, Elizabeth. I always used protection.'

She flipped her slim hand as though to toss away his

statement. 'A sheep's gut, Hugo? Don't be ridiculous. Those things are not to prevent conception, and if you thought they did, you deluded yourself.'

'You speak from much experience?' he said, acidly, unable to let her words go unchallenged.

The last thing he wanted was to be the father of her child—if she was with child. That was one part of his father's life that he had no desire to emulate. He did not believe he had any children by any of the women he had enjoyed.

He knew himself well enough to know that if such a thing happened, he would keep the child rather than giving it to some farm family to raise. He also knew his decision might be a mixed blessing for the child, as his father's had occasionally been for him.

Elizabeth's left foot began to tap, a habit he knew arose when she was agitated. He put aside his memories.

'You were not my first lover, Hugo. I was married.'

'And Mainwaring used sheaths?' He allowed the sarcasm he felt to drip from every word.

She flushed so quickly, he was not sure he had seen it. 'No.' She turned away and turned back as quickly, clearly anxious. 'No, but I was no innocent when you met me. I know those things do not work. They were never meant for the purpose you put them to.'

'True. But to the best of my knowledge, Elizabeth, I do not have any bastards, and I have never hesitated to do as I pleased.'

She glared at him. 'Perhaps one of your former lovers did not tell you?'

His stomach twisted at the thought before he thrust the possibility away. 'I cannot imagine a woman keeping that to herself. As you know, I make it plain from the beginning that I will provide for any child.'

'So you say.' Her full red lips curved down. 'But even

a woman's husband has been known to refuse to acknowl
edge a child borne by his wife.'

He had heard rumours that she had borne a babe during
her marriage, and she had no children now. He had never
asked her about it, respecting her privacy as he had ex
pected her to respect his.

'That is rare, Elizabeth, and you know that.'

Now she did flush and the colour stayed on her high
cheekbones. 'Yes. You are very eloquent, but I am ada
mant.' She raised her hand to keep him from responding.
'No more, Hugo. Suffice it that I know those flimsy things
do not work. I carry your child.'

It sounded as though rumour was truth. He did not push
her. Her past was not his concern. If she had truly carried
a child during her marriage to Mainwaring and given the
babe to some country family to raise as their own, then so
be it. It was not unheard of in their circles. And it was still
none of his business except in the way it affected her now.

Nor would fighting her change anything. He knew her
well enough to recognise that she was determined to lead
him to the altar, no matter what her true motive was. And
he knew himself well enough to know he would not refuse
when an innocent child was involved.

'I will not continue to argue with you, Elizabeth.'

'I do not want to bear a child without a father, Hugo.'
Her posture turned defensive. 'You of all people should
know how difficult that is. Even though your father claimed
you and provided for you, you must have suffered some
ridicule. In school if nowhere else.'

He had. And it had been difficult. Young boys could be
cruel. He had thought himself beyond the hurt of the teasing
he had received at school, matured. He was surprised to
find the wounds could be so easily dredged up. He had been
too sensitive.

Although he had been dearly loved, he had been a bas
tard. He knew several of his contemporaries were not their

fathers' children, that their mothers had conceived with a lover, but the children had been born in marriage and everyone accepted them as the legal children with no shame attached. He would prefer any child of his be born in wedlock.

'Yes, Elizabeth, I do.' He did not try to hide the weariness weighing him down along with the knowledge of what he must do.

'What about St. Cyrus?' he pursued. It was one thing to let her deny the connection when there were no consequences, it was quite another to let her foist another man's babe on him.

She stiffened. 'I told you before, Hugo, you are the father.'

She sounded so certain that his heart lurched. He had been so careful, but he knew, as she had pointed out, that his method of protection was not foolproof. Most men of his station used them to protect themselves from disease when they bedded prostitutes. They did not care if the things kept them from impregnating the women. The suppliers did not care either.

'How can you be sure? We have not been together for nearly three months. Surely you would have contacted me sooner if I had caused your condition.'

Her anger of seconds before melted away. Now she was all softness and vulnerability. He mused cynically that she should have been an actress.

She knelt before him and rested her head on his knees. 'I wanted to be sure. I might…I might have lost the child.'

He did not touch her. Nor did he push her away. 'But you did not.'

'No, I did not.' She lifted her head to look at him.

He returned her look, wondering what he was going to do. His heart rebelled at what she wanted. His honour said he must do the right thing.

'Are you sure?' he asked, knowing she would tell him

once again that he was the father. But he wanted to hear her say it again and again, until, maybe, she might say he wasn't.

'Yes.'

He searched her eyes for a lie, wanting to see them shift away from his scrutiny. He wanted to see the corner of her mouth twitch from nervousness, from the fear of being caught in a lie. Neither happened.

He pushed her gently away and stood. 'I will send the announcement of our engagement to *The Times*.'

She stayed kneeling, but such a look of triumph lit her face that for an instant Hugo knew she had lied. He was not the father, he was simply her dupe. Then the look was gone and all he could discern was relief, as though she had thought he would refuse. He would have if he could have proved St. Cyrus was the one, but he could not. He would never know for sure unless the child was born several months early or late, proving it was conceived when they were not together. By then it would be too late for him, they would be married.

'I will call on you tomorrow afternoon.'

She finally stood. 'As you wish.'

He forced his shoulders to relax only to have his hands clench. He had to clarify things from the beginning. 'This is only a marriage of convenience, Elizabeth.'

'Surely you jest, Hugo.' She took a step toward him. 'Why should we deny ourselves the pleasure of each other's body?'

And why? he asked himself. She would be his wife and, after this fiasco, he would be lucky if Annabell even spoke to him, let alone let him touch her. Still, Elizabeth had won, but he was no longer interested in her as a woman. He would not do still another thing he did not wish to do.

'Because I am marrying you for the child's sake. Nothing more.' He eyed her coolly. 'And you may continue to see St. Cyrus after the child's birth.'

She reared back, her sensuous body poised like that of a hissing cat's. 'You are not making this any easier.'

'I did not intend to.'

He turned and got to the door before she spoke.

'Hugo, what is her name?'

He stopped an instant, no longer, and then was gone.

The next day he entered a jewellers, his hat tilted rakishly, ebony cane clicking on the flooring. Just below the surface veneer, anger simmered in him. The last place he wanted to be was here, choosing an engagement ring for Elizabeth. The only consolation was that he would not give her the Garibaldi sapphire. While it was not the traditional engagement ring given to the Fitzsimmon bride—Joseph would give the Fitzsimmon engagement ring to his bride— it was a ring left to Hugo by his Italian grandmother. It had been in her family for ten generations and went to a true love. He would not give that to Elizabeth.

A clerk appeared immediately. 'May I help you, sir?'

Hugo looked at the man, resisting the urge to snap. The situation wasn't this man's fault. 'I need an engagement ring.'

'Is there a particular type?'

Hugo paused. He had not considered what to get, only that he had to find something to replace his grandmother's ring.

He obviously looked undecided for the clerk said, 'Might I suggest this tray over here? They are already made so you can see immediately what they look like.'

Hugo followed the man and studied the rings displayed on a black velvet background. 'I want something more elegant than these. Nothing ostentatious.'

'I understand, sir. If you will give me a moment, I will go to the safe.'

Hugo cooled his heels reluctantly. The sooner this was

over, the sooner he could give it to Elizabeth and be on his way back to Rosemont and Annabell.

Annabell. What was he going to tell her?

'Ahem…' The clerk cleared his throat. 'I believe I have just the thing, sir.'

Hugo wished he had just the thing to turn this fiasco into a silk purse, but there was no way that he could see. Frustration made him brusque.

'I hope so.'

The man paled, but stood his ground, a tray in one hand. Hugo looked down and his eyes widened.

'It is a cabochon aquamarine, sir, circled by diamonds of the first quality.' He smiled proudly. 'We also have a necklace and drop earrings to match. They would make a stunning bridal gift, if I say so myself. The lucky woman could wear the engagement ring daily and the other pieces as she wanted.'

'They are very striking.' They would look perfect on Annabell with her silver-blonde hair and navy blue eyes. 'I will take them.'

The man bowed. 'I will have them wrapped.'

'And,' Hugo said just as the man stepped away, 'I still need an engagement ring.'

The man stopped, seemed to rearrange his thoughts and turned back. 'Let me see what else we have, sir.'

He left and Hugo wondered what he had done. Annabell did not wear jewellery. He doubted it was for lack of the baubles, since she was wealthy. Possibly she did not care for it. Still, he wanted to give her something, and most women enjoyed getting the things.

The clerk returned. This time, the tray held a large opal and diamond ring. It was lovely, but not striking. It would do.

'We only have the ring in this style, sir.' The clerk's tone was apologetic.

'I will take it.'

'Yes, sir.' The clerk bowed once more. 'I will have it packaged with the other set.'

'No, I want them separate.'

The man's eyes widened a fraction, but otherwise his face remained noncommittal. 'As you wish, sir.'

Not long after, Hugo left, as satisfied with his purchases as was possible. He didn't much care how Elizabeth felt about the ring, but he cared a great deal about what Annabell would think of her gift. Surely, a parure of jewellery like the aquamarines and diamonds would bring her enjoyment.

Trinkets had always been enough before, but no matter what he told himself, somehow he did not think they would suffice now. Before, his liaisons had been for pleasure and passion only. What he shared with Annabell was more, much more.

His stomach knotted. Dread such as he had never experienced before tensed his shoulders. He had not wanted to come to London, had not wanted to leave Annabell. More than anything he wanted to return to her, her warmth, her stubbornness and her passion. But things were different now.

She might leave him. And for the first time in his life, he understood what it was to know another person held the power to hurt him. It was not a pleasant sensation.

He signalled his coach. The sooner he gave Elizabeth the ring, the sooner his business here was done and he could return to Annabell. He had to convince her that they could stay together even if he did marry Elizabeth. An arrangement like that was not unheard of, just rare. It was the best he could offer now, but he had an awful feeling it wasn't going to be enough. She might have done it had he been single. But he had to try.

He should let Annabell go, but he was too selfish. It would hurt too much.

* * *

Annabell strode across the grass toward Rosemont, stopping to look at the daffodils beginning to turn brown. Soon the roses would begin their procession of colour and scent. Hugo's lawn would be full of blooming flowers. It would be lovely.

She entered the hall and handed her coat to the butler who appeared as though by magic. 'Thank you.'

He bowed, his demeanour everything that was precise. His gaze did not even stray to her unconventional attire.

She glanced down at her harem pants and boots. The hems of the pants were damp, but they weren't muddy. Neither were her wellingtons. She would get a book from the library to keep her company before going upstairs to change.

Hugo's absence had been harder on her than she had expected. The two nights had seemed unending; her bed cold, her body colder. And she did not know when he would return. How long did it take to give an old mistress her *congé?* She should have asked her brothers who certainly had plenty of experience in that area.

She pushed open the library door and entered, glanced at Hugo's favourite chair and froze. Someone was in it. She moved closer.

'Hugo?' She did not try to disguise her joy. 'Hugo, when did you return?'

He rose and turned to face her. A glass of brandy listed in his hand. His hair was disordered. His eyes were bright. His shirt was open at the collar. He was foxed.

She closed the distance between them and took the glass from his hand. 'What are you doing?'

'Drinking myself to the point of courage.' His words were only slightly slurred. 'That should be obvious.'

She would not have noticed if she had not known him so well. He held his liquor as well as Guy and Dominic and there were times when even she could not tell if her brothers were inebriated.

'Why do you need courage?'

Even as she said the words, her stomach tightened. He had no need of courage with her, unless he had something to say that would be unpleasant. Something like… She refused to finish that line of thought. Hugo would never do that after telling her he was going to break off his liaison with his former mistress.

He reached for the glass she still held, so she put it behind her back. Something was wrong. Badly.

He shrugged and sank back into the chair where he sprawled with one ankle over the opposite knee. 'Keep the drink. You might want to imbibe it, *bella mia.*'

He had never used that term of endearment. She frowned and set the glass down out of his reach. 'Why is that?'

He stared at the roaring fire as though trying to find answers to some world-shattering question. He looked utterly sad, as though he'd lost something he prized above all others.

She watched him without saying anything. Apprehension began to crawl up her spine. He had only been gone three days, but his behaviour made it seem as though the world had changed in that time. She sat gingerly in the chair beside him, wondering if she should run instead of stay. There was something about his whole demeanour that spoke of disaster.

Still he said nothing. She waited him out. One thing she had learned with her brothers and later her husband was that waiting was the best option when dealing with a man who had drunk too much. They would tell you what they wanted to tell you when they wanted to tell you. Most of the time, she hadn't wanted to hear their reason for drinking. Her heart told she didn't want to hear Hugo's either.

'Give me back the drink, Bell,' he said without looking at her.

'Not until you tell me what is wrong. Nothing should be

so bad that you could return home without coming for me and instead drink yourself nearly into a stupor.'

'You think so?' There was a flat tone in his voice that she sensed hinted at emotions too powerful to release.

'Yes, Hugo, I do. I thought we had reached an agreement with one another.' She paused, trying to think of how to say what she thought their relationship was. It was difficult. 'Not a legal commitment, but…but an emotional one.' When he continued to remain silent, she added awkwardly, 'For now at least.'

He angled his head to look at her. His gaze roved over her, making her hot, then cold, then hot again. He made her think of a condemned man looking at his last meal. Her imagination was running wild. She chided herself.

'What is wrong?'

He sighed and looked back at the fire. 'Would you be my mistress?' His voice was deep and raspy, nearly painful sounding.

Her chest contracted painfully. The word mistress was so demeaning. It made her remember how her brothers took mistresses, women they used, paid well and discarded. Although Guy no longer did so since marrying Felicia. But still, the word left a sour taste in Annabell's mouth.

Until he asked the question, she had not really thought about the reality of their relationship. She had already made love with him, numerous times. They weren't married and neither one of them had spoken of marriage. That made her his mistress already. She had thought it didn't matter to her. Now she wondered if she had been fooling herself.

'I thought I already was,' she finally said.

His laugh was harsh and bitter, seeming to rip from his chest. 'I suppose that literally you are right. But it never occurred to me to think of you that way.'

'Then why now?'

Her voice was low and careful, under control, or as much control as she was capable of. A sense of impending doom, unbearable hurt hovered on the edge of her consciousness. Something terrible had happened and it was going to change everything between them. She knew it.

He rose and came to stand in front of her. His beautifully formed mouth was a thin slash in a face white from strain. Before she realised his intent, he reached down, grabbed her upper arms and pulled her to her feet. His force was such that she stumbled against his chest where he held her.

His breath smelled slightly of rich, sweet brandy. His body smelled of cinnamon and musk. She had missed him so much. Even now, knowing he was somewhat inebriated and that he was about to tell her something that would hurt immeasurably, she wanted him. She wanted all of him: his mind, his body, his heart.

She was a fool.

'Ah, Bell,' he said, his voice an agonised groan, 'make love to me.'

She blinked, wondering where this was leading, then no longer caring when his lips touched hers. She sank into his embrace as they sank to the carpet. Nothing mattered but his mouth on hers, his hands undoing her garments, his body pressing her to the floor.

He cursed her harem pants and nearly ripped them as he pulled them down her legs. She was barely out of her garment when he opened his breeches. He sucked her tongue into his mouth and plunged his body into hers. It was a quick, sharp thrust that she rose to meet with all the passion in her soul.

'Bell, Bell,' he said over and over again.

His lips kissed hers, his tongue danced with hers. He shuddered. He swallowed her moans of pleasure and returned them to her with his own release.

She clutched him to her, her nails digging into his flesh, her back arching. Her body spasmed.

They collapsed with him still sheathed in her, her muscles still gripping him, her legs still cradling his hips. He looked down at her, his eyes deep green pools of pain.

'I have missed you so much. You will never know.'

She lifted her head to kiss him softly on the lips. 'I know, Hugo, for I feel the same.'

They stayed in each other's arms until their bodies cooled. Hugo finally rolled to the side and buttoned his breeches. She pulled her harem pants back on and secured them.

'Will you tell me now?' she asked quietly.

He gave her an inscrutable look. It was as though their passion had burned to ashes whatever had held him in its grips. Her chest clenched.

He stood and gave her a hand. She took it and he pulled her up. One arm cradled her to his heart while the other smoothed the tendrils of hair that had come loose from her braid during their lovemaking.

'You mean more to me than anything.'

She looked at him. He had not said he loved her. It was as though he could not say the word, but then neither could she. She understood his reticence. To love someone was to give yourself into that person's power. Neither of them wanted that. Or so she told herself.

He took a deep breath and let her go. She stumbled when his arm left her and he stepped away so he no longer supported her. She grabbed the back of the nearest chair, the one Hugo had been sitting in when she found him.

He shifted to the fireplace. Whatever he had to say, bothered him greatly.

He looked at her, looked away. 'I…I did not end it with Elizabeth, Bell.'

Her stomach lurched. 'You are going back to her.' Her words were flat from pain and disillusionment.

'I have to.' He reached for his nearly full glass of brandy that still sat on the nearby table and downed it in one gulp. 'She is carrying my child.'

Annabell reeled under the words. 'Surely not. You always use protection.'

His mouth twisted bitterly. 'She says so and I have no way of proving her wrong.' He closed his eyes as though in pain. 'Oh, Lord. I did not use protection just now.' He opened his eyes and looked at her, his countenance twisted as though he were being tortured. 'I am so sorry, Annabell. I did not mean to lose control like that. I have never done so before.'

He took a step toward her, his arm out to gather her to him. She moved backwards, her hand out to stop him. The bitterness of betrayal created a sour pit in her stomach. She felt as though she was in a nightmare, but knew she was awake.

The words spilled from her lips. Words meant to hurt him as he had hurt her. 'And if I get pregnant, Hugo, will you marry me as well?'

Chapter Twelve

Annabell curled into the sanctuary of the chintz-covered chair in her bedchamber. She had walked out on Hugo before he could answer her question. She had not wanted to know what he would say, knowing it would be too painful to bear. She felt as though someone had taken away her world. Tears tracked down her cheeks and she ignored them. Her chest was tight with pain.

Annabell gulped back an hysterical giggle. He was going to marry his former mistress. How ironic. How funny. How painful.

And she might be pregnant from their lovemaking in the library earlier. Her life could not be worse.

She dissolved into fresh tears.

A long time later, she stared into the dying fire. Surely she would not become pregnant from one time. Fenwick-Clyde had never done anything to protect her during their years of marriage and she had never conceived. She doubted she would now. It was some comfort.

But no matter what happened to her because of their lovemaking, she could not stay here. It would be too painful to see him daily and know he was going to marry someone else.

Not that she wanted to marry him, she told herself. She had made a vow after Fenwick-Clyde's death that she would never put herself in a man's control again. That meant never marrying. Yet…

He had asked her to stay, to be his mistress. His marriage was not a love match. Elizabeth Mainwaring carried his child. That was all. That was enough.

Annabell had thought her pain was too intense to worsen. She was mistaken. Her heart thudded, skipped a beat and her stomach twisted.

She could not ever remember feeling this devastated, not even on her wedding night. Fenwick-Clyde had demeaned her in ways she would not have imagined possible until they were done to her. But he had not broken her heart.

At the time she had decided she was in hell and death would be preferable. Now she knew better. Hell was losing the only man she had ever loved. No matter what Hugo said, she could not be his mistress. She could not do to another woman what had so often been done to her.

She would have to relocate to the inn that weeks ago had been full with sportsmen come to see the prizefights. Hopefully there would be room for her and Susan now. If she stayed here, she feared her resolve would weaken.

She struggled to her feet, feeling as though her body had aged fifty years in the past several hours. She would start packing. She usually packed her own things. The places she went often did not have servants. The activity would give her something to do. She didn't think she could sleep and she couldn't stand to keep thinking about what had happened.

Every piece of clothing had a memory of Hugo attached. Her brown harem pants. She folded them carefully and put them on the bottom of her portmanteau. She had worn them the first time she met Hugo. He had come upon her at the villa, and she had not known who he was. He had kissed her. She should have known from her reaction that he would mean more to her than she could ever have imagined. But she had not.

Her mauve silk evening gown. She had worn it the night she first went to Hugo. He had made love to her the entire night, erasing from her mind the horror of Fenwick-Clyde's groping hands and slobbering mouth. Hugo had shown her how wonderful the joining of a man and woman could be. She trembled with the force of the memory, her fingers stilled, the fine muslin crushed in her grasp.

Her head dropped and she shut her eyes, wondering why it was so difficult to shut out the memory of that night. But she could not forget his touch any more than she could forget to breathe.

Finally, exhausted from crying and from memories she could no longer endure, she collapsed on to the bed. Someday she would be over this. She had survived Fenwick-Clyde. She would survive Hugo Fitzsimmon.

Annabell woke the next morning to knocking. She felt groggy and disoriented, as though she had been the one consuming untold amounts of brandy. She didn't remember falling asleep. Finally, when the knocking became louder, she sat up abruptly then had to stay still until her dizziness abated. She fingerbrushed the hair from her face. She was still fully clothed, wrinkles and all. She grimaced.

She pushed off the bed and made for the door, her path only a tiny crooked. She was exhausted.

She did not open the door. 'Who is it?'

'Susan, Annabell. Let me in.'

Annabell groaned silently. Her companion's voice sounded more frazzled than usual, if that were possible. She must know about Hugo.

Annabell was tempted to tell Susan to go away, but knew it would only postpone the inevitable. 'Come in.'

She moved back to the bed and sat down. Her head ached and her mouth felt like it was stuffed with cotton. Briefly, she wondered how Hugo felt, but quickly pushed that traitorous thought away. She could no longer afford to care how Hugo felt.

'Annabell,' Susan gushed, slipping into the room and closing the door solidly, 'you'll never guess who just arrived. I nearly fainted. I could not believe my eyes. You know my sight is failing. I just know it is, but there he was. The last person I ever expected to see here. I mean, who would have thought he and Lady Fitzsimmon even knew each other, let alone well enough for Sir Hugo to invite him to stay.' She paused for a breath. 'Why, I never. You will never believe—'

Annabell put her hand to her throbbing forehead and closed her eyes. The absolute last thing she needed this morning was this chattering on about something that very likely didn't matter.

'Susan, please. I have a splitting headache. Just tell me and be done.'

A sigh gusted from the other woman's pinched mouth. 'Lord Fenwick-Clyde. He's here. Courting Lady Fitzsimmon, I swear, or I just fell off the turnip wagon, which I know isn't so. I'm all of thirty and five.'

Annabell groaned. 'Surely you're mistaken, Susan. Timothy doesn't know Lady Fitzsimmon. She is a widow of the utmost respectability. He is at least five years her junior, maybe more.' She shook her head, only to gasp at the pain caused by the motion. 'You must not have had your spectacles on.'

Susan sniffed. 'I most assuredly did have my spectacles on, Annabell. As for Timothy being too young, he is so starched and pompous one would think him a hundred. He is high in the instep and looks down his long nose at everyone. It was his father who was a lecherous old sot, not him.' She crossed herself. 'Forgive me for speaking ill of the dead, but truth is truth.'

This couldn't be happening. Annabell wondered if she

had died from the agony of losing Hugo and was now torturing herself with even more difficulties. But she knew better.

She stood, keeping one palm on the high bed for balance. 'When did Timothy get here?'

'Not more than thirty minutes ago. Lady Fitzsimmon is with him. Sir Hugo isn't to be found.' She gave Annabell a speculative look, her eyes bright like a bird's, but didn't ask anything.

'Does Timothy know we're here?'

Susan shrugged. 'Not unless he saw me or you told him.' She giggled. 'But I don't think he came here for us. He was bowing over Lady Fitzsimmon's hand when I saw him. The children were just going into the room, too.'

Annabell nearly smiled. She had never thought Timothy was taken with children, but it seemed he could be persuaded. The situation was nearly comical, but her head still ached and her entire body still felt as though she had abused it.

'I had planned on our leaving today.'

'Oh, no. Never say so.' Susan's voice was high and tight.

Annabell nodded and instantly regretted it. 'I think it for the best. Or had thought so until this. Surely Timothy is not here to court Lady Fitzsimmon, but then why not?'

She needed more time to think things through. Her stepson was here. Before she knew it, Hugo's future wife would be here. This was worse than any picture of Hades she could ever have created.

'We were leaving?' Susan sounded as though she fought back disappointment. 'I thought you and Sir Hugo had come to an understanding.'

The woman looked frazzled. Her pale blonde hair, turning grey at the temples, was crimped around her narrow face. Her big blue eyes were wide and startled, seeming larger because of the spectacles she seldom wore. She looked as though someone had taken away her most prized possession. She reminded Annabell painfully of the way Hugo had looked last night.

Annabell sighed. 'Is there something you wish to tell me, Susan…a reason you don't wish to leave?'

Even though she asked the question, Annabell knew the answer. Mr Tatterly had been courting Susan since they first came here nearly three months before. Even Susan had finally realised what was happening and, it appeared, welcomed the attention. But Annabell wasn't going to tell her companion she already knew what was happening. It wasn't her place. Not yet.

Susan's pale skin turned beet red. Her gaze fluttered away and she put one hand to her throat. 'I…I am not sure, Annabell. That is, I think perhaps, but he has not said a word. I believe that just possibly.' She paused and blushed even more if that were possible. 'I don't mean to sound vain, you understand. Ordinarily I would never say, never think such a thing. But I believe—just possibly—that, ahem…'

Annabell took pity on her companion of many years and said gently, 'That Mr Tatterly is showing a marked interest in you?'

'Yes.' Susan pinched her lips together and collapsed on to the nearest chair, obviously overcome by the effort of being so concise. 'I think.'

Annabell went to her and took her cold hands into her own. 'My dear, he is besotted with you and makes no effort to hide his feelings.'

Susan looked up at her with eyes so full of longing that all Annabell could do was hope her friend would not be disillusioned and hurt. She knew how painful that was. She squeezed the other woman's fingers and let go.

'I wager that, given enough time to screw up his courage to the sticking point, to borrow one of my brother's less ladylike sayings, Mr Tatterly will announce his intentions.'

'Do you really think so?'

There was so much vulnerability in the question that Annabell's heart went out to her friend. 'Yes, my dear, I do.'

Even as she said the words, Annabell knew she could not move to the inn for she would have to take Susan with her. Mr Tatterly might call, and he might even still court Susan. But he was a timid man. He might just as easily think Susan did not care for his attentions if they moved. Mr Tatterly was nothing like his employer who would pursue the woman he loved to the ends of the earth. Would that Hugo had loved her. She chided herself for wanting, however briefly, something that was so impossible.

Annabell turned abruptly away, not wanting Susan to see the moisture threatening to spill from her eyes. Besides, how had she got from Susan's possible happiness back to her misery? Her self-centred selfishness.

Then there was Timothy. Surely he wasn't courting Hugo's stepmother. But maybe he was. She had never known him well. He had already been on his own when she married Fenwick-Clyde. Timothy had visited infrequently, and it had been obvious that there was no affection lost between him and her father.

Her voice was heavy. 'I think we will not move to the inn after all, Susan. Not today.' She took a deep, shuddering breath and made herself smile. Nothing would come of this self-pity and moping. 'Also, would you please have a servant bring up hot water so I can wash? I think it best if we let Timothy know we are here sooner rather than later.'

'Yes, yes, you are right, as usual.' Susan stood and scurried to the door, her former despondency gone as though it had never existed. She paused with her hand on the knob. 'Mr Tatterly has asked me to go into the village with him this afternoon. He has some errands to run for Sir Hugo and Lady Fitzsimmon. I did not think you would need me this morning. That is, I thought you would be at the villa, but that the village men would be there to help. If it is not convenient, then I will tell him no.'

Annabell blinked as she followed the rambling, contra-
dictory words with an ease honed by experience. 'No, Susan. You go with Mr Tatterly. It will be much more fun
than digging around in the dirt. And I haven't any new finds
for you to draw.'

She gave Susan her best smile, knowing it didn't reach
her eyes but also knowing Susan would not notice it. The
other woman was caught in the throes of her first love.

Better to keep her pain to herself.

Dressed in a very proper white muslin morning dress
with blue ribbon trim and a deep flounce around the hem,
Annabell descended the stairs and headed for the salon. She
even wore her widow's cap of white muslin trimmed with
Brussels lace. Before last night, she would have gone to the
library, hoping to see Hugo. Just the thought made her falter
before she regained her composure. All she wanted to do
now was avoid him, but she had to meet Timothy.

She slipped into the large, rectangular room and stopped
to get her bearings. She had not been in here much. It was
a cold room with two fireplaces that did little to ease the
discomfort. The furniture was formal and grouped in precise
little groupings. No, this had not the warm cosiness of the
library, nor was Hugo here, she noted with a relief that
seemed suspiciously like disappointment.

Juliet Fitzsimmon sat daintily on one of the bigger-than-
life chintz-covered sofas with her hands folded demurely in
her lap. As always, she was the height of fashion, from her
Titian-red hair to the tips of her elegant little kid slippers.

Across from Juliet, in a stiff-backed wing chair, was Timothy Simon Fenwick-Clyde, the only son and heir of Annabell's deceased husband. She studied him dispassionately.

He was pale and slim, with hair the colour of weak sunlight cut into a Brutus. His eyes were a light grey, his lashes
lighter than his hair and his brows a startling contrast of
deep brown. His mouth was thin, but finely formed. His

chin had a cleft. His hands were long and elegant. He was much like his father physically.

He was immaculately dressed in a navy morning coat and grey pantaloons. Had it been evening he would be in breeches. He had always followed fashion, unlike Hugo. She sighed and continued her study of her stepson. Timothy's boots were polished to a shine that reflected the nearby flames. He was never less than perfectly turned out. In this area he was totally at odds with Annabell's dead husband. Fenwick-Clyde had been more interested in his pursuits than his person.

'How do you do, Timothy?' Annabell strode towards the couple.

Timothy, Lord Fenwick-Clyde, started and jumped to his feet. 'Annabell.' His fair complexion reddened. 'I did not know you were acquainted with Lady Fitzsimmon.'

Annabell smiled and took the seat Juliet waved her to. 'I was not until recently. I am here to excavate a Roman villa.'

'Ah, I should have known.' The present Lord Fenwick-Clyde barely concealed his disapproval as he sat back down. 'You took up that hobby after my father died.'

Annabell nodded. 'It harms no one, gives me great pleasure and preserves our history for posterity. What more could one want in a hobby?' She was careful to keep her hackles over his attitude from showing in her voice.

As though sensing unease, Juliet waved one delicate white hand to indicate the tea table. 'Would you care for something, Annabell?'

Annabell, not wishing to fight with her stepson or cause her hostess discomfort, accepted. 'That would be wonderful, Juliet. I must confess that I have not broken my fast yet.'

'Then you most definitely shall have something to eat,' Juliet said in her light, clear soprano as she rang for a servant. 'Hugo would be appalled to know a guest of his was going hungry.'

The last was said teasingly, but Annabell didn't have the fortitude to smile. Just the mention of her former lover was enough to make her appetite flee.

'So,' Fenwick-Clyde said, 'Sir Hugo is in residence.' He cast a quick look at Annabell. 'I had thought he was still on the Continent, particularly since my stepmother is here.'

Juliet sat a little straighter. 'Annabell is my guest, Lord Fenwick-Clyde, and I imagine that I am ample chaperon for anyone and particularly for a widow.'

This time Annabell did smile. She had not thought Juliet Fitzsimmon had the wherewithal to speak her mind so forcefully. She was glad she had been wrong.

'My pardons,' Fenwick-Clyde said hastily. 'I did not mean to imply anything out of the ordinary.'

Annabell gazed at him. Susan had been right when she had described him as high in the instep. There were times he was insufferable. This had boded ill to be one of those times. Fortunately, Juliet had nipped him in the bud. She stole a glance at her hostess. Juliet might be good for Timothy. The real question would be whether or not he was good for Juliet.

To turn the focus from proprieties, Annabell asked, 'What brings you to Kent, Timothy? I don't recall any property in this area.'

Her stepson flushed deep scarlet before seeming to regain his composure, yet during it all he kept his attention on Juliet. 'I came to pay my respects to Lady Fitzsimmon. We met during the Season and have maintained a correspondence since then.'

Faint pink tinged Juliet's cheeks. 'Lord Fenwick-Clyde has been very generous with his time. I felt it only right that he be invited to visit. Hugo agreed.'

Annabell dropped her eyes to give the couple a moment of privacy and took a long drink of hot tea, laced with cream and sugar. It was hard not to smile at them. They were so obviously interested in each other and trying so very hard not to be obvious. Fortunately for them, nothing stood in their way. Timothy was too much of a prig to have had a mistress to get pregnant. He would be free to marry where he chose. And the age difference was not unheard of.

Not that she wanted to marry Hugo, she told herself sternly. She merely wished their relationship had not changed by his having to marry someone else. That was all. Nothing more.

She followed the tea with some toast just brought by a maid.

'How long will you be staying?' she asked her stepson.

Having never taken his attention from his hostess, he raised one sandy eyebrow. 'I don't know, Annabell.'

'As long as he likes,' Juliet said before he finished speaking. 'The children adore him.'

Somehow, Annabell could not imagine her starched stepson gambolling with Joseph and Rosalie. She could barely picture him unbending enough to kiss Juliet. And she could never think of him as passionate, although he had had a wife and had got her in the family way. She said nothing.

'Here you are,' Hugo's deep voice drawled. 'Butterfield told me Fenwick-Clyde had arrived. I see you have been entertaining him.' He strolled into the room. 'How do you do.' He held out his hand. 'I'm sorry I missed you when I delivered the invitation.'

Fenwick-Clyde rose and extended his hand. 'Sir Hugo.'

Annabell tried to surreptitiously study Hugo. He looked haggard, as though he had had a bad night. His hair was rumpled and his eyes were bloodshot. The lines around his beautiful mouth seemed deeper. His swarthy complexion looked sallow in the pale light coming from the many-paned floor-to-ceiling windows. She was not surprised to see him position himself close to the fire with just a barely perceptible hitch in his walk.

It hurt her to see that his thigh with the wound seemed

o pain him, making him hesitate in his walk, although she
doubted anyone else had noticed. He was a naturally graceful man, but she knew him intimately now, and could see
ne did not move with his usual smoothness.

She forced her attention back to the other couple. They
were much safer to her emotional well-being.

'Do you plan on staying long?' Hugo asked.

His tone implied that he didn't much care what Timothy
intended to do, but Annabell knew better. She had learned
that Hugo didn't ask unless he was interested in the answer.
Otherwise he would keep his own counsel. She wondered
if he worried that the old adage, 'like father like son', held
true for Timothy. She would have to reassure him, for Juliet's sake, that to the best of her knowledge it did not.
Timothy was the antithesis of his deceased father.

Again, Timothy hesitated as though he did not want to
give the wrong response, and Juliet answered for him. 'Lord
Fenwick-Clyde is free to stay as long as he wishes. Did you
not tell me that, Hugo?'

Annabell shifted her attention to Juliet, amazed. That was
twice in a matter of only minutes that the normally reserved
and utterly polite Juliet had spoken with the intention of
setting the record straight, so to speak. She began to see
Hugo's stepmother in a new light.

'Of, course,' Hugo said. 'I did not mean to imply anything different, Juliet. I merely inquired so that I could pass
the information along to Butterfield.'

He spoke so innocently and his face was so bland that
Annabell nearly believed him. But she saw the hand that
he rested on the marble mantelpiece tense. He was definitely not comfortable with Timothy's visit. The small
frown on Juliet's normally smooth brow told Annabell the
other woman also realised Hugo was not perfectly sanguine.
Timothy seemed unaware of any tension, but he did not
know Hugo as the two women did.

'If it is not convenient, Sir Hugo, I can stay at the inn in the nearby village.'

'Not at all.' Hugo pushed away from the mantel. His gaze roved over the three of them, lingering briefly on Annabell. 'I hope to see you at dinner, Fenwick-Clyde. Right now, my estate manager is waiting.'

He made an inclusive bow and left. Annabell watched him, wishing she were going with him and knowing she never would. She turned back to the couple.

'Sir Hugo isn't the only one with things to do.' She smiled, a tight movement of her lips that did not reach her eyes. 'I must continue my work. The more time I spend at the dig, the sooner I will be finished, or...' she paused as she realised what she intended to do '...the sooner I will be able to turn it over to someone else to finish excavating.'

'Never say you are thinking of leaving?' Juliet said, genuine dismay in her light voice.

'I must some time, but not today and very likely not this week.' She rose. 'If you will excuse me?'

Both nodded, but it was obvious neither one cared. They were more involved in watching each other and discovering just how far they were to go.

Annabell walked from the room, envying them with all her heart.

Chapter Thirteen

Dinner that evening was uncomfortable in the extreme. Annabell nearly went so far as to excuse herself during the dessert course. Hugo watched her the entire time with a look of brooding awareness that made her stomach do cartwheels and her palms moisten. His attention was so marked that several times Annabell caught Timothy looking from Hugo to her and back again. She did her best to ignore everything, but could not stop her awareness of her host.

Finally Juliet rose and she and Susan followed suit. They escaped to the salon.

'Please excuse me, Juliet, Susan,' Annabell said before the other two had barely sat down. 'I don't feel well. Too much sun today, no doubt since I forgot my bonnet. I think I will retire early.'

Both women were glowing with pleasure at the knowledge that the men they were interested in returned their regard, but Juliet looked disappointed at Annabell's request. Still, always gracious, she said, 'Of course, Annabell. I will explain to the gentlemen.'

'Thank you.' Annabell smiled at Susan. 'I will see you in the morning.'

Susan nodded. 'Have you found something?'

'A pot, nothing fancy, but I think we should record it. I

don't think it is native to this part of the world. Possibly from Greece.'

'Oh, how exciting.' Susan clapped her hands. 'I shall be prompt.'

Annabell's smile softened. 'I know you will.'

But she did not want to linger. She did not know how long the men would spend with their port. She doubted it would be long since two of the three would be anxious to join the ladies. Before Susan could continue on or Juliet say anything else, Annabell left.

She fled, wondering if she was making a mistake by not moving to the inn. She reached her room and closed the door securely. Perhaps she would leave when Lady Mainwaring arrived. She did not think she could stand to watch Hugo with his future wife, no matter that Hugo did not love the woman. He was still marrying her. Lady Mainwaring still carried his child, begotten in passion.

The picture was too painful.

Annabell managed to undo the top buttons of her dinner gown so she could twist it around to the front and undo the rest. She slipped out of the thin muslin, shivering in the chill air, and left it wrinkled on the floor while she went for her robe. She looked back at the dress and decided to hang it in the wardrobe.

She had her head stuck in the recesses of the mahogany-and-sandalwood inlaid wardrobe when someone knocked. It was probably Susan come to talk about tomorrow.

'Come in,' she called, making room for the dress.

She heard the door open and shut, and expected to hear Susan. Instead cinnamon reached her. A *frisson* ran the length of her spine down to her toes. She pulled her head and torso out of the wardrobe.

'Hugo,' she murmured, turning around to see him standing too close for comfort. 'What are you doing here? Someone will see you.'

'No one saw me.'

He was magnificent. His too-long hair tumbled over his forehead and curled around the modest collar of his shirt. His black evening coat was unbuttoned and his black satin breeches were snug to his thighs and hips. His clothing left nothing to her all too active imagination. He was a man in all his glory.

She swallowed and looked at his face, only to see he was studying her as she had done him.

He gazed at her, taking in her dishabille. Self-consciously, she brushed the loose hair from her face. His attention lowered and she belatedly remembered she wore nothing but her chemise.

Hunger sharpened the angles of his face. 'I brought you something.'

She reached behind her and grabbed the first garment her fingers touched. It was a cape. She dragged it around her shoulders, embarrassed by her near nudity as she had not been before with him.

She spoke harshly. 'I don't want anything from you. Please go before someone finds you here. The last thing I need is to be linked with a man who's about to marry another woman.'

Even as she said the words, she realised their illogicality. The last thing she needed was to have *any* man in her bedchamber. The fact that it was Hugo only made it slightly worse.

His eyes narrowed. 'I want you to have these.'

He held out a square black velvet box. She knew it must be jewellery. The hard knot of pain in her chest slowly turned to steam.

'I am not your mistress, Hugo. I don't want jewellery from you, even if it is only a token of your appreciation for past favours. I know when men give gifts such as that to women. My brothers have done it enough. I don't want it from you.'

He opened the box to show the parure of aquamarines

and diamonds. The stones sparked with fire even from the distance separating her from them. It was a stunning set of necklace, drop earrings and bracelets.

'I bought them to complement your beauty.'

'You bought them to pay me off.' She took a deep, steadying breath and met him squarely. 'Get out.'

His face darkened and there was a dangerous gleam in his eyes. He set the velvet box down carefully. Too carefully.

She edged back.

He closed in on her.

She stepped back until the wardrobe stopped her. She put her hands up to ward him off. It was no use.

He pressed her to the hard wood, a hand on either side of her head. His face was too close.

'Don't send me away, Bell. I want you too badly to leave.' He took a deep breath. 'I won't leave, not while you look at me with desire as you just did.'

She closed her eyes to the ardour he radiated. 'You are mistaken. I don't desire you, Hugo. I am mad at you for your effrontery in offering me the same gift you would give a discarded mistress.'

'They are a gift, Bell. Nothing more. They belong on you.'

'I don't want them,' she repeated for what felt like the hundredth time. 'Take them and get out.'

'I have tried to be gentle with you, Bell, to woo you the way women want. Talking of emotions, finding out your likes and dislikes. Now I am going to seduce you with no regard for anything but your body and mine.'

She gasped, her eyes flying open. 'How dare you!'

He laughed, hard and sharp. 'I am desperate. I dare a great deal.'

His hand left the wardrobe and gripped her face. He held her for his kiss, his body pressed to hers. His lips met hers, hard and demanding, unlike any kiss he had ever given her.

His tongue forced her mouth open and plunged in. His fingers undid her braid and caught thick strands of hair, pulling her head back to expose her neck.

The pulse beat just where her collarbone showed. He moved his lips there and sucked. Shivers broke out on her skin.

Still holding her head back with one hand so her neck arched to give him access, he used the other hand to sweep off the cape she had so hastily donned. It fell from her shoulders to puddle in a brown heap on the floor. He pushed the chemise off one of her shoulders and down until her breast jutted exposed above her corset.

He lifted his head long enough to gaze at her exposed flesh, then he bent down and took her nipple into his mouth and sucked. She gasped and her back arched against her will so he had better access to her flesh.

Her hands, which had so recently pushed him, gripped the lapels of his coat and she hung on as though a storm raged through her body, pummelling her with its intensity. She could no longer resist him.

Sensing her surrender, he freed her hair and used the other hand to push the chemise off her other shoulder so that both her breasts glowed in the light from the fire. He raised his face and looked at her. She met his eyes, unable to turn away.

He took a deep shuddering breath. 'Tell me to leave now, and I will go.'

She gazed at him, seeing his need even as her own devoured any words of refusal she might manage to utter. 'I thought you intended to seduce me without regard for my wishes.'

His voice was deep and resonated with his arousal. 'I did, Bell. I did.' Pain twisted his mouth. 'But I cannot do that to you. You value your independence too much for me to take it from you simply to satisfy my appetites.'

She groaned, knowing his words had slipped between the

widening cracks of her emotional barrier. 'You have won,' she whispered.

'We both have.'

She closed her eyes, wanting what he was about to do to her, wanting him so badly she hurt with the need. When one of his arms went around her shoulders and the other behind her legs and he swung her up, she didn't protest. Let him take her where he willed, let him do to her what they both wanted.

He laid her on the bed and stepped back. 'Look at me, Bell.'

She didn't want to see him. She wanted only to feel him. Looking at him would be more than she could stand, for then she would have to admit to herself that she loved him. Had loved him from the first moment he kissed her. Her mouth twisted in bittersweet memory.

'Just kiss me and be one with it, Hugo,' she said, her voice hoarse with desire and denial and a loss that penetrated to her soul.

She heard him moving and the sound of cloth and knew he was undressing. The part of her that always revelled in his masculinity made her open her eyes. He stood naked.

The fire was behind him so the orange glow lined him, but she could still see him well enough. Dark hairs, crisp yet silky, covered his chest, circling his nipples. They formed a trail down the hard planes of his stomach past his stomach and lower. He was ready. She looked at his face and saw the tight line of his mouth and the blade edge of his jaw.

She lifted her arms to him.

He lowered himself to her so they lay side by side. His hands skimmed her bosom and stomach, his fingers touched her softly. She sighed as his mouth met hers. His kisses tantalised her, light then hard, shallow then deep. His fingers moved in unison. Her hips matched his ministrations. She gripped his shoulders, shivering with need as he moved. She felt his muscles tense and knew he was holding himself back.

She tore her mouth from his. 'Now, Hugo. Enter me now.'

He licked his lips. His pupils were so dilated that she could see her face in their black depths. She met his gaze without flinching even as her body pulsed from his attentions. He smiled, a look of power and barely suppressed passion.

And still he would not take her.

Her breathing increased. Her eyes closed and her back arched. She dug her nails into his muscles and rode the release he gave her.

When she could finally speak, she asked, her voice hoarse and weak, 'Will you take your pleasure now?'

He gave her an inscrutable look and, instead of moving between her legs, slid from the bed. Her eyes widened as she watched him go to his knees so that his face was level with the top of the mattress. The look he gave her was wicked and sensual. His lips parted and his tongue appeared.

He gripped her hips and positioned her for his deep kisses. She gasped with pleasure even as she tried to push him away.

'Stop, Bell. Let me give you this gift.'

She barely heard him over the rushing of blood in her ears. She had never experienced anything like this before. It was strange and embarrassing and—she gasped when he hit a sensitive spot—arousing her beyond her wildest imagination. He licked and sucked and used his mouth and tongue as he had his fingers and hand.

She writhed in exquisite torture. Just as she thought her body would explode, he withdrew only to return before she had completely calmed. He played her like a musician plays his instrument. He wrung from her every sensation her body was capable of giving.

Her soft moans and small gasps of pleasure filled the darkness in the room. She felt transported to a place where anything was possible. His mouth finally left her and she whimpered with frustrated need.

'Shh,' he murmured. 'I won't leave you like this. I promise, Bell.'

On one level she heard his reassurance, on a deeper level her body burned with desire not realised. Her nails clawed the sheet beneath her throbbing body.

'Look at me,' he ordered.

She opened her passion-heavy eyes to see him standing between her thighs, his masculinity firm and ready. He had already put on his protection. She reached for him and he caught her hands with one of his. With the other hand and his hips, he opened her wide. She finally realised what he meant to do.

He released her hand to grip her hips and hold her still. Then he thrust deep inside her. One strong, intense penetration and she exploded. She screamed with released tension as her body pulsated, and his hips pushed deeper and deeper. He seemed to touch something deep inside her that was both pleasure and pain. It was like nothing she had ever experienced.

Her mind numb, her body tingling, she hung on as he pounded into her. Suddenly, it was as though he had not already brought her twice to climax for she shattered again and again.

She gasped and sucked in deep gulps of air, her hips continuing to move with his. She was in a daze of satiation, yet still saturated with desire for this man who continued to move inside her as though he had just begun.

Suddenly, she felt him stiffen. He groaned, then spasmed.

Long minutes later, he still lay half on her, his feet on the bare floor, his chest covering hers. He kissed the side of her neck and smoothed the damp hair from her forehead. She turned to catch his lips with hers.

'I love you,' she whispered, not realizing she meant to say the words until they were out.

He looked sombrely at her. 'I know, Bell. I know.'

Annabell woke, wondering why she felt cold and bereft. Then remembered. Hugo had made love to her, such as he had never done before. In hindsight, it seemed he had taken her with desperation as much as passion.

She turned from side to side and swept her arms over the covers, hoping he was still with her and knowing he was not. He had been saying goodbye with his body.

Her mouth twisted. He had been showing her what she could never have. A lover who cared enough about his partner's pleasure that he would take himself to the limit in order to turn her inside out. But he was more than that to her.

He was the man she had fallen in love with despite her better judgement. In spite of everything she had ever told herself, her heart was his. She had not given it to him, he had taken it. And now he had returned it because he did not want it.

She curled into a tight ball as though she could shut out the pain. It was a futile action and she knew it, but there was nothing else she could do. He was gone and she loved him.

Hugo sat in the chair he had moved closer to the fire in his bedchamber and stared at the flames, seeing Annabell's face in each leaping glimmer. In another, he saw the curve of her breast. In another, the light in her eyes when he sheathed himself inside her body.

He would never touch her again. She wouldn't let him.

He emptied the last of the brandy into his glass. Instead of drinking the liquor, he threw it on the flames so they danced and reared to the top of the fireplace.

When she woke, she would find the aquamarines. He

should have taken them because she would despise him for
leaving them, but they were for her. He had bought them
for her, hoping she would remember him every time she
looked at them. Hoping she would remember his touch
every time she wore them. If she wore them.

He rose naked from the chair, his body exhausted but far
from satiated. He could have made love to her all night.
Even the thought of it aroused him. But he had not.

Tomorrow Elizabeth Mainwaring arrived.

The next morning, Annabell looked up from the piece of
mosaic she was carefully uncovering. A post-chaise rum-
bled down the dirt road that skirted her dig on its way to
Rosemont. She caught a glimpse of a crest. Lady Elizabeth
Mainwaring was arriving.

Annabell slumped to the ground, careful even in her misery not to sit on something important. She pulled her knees
up and hugged her arms around her calves, eyes staring at
nothing. She had known this was coming. No one had made
a secret of the fact that Hugo's future wife was arriving
today. She should have moved to the inn, but that would
have meant taking Susan from Mr Tatterly. A single
woman, widow or not, did not stay in a public inn alone.
And what if Mr Tatterly had stopped seeing Susan because
of the relocation? She couldn't chance that just because she
was not happy.

Nor could she leave the area completely and return to
her brother's town house. That would mean leaving the dig
before she was ready. She had decided long ago to devote
herself to uncovering the past and exploring different lands
and cultures. Not even the pain caused by her ended liaison
with Hugo was going to change that. If anything, her heart-
ache was going to make her vocation even more important.

But not this instant.

For a few moments and a few moments only, she was
going to wallow in her misery. Elizabeth Mainwaring was

going to get the only man Annabell had ever loved or ever
would love. It didn't seem fair, but then she had learned
long ago that life rarely was fair.

Her vision blurred. Eternity passed and was gone.

Annabell pulled herself together. Enough self-pity. She
had work to do. The sooner she finished here, the sooner
she could leave. The sooner she left, the sooner she would
not have to see Hugo every day and know he would never
be hers.

She jumped to her feet and swiped at her eyes.

A little more and she would have another mosaic un-
veiled. This one seemed to be the floor of what was probably the winter dining room. She thought it even had heat-
ing under the floor. Tomorrow she would need Susan to
sketch it.

She bent back to her task, humming a country ditty. Anything to make herself feel less melancholy.

'Why don't you sing the song?'

She started, dropped the fine brush she had been using
to remove dirt and craned her neck around. Hugo stood in
the clearing. She hadn't heard him.

'I didn't hear you.'

He shrugged, his broad shoulders moving eloquently in
the loosely-fitting brown jacket. 'You were entertaining
yourself.'

'What brings you here?'

She turned back to her work. The last thing she intended
to do was to let him upset her or, worse yet, to entice her.
She didn't care that he was willing to carry on their liaison.
She was not.

'Elizabeth just arrived.'

'And?' She was not about to tell him she had seen his
future wife drive by.

'I wanted you to know so you would not be taken un-
awares.'

'That was nice of you.'

She was proud her voice was cool and nearly mocking. He would never know how much this hurt her. Never.

'You don't make anything easy, do you?'

She stopped swishing the brush, but did not look at him. 'Why should I? I didn't cause this situation.'

'Dammit, Annabell.'

She turned at that. He stepped toward her, and she put out her hand to stop him.

'Don't come near me, Hugo.'

His eyes smouldered. 'Why not? Don't you trust yourself with me?'

She stood so as not to feel overwhelmed by him. 'If you must know, then no. I don't trust myself with you. Or you with me. You are engaged to someone else, but you make no bones about the fact that you still want to bed me. I won't do it, Hugo. I won't. Not again.' Her voice cracked.

'Why not, Annabell? You enjoyed last night, I have the scratches to prove it,' he ended with a wry twist of his beautiful lips.

'I told you.'

Anger darkened his face. 'You told me you wouldn't do to another woman what was done to you. But that isn't your real reason, is it?'

She shrugged and pushed back a thick strand of hair that had come loose from the bun at her nape. 'Of course it is.'

'Very noble,' he said sardonically. 'Then if that is part of your reason, it isn't all.' He moved a step closer. 'It isn't as though you wanted to marry me yourself. Is it?'

'Not wanting to marry you myself and having you marry someone else are two totally different things.' But how could she explain something to him she didn't really understand herself. 'Had you remained single, we could have continued our liaison indefinitely.'

'We can continue it once I'm married.'

All she could do was look at him. Why didn't he understand? She had told him last night that she loved him and regretted having done so more than she could say. At least he hadn't thrown that at her. But neither had he told that he loved her in return.

'I thought last night was the end,' she finally said. 'I thought you came to me to say goodbye.' Her hands clenched. 'You left me those jewels.'

'I bought them especially for you, Bell. I would have bought them for you if Elizabeth had never existed. They are my gift to you.'

'I told you I didn't want them, but you left them. I told you I won't continue our liaison, yet you persist in hounding me.' Her voice rose in anguish. 'When will you listen to me and leave me alone?'

He stared at her, his shoulders tense, his mouth thin. 'I don't know, Bell. I can't seem to stop myself. No matter what has come between us, you are all I think about. All I want.'

She twisted around, her fist ground into her mouth to keep from sobbing. Her shoulders hunched. 'Please go, Hugo. Just go.'

Her misery must have reached him. She heard his footsteps and then Molly snorting, followed by the clop of hooves on the damp ground and then the dirt road. Annabell took a deep breath and willed herself to relax. Her shoulders slumped, her fist fell from her mouth and she turned.

He was gone. It was just as well. She had things to do. Thank goodness she had work.

Hugo rode away.

Why had he confronted her? Why was he provoking her? He was the one who had offered for another woman's hand. He was the one who had broken Annabell's trust even though neither one of them had ever promised the other exclusivity. He had never said *I love you*.

But she had. He had not answered her. It didn't matter what he thought. He was engaged to Elizabeth Mainwaring.

He must have yanked on the reins for Molly shied. He soothed her. 'Easy, girl. I didn't mean to do that.' She responded to his voice and calmed.

And why had he brought up marriage to Annabell? What good would it do either of them if he forced her to tell him she wanted to marry him? Nothing. In his rational moments he knew that. He had never intended to marry her in the first place, just as she had never wanted to marry him. So what was he doing now?

He didn't know...but he didn't want to go home to Elizabeth.

He whistled to Molly, their signal for a good run. The exercise would do them both good. He aimed her away from Rosemont.

Chapter Fourteen

Annabell studied herself in the full-length bevelled mirror. She was not a beauty. Never had been, and her silver-londe hair was too out of the ordinary. Normally it didn't other her. Hadn't bothered her until she had entered the all and caught a glimpse of the sultry beauty Hugo was to narry. Even now, hours later, she could see Elizabeth Mainwaring in her mind's eye, and the scent of tuberose eemed to hang heavily in the air.

She made a face at herself. She had nearly worn the mauve gown, but the memories had been too fresh, too nsettling. Instead she had settled on this simple dinner ress of white gauze striped with blue. It was fancier than hey had been wearing, but she sensed Lady Mainwaring vould be dressed much more glamorously.

Unable and unwilling to do ringlets, she had braided her air and wrapped it around the back of her head. She jabbed small spray of diamonds into one side.

Against her earlier better judgement, she had even onned the aquamarines. They sparkled and shone in the ght from the candelabra. Hugo had been right. They com-lemented her skin and hair colouring. They looked good n her.

But she hadn't wanted them. Had threatened to return

them. She even considered them an insult. Yet, in a moment of weakness she had put them on. She had wanted to wear something Hugo had given her when she met the woman who had taken him from her, who would likely be wearing his ring. Stupid and silly, but there it was.

She sighed and turned away.

She thought briefly of sending her excuses, then chided herself for a coward. She had never run from adversity or pain. Even when Fenwick-Clyde had been at his worst, she had faced him and lived through the ordeal. She might have cried later, but he never knew.

Nor would Hugo know.

Taking a deep breath, she lifted her chin and squared her shoulders. After she was through this, nothing would ever be hard again.

She made her way down the hall to the stairs and down to the salon where everyone gathered for a drink before dinner. A footman waited to announce her. She shook her head. The last thing she wanted was to draw attention to herself. Better to see what was going on before anyone knew she was here. More than anything, she wanted to see Hugo with his fiancée before he realised she was there. She just hoped he would not be hanging on Lady Mainwaring's every move or admiring her every gesture and ample curve.

Annabell sighed and passed one gloved hand briefly over her eyes, wishing she could shut out the world as easily as she could block her view.

She paused in the doorway to the salon. She had made sure she would be the last to arrive so she would have the least amount of time to mingle with the other guests before dinner was served. Seeing Elizabeth Mainwaring practically draped across Hugo's right arm made her heart ache and confirmed the intelligence of her decision. She had a long, miserable meal ahead of her.

Susan immediately bustled in her direction. 'Annabell, what took you so long? You are usually the first to arrive and tonight you are the last. I had begun to think I should send a servant to see if you were unwell.' She paused long enough to take a breath. 'You are very handsome tonight. The white and blue becomes you enormously. And the aquamarines. They are *magnificent*.' Her eyebrows rose, for she knew Annabell did not own such jewellery. When Annabell refused to answer her companion's silent question, Susan turned slightly. 'Don't you agree, Mr Tatterly?'

Tatterly, his square face looking frazzled, nodded. 'Very fine, Lady Fenwick-Clyde. You are absolutely correct, Miss Pennyworth.'

Annabell swallowed a groan. Leave it to Susan to mention the aquamarines. Silly as it now seemed, she had hoped no one would mention them. And Juliet and Timothy might not have. But Susan knew exactly what she owned right down to what she had brought with her. There was no help for it but to brazen it out.

'Thank you, Susan. Mr Tatterly.' She smiled at the footman who extended a tray of sherry. 'I was detained because I spent longer than normal today at the site.'

Juliet drifted over, a smile making her face radiant. 'Did you find something new?'

Annabell shook her head. 'Not really, but I am still uncovering my latest discovery. I want to be very careful not to damage anything.'

Timothy, who had followed Juliet, frowned. 'Do you think it is safe to stay so late? A woman alone?'

Annabell swallowed a sharp retort. That was just the thing she expected from him. He didn't mean any disrespect, he just considered women to be the weaker sex.

Patiently, she said, 'I am well able to care for myself, Timothy, but I thank you for your concern.'

'Oh, dear, yes,' Susan said. 'The places we have travelled. Why, we met on a packet ship coming home from Egypt. Annabell was the kindest possible, taking me under her wing when it became obvious I was having trouble with my lively charge who had decided she was enamoured of a gentleman. When he turned his attentions to Annabell, she made short shrift of him.'

'Really,' Hugo drawled, having wandered over with Elizabeth Mainwaring still draped across his arm like a serving towel. 'In what way, if I may be so bold as to inquire?'

Annabell pressed her lips together and forbore to give Susan a minatory look. The woman had no idea the trouble she caused when she tried to help.

'Oh, nothing out of the ordinary.' Annabell waved a hand as though to negate the story.

'Oh, no, it was more than that,' Susan interposed. 'Why, I saw Annabell push him over the railing and into the Nile. Nasty, dirty water it was too.' She laughed. 'When they fished him out, he was none too happy, but there was nothing he could do.'

'Indeed?' Hugo's eyes had an unholy gleam in them. 'Was he being impertinent?'

'No, really, Annabell,' Timothy Fenwick-Clyde said before she could reply. 'That is too bad of you. Surely there was another way to curb him. Wasn't there a British gentleman to protect you? Or was this one of your wild trips you took after m'father's demise?'

Annabell looked from one man to the other. Each wore a totally different expression, but she didn't appreciate either one. The urge to give them both a set down was strong.

'I may be *only* a woman, but that does not mean I am incapable of taking care of myself. That particular malady is more often than not a myth perpetuated by the male gender in order to keep the female subservient.'

The scent of tuberoses filled the air. 'A veritable Amazon,' Elizabeth Mainwaring drawled in her raspy, provocative voice.

The sensual sound reminded Annabell of a cat that was being scratched by a besotted owner. She wondered if it reminded Hugo of a woman who has been well bedded.

Her throat closed on the thought, and she had to consciously make herself relax. It would do her no good to dwell on Hugo and his sexual liaisons.

She looked at the woman. Elizabeth Mainwaring was provocation personified. She wore an evening gown in the latest London fashion, very high waisted and very low in the décolletage. The black satin, to differentiate it from the matte crepe of mourning, became her pale complexion and creamy bosom. The magnificent diamond necklace that seemed to drip like stars between her full breasts shone to perfection against her skin and gown. Her honey-blonde hair was curled around her perfectly oval face, accentuating her large blue eyes, before being braided around the back of her head. Her waist was small and her bosom and hips fully rounded. She was—stunning.

No wonder Hugo had made her his mistress and now his future wife. For the first time in her life, Annabell felt inadequate. Always before she had known she was tall and elegant with an adequate figure and with a mind that held its own in any company. Now, she appreciated painfully how a beautiful woman could mesmerise with nothing more than her body.

And there was the engagement ring, an opal surrounded by diamonds, not too big and not too small. The setting was modern, as though Hugo had recently purchased it. Annabell swallowed hard.

'Yes,' Hugo drawled. 'Lady Fenwick-Clyde is very like those mythical female warriors.'

His voice brought Annabell back to the conversation. She dragged her attention from the woman still curled around him. That sight only worsened her already sore heart.

She made her eyes meet Elizabeth Mainwaring's before moving on to Hugo's. 'A woman has many weapons in her arsenal to achieve what she wants. I choose to use my hard-won independence.'

Lady Mainwaring's blue eyes narrowed. 'And others do not?'

Annabell shrugged, regretting her hasty words. She didn't even know this woman, only by gossip and the picture she presented this evening. She had no right to judge her or to make veiled aspersions against her.

'Women are powerless in our society unless they are widows or dearly loved by the men in their lives. Any means to achieve happiness is worth using. I have chosen to use my independence since Fenwick-Clyde's demise to ensure that I am able to do as I wish.' She gave Timothy an apologetic look. 'I do hope you understand, Timothy.'

He nodded, but his complexion was pale. 'Perfectly.'

'Dinner is served,' the butler intoned, breaking the tension that had developed.

Hugo took his stepmother's arm and escorted her to the dining room while Timothy took Lady Mainwaring on one arm and Annabell on the other. Miss Pennyworth followed happily with Mr Tatterly.

Annabell heard Susan chattering on behind them. Thankfully someone had been unaware of the storm brewing so recently. Which was usual, since Susan had started it without any wish to cause trouble. It was simply her personality.

'How very difficult it must be for a gentleman of your sensibilities to have a stepmother of such independence,' Lady Elizabeth Mainwaring said in dulcet tones.

Annabell felt Timothy's muscles tense under her fingers. The other woman had hit the bull's-eye with one shot. That always had been the major source of friction between the two of them. They had finally reached a tacit agreement to smile politely, inquire about one another's health and then go their separate ways.

'Annabell more than earned her independence,' Timothy said. 'I am happy she values it.'

Annabell nearly stopped in her tracks. That was the nearest thing to an acceptance of her that she had ever heard her stepson say.

'Why, thank you, Timothy.'

He looked down at her, his eyes turbulent. 'You are welcome.'

He led each of them to their seats. Lady Mainwaring sat to Hugo's right in honour of her engagement to him. Lady Fitzsimmon sat at the opposite end of the table from Hugo as befitted the current Lady Fitzsimmon. Annabell sat on Hugo's left, a position she found disturbing, but could do nothing about. Her stepson sat beside her with Mr Tatterly across from him. Susan sat beside Mr Tatterly. They were an uneven number.

The first course began. Turtle soup and fish.

Annabell found she was not hungry, even for the turtle soup, a delicacy she normally relished. Across from her Lady Mainwaring ate sparingly, all the while keeping a light chatter going that included Hugo and Mr Tatterly. Both men looked interested, although Mr Tatterly made a point of trying to include Susan.

Annabell fiddled with her spoon and declined the salmon. Instead, she sipped steadily on her wine. She noticed everyone else also imbibed freely, particularly Hugo.

'Would you like some turbot?' he asked.

She looked directly at him for the first time since sitting down. He looked far from happy. Comfortable, yes, but then he was very experienced.

'No, thank you.'

'As you wish.'

His voice was bored and dismissive. It hurt. She took another sip of wine.

'Lady Fenwick-Clyde,' Lady Mainwaring addressed her. 'Do you find that London is quite flat with everyone on the Continent?'

'Not everyone is there and the Season is barely started.'

'True.'

Inanities, Annabell thought. A way for two women who want the same man to pass the time without being at each other's throat. And they still had several courses to go before dessert, after which she could plead a headache and escape to her room. *As she had done last night.* Only Hugo would not follow her tonight—or any other night.

The conversation buzzed around her. Her stepson, Timothy, concentrated almost exclusively on his hostess. A pretty flush made Juliet's skin glow. Her gown of a white muslin slip overlaid by a celestial-coloured netting further complemented her blue eyes and blush-red hair. She was pretty and gentle.

Annabell felt Hugo's attention on her. Heat crept from her stomach to her face. Fortunately the table was large enough that they were too far apart for him to touch her even by accident.

She finally turned to look at him, determined to act with more spine. 'Do you wish to say something to me, Sir Hugo?'

'You are wearing the aquamarines.'

Her flush deepened. 'Yes. They go perfectly with this gown.'

'They go perfectly with you.'

His brooding gaze rested on her like a heavy mantle of fur, warm and nearly suffocating. She glanced away from him and saw Lady Mainwaring look from him to her. She made herself smile at the other woman who merely looked at her for a long moment before turning her attention to Hugo.

'Hugo, my dear, please pass the salt,' she purred.

Annabell noticed every man at the table look at Lady Mainwaring as though unable to resist the call of her voice. The lady's smile was self-satisfied as Hugo acquiesced. She picked daintily at her food.

Unable to tolerate much more, Annabell was glad to see

the footman remove the dishes. The next course had to be better than this last one. It was not.

Annabell sat through dinner, feeling as though she were being tortured for wanting something she could not have. If she had never loved Hugo, she would not be suffering now.

The next course was removed. And so it went.

Juliet finally rose and Annabell followed suit with an alacrity that threatened to topple her chair. Without a backward glance, she followed her hostess from the room. They trooped back into the salon, a large rectangular room that never seemed warm.

Before the tea tray was brought in, Annabell rose. 'Please excuse me, Juliet. I have the headache and plead exhaustion.'

Juliet stood immediately, went to Annabell and took one of her hands. 'You poor thing. You have been working too hard trying to finish your excavation. Of course you are excused. I will send a maid up with tea and some laudanum to help you relax.'

Annabell smiled. She could easily understand what her stepson saw in this woman five years his senior.

'Thank you, but I don't need anything. I am merely tired. After a good night's sleep I will feel right as can be. I will probably miss breakfast too since I wish to spend every minute at the villa so I can finish this as quickly as possible and intrude no longer.'

Juliet shook her head. 'You are more than welcome here, Annabell, with or without the Roman villa.'

Annabell's smile deepened. 'You always make me feel warm and liked. Now, if you will excuse me.'

Susan, realising what was happening, scurried over. 'Oh, dear, oh, dear. I knew you were working too hard. Tomorrow you must rest instead of going out there. The men from the village will be able to carry on for a day without you. You know they will. I will go up with you and make sure that you get your tea and laudanum.' She turned to Juliet Fitzsimmon. 'What a perfect idea, Lady Fitzsimmon, to have laudanum sent up. Annabell does not have any with her. She does not like to take drugs of any sort, but she does look peaked. A good night's rest will be the best thing for her and laudanum will ensure that she gets it.'

Annabell nearly groaned. The last thing she needed was Susan's over-solicitousness. Her companion always meant well, but she could be exhausting.

'I will be perfectly fine, Susan, dearest. You stay here and enjoy yourself. The gentlemen will be arriving shortly.'

'Oh, no, I couldn't let you go up all by yourself.'

'Of course you can. I will be fine. A maid will bring the tea and laudanum, which I will take.' Susan raised both brows. 'I promise.'

'Well—'

'Oh, stop,' Lady Mainwaring's smoky voice interrupted. 'She has said she will do it. She is a grown woman with a penchant for exerting her independence. Let her be.'

Annabell's eyes widened slightly. She looked at the rival who had won the match and very likely didn't even know there had been a contest. Lady Mainwaring shrugged her delicately rounded white shoulders as though to say, what a fuss.

More flustered than ever, Susan said, 'Oh. Yes. I know that, Lady Mainwaring. I had just thought to help. Nothing more.'

Annabell, whose hand had been released by Lady Fitzsimmon, moved to touch Susan. 'It is all right. I know you only meant to help. You always think of others before yourself, dear Susan. But, as Lady Mainwaring said…' she cast a considering glance at the other woman '…I am fully capable of taking care of myself in this matter.'

'What matter is that?' Hugo's voice preceded him through the door.

'Nothing that need concern you,' Annabell replied

quickly. Then added, 'Sir Hugo. But thank you for your concern.' She turned to the other women. 'Goodnight.'

She felt Hugo's gaze on her as she left. Heat crawled up her back and made her head ache even more. She wished the excavation was done and she could leave. She would go join Guy and Felicia in London and Susan could remain here if that was acceptable to Juliet. That would give Susan more time with Mr Tatterly.

Annabell reached her room, closed her door and locked it, leaving the key in the hole so no one with another key could unlock it. She did not think Hugo would follow her with everyone here, but there were times when his passion was upon him that proprieties were the last thing on his mind.

She managed to undo her dress and let it fall to the floor and left it. She would wait till morning to hang it in the massive wardrobe. She would feel better then. She left the jewellery on.

Moving toward the mirror on the dressing table, she picked up a candelabra. She set the candles down and sank on to the chair. Her reflection, morose and exhausted, looked back at her from the mirror. Instead of unfastening the jewels as she had intended, she studied them. The flaw-less watery blue of the aquamarines were complemented and lent added sparkle by the circling diamonds. The white gold the gems were set in looked good on her pale skin. Hugo had picked well, so well that he might have had them specially made just for her.

Slowly, she unfastened the necklace, next the two brace-lets and lastly the drop earrings. She picked up the box they'd come in from amongst the scattered bottles and vials. She carefully arranged them on the black velvet. She would not wear this gift again.

When the maid came with tea and laudanum, Annabell unlocked the door, and the maid saw that she was already dressed for bed. 'Thank you,' she told the young girl, who bobbed a curtsy. 'You may go.'

The girl bobbed another curtsy and scuttled back out the door. Annabell relocked it. That would keep Hugo out, but would it keep her in? In spite of everything, she longed to go to him, to touch him, to have him hold her. She was hopeless.

She drank the tea and left the laudanum. The opiate always left her feeling muddled in the mornings after she'd taken it. She would need her wits about her tomorrow.

Annabell rose earlier than was her habit, dressed and went downstairs. She doubted that her daily provisions were ready yet or that breakfast had been set out so she would go to the kitchen and get a bit of toast and some tea. She moved quietly on the carpeted hall and was just about to round a corner when she heard voices. She stopped.

'Miss Pennyworth,' Mr Tatterly's solid voice said, 'you are up early.'

'Yes, Mr Tatterly. I have chores to finish before I can join Annabell at the villa.'

Susan's voice was even more breathless than normal. Annabell smiled.

'Perhaps if I helped you, you would have some time to take a stroll through the gardens with me? They are very nice this time of morning.' There was a hesitation to Mr Tatterly's voice, as though he were not sure of his ground.

'Why, thank you,' Susan said.

Annabell could imagine the smile on her companion's face. Things were progressing nicely between the couple. She would find another way downstairs to give the two some privacy, but the next words stopped her.

'I have something I wish to ask you in private.'

Tatterly sounded as though his cravat was too tight and he had to force the words past the constriction. Annabell sympathised with his nervousness. She anticipated that he wished to ask Susan to marry him, and that would make any man nervous, let alone one as shy as Mr Tatterly.

'Oh, my.' Susan, on the other hand, sounded thrilled. 'Of course I will walk with you. Shall we go now?'

'What about your chores, Miss Pennyworth? I don't wish to interfere with them.'

'You shan't, Mr Tatterly.'

Annabell walked back to her chamber door to give the couple time to get down the stairs. She would soon lose her companion, but while she was sad she was also glad. Susan would be happy with Mr Tatterly.

After several moments, she retraced her steps to find them gone. She descended to the ground floor. The delay had been long enough that her food hamper stood in its regular position by the front door. She fetched it and started out only to see Lady Mainwaring on the front steps dressed for riding.

Annabell paused for an instant before nodding. 'Good morning, Lady Mainwaring.'

'The same to you, Lady Fenwick-Clyde. I hope you are feeling better today.'

Her sultry voice seemed to cling like honey to every word. No wonder Hugo had taken her as his mistress. And that was without taking into account her considerable beauty. Her rich gold hair was swept up and under a navy blue velvet hat with a single ostrich plume that curved so the end tickled her flawless cheek-bone. Her lips were full and red as the evening sun. Her figure was outlined to perfection in a tight-fitting habit. A waterfall of fine lace spilled from her jabot to draw attention to her voluptuous bosom.

Annabell felt completely inadequate in her practical harem pants, man's plain white shirt and loose-fitting jacket. She felt absolutely clumsy in her wellingtons. Well, there it was and nothing she could do about it. She and Lady Mainwaring were the complete antithesis of one another.

With only a tiny pang of jealousy, Annabell replied, 'I am much better today, thank you. A good night's sleep is the best cure for ailments.'

'Generally.' Lady Mainwaring laughed and a wicked gleam entered her eyes. 'Are you off to your Roman villa?'

'Yes.' Annabell wondered what the woman was up to. She couldn't be interested in something so unfashionable as an excavation.

'Hugo has told me a little about what you are doing. Very commendable.' She flicked the riding crop against her lower leg. 'But what I find utterly fascinating is your independence. I don't know another woman who would do as you are.'

Annabell studied the other woman's face, looking for derision or malice. There did not appear to be either.

'I do as I please and have done so since Fenwick-Clyde's death. If that is independent, then so be it.'

'Do you follow your own desires in everything?'

Now there was a hint of something more than interest in the lady's voice and expression. Annabell wondered if she was prying into her personal life. It was none of her business if that was the case.

'I do as I see fit, Lady Mainwaring. Nothing more and nothing less.' She picked up the wicker basket she had set down when the two of them had started talking. 'Now, if you will excuse me, I have work to do.'

'Of course,' Lady Mainwaring murmured. 'And I have a ride to enjoy. I look forward to seeing you at dinner.'

Annabell smiled but said nothing. She did not look forward to seeing anyone at dinner tonight. Perhaps she would plead another headache and have a tray sent up to her room. That would be easier.

Every time she saw Hugo's former mistress and soon-to-be wife, she felt a pang of jealousy and pain that was far from pleasant. She had never considered herself a petty person, but she did not enjoy seeing Lady Mainwaring's extraordinary beauty or hearing her sultry voice. She had to let that go. She could change nothing.

And for now, she had work to do.

Chapter Fifteen

Annabell slipped on to the veranda while everyone else was in the salon talking or playing cards. She had been unable to continue seeing Lady Mainwaring draped over Hugo's arm and hanging on every word he said. Weak and petty, but she was rapidly learning that where he was concerned she was not as strong as she had always thought.

The scent of roses reached her. The moonlight showed a gravel path through the gardens. A walk might calm her down, help her regain her equilibrium.

She moved down the steps, smiling at the lion rampant that guarded the entrance to the rose walk. To her fanciful imagination, he was a large tabby cat rearing on hind legs to catch a butterfly. She smiled and realised with a start that it had been a long time since she had seen anything whimsical in life. If nothing else, falling in love with Hugo had given her a deeper appreciation for everything around her.

She stopped and cupped a large red rose to her face. She inhaled the intoxicating scent.

'They are most beautiful in the moonlight,' Hugo's voice said from behind her. 'But their smell is strongest in the full afternoon sun.'

She started and moved away. 'I did not know you were behind me.'

She did nothing to keep the accusatory tone from her words. She did not want him here. It was too painful.

He stretched his lips, showing white teeth. It was a predatory action. She took a step back and caught herself. She was not going to turn tail and run from him.

'Why are you here, Hugo?'

He gazed at her, his eyes brooding. 'Because of you, why else?'

'Then leave. I don't want you here.'

He closed the distance between them. 'Don't lie to me, Bell. Lie to yourself if you must, but not me.'

Her heart thumped painfully. 'I am not lying.' But she was.

He grabbed her upper arms and pulled her to his chest. 'You want me here as badly as I want to be here.'

She stiffened and flattened her palms on his chest and pushed. She didn't move an inch, he held her so tightly. 'Have you been drinking?'

He laughed harshly. 'A little. But that is not what runs hot in my blood.'

The moonlight turned his swarthy complexion sallow and accentuated the hollows of his cheeks. It made his eyes dark pools of passion and pain, his sensual mouth a slash of promised delights.

She drew a shaky breath. 'Let me go, Hugo. This is not right.'

'Right?' His voice was hard. 'What is right? My engagement to Elizabeth?'

'No, but necessary,' she said, her voice weaker than she liked. 'You must pay the piper for your actions.'

'Or another man's,' he said bitterly.

'You can't change the situation,' she managed to say, through lips gone numb with pain. 'You agreed to this marriage.'

He groaned, his fingers tightening until she knew she

would have bruises the next day. 'I have to, Bell. I couldn't
let her deliver a child out of wedlock.'

'Why not?' Even as she asked, she knew why. And she
would have thought less of him if he had.

He set her away. 'Because. Because as much as my father
protected me, there were still the sly glances and quickly
hushed words. My father loved me dearly, but I knew with
a small boy's insecurity that my father had not married my
mother. I might be in much different circumstances if he
had married and had another child sooner than he did. As
it was, I was his only child for many years.' He turned his
back to her so she could barely hear him. 'I would not do
that to another child.'

'Even though you do not love the mother?' The words
were a cry from her heart.

He rounded on her. 'Even though I do not love Elizabeth
Can you understand?'

She nodded. The hurt he had inflicted did not keep her
from understanding what he did and why he did it. But it
didn't make it easier to watch him and Elizabeth Mainwaring together either.

'Yes,' she sighed. 'I can understand.' He took a step
toward her. She put her hand up. 'Please, Hugo, no more.
While I can understand, it still hurts. Please, leave me
alone.'

She thought he would refuse, but then he bowed his head.
'You are right. My pursuing you only makes it harder.'

'Yes,' she murmured.

Without another word, he left, taking her happiness with
him. Something was going to have to change. She couldn't
take much more of this. With feet that felt leaden, she made
her way back to the veranda, her pleasure in the rose garden
gone like it had never been. She climbed the shallow steps
and saw a shadow moving, sensed another person.

'Lady Fenwick-Clyde?' Elizabeth Mainwaring's rich,
honeyed voice penetrated the darkness of the veranda.

Annabell faced the other woman. 'Yes, Lady Mainwaring?'

For an instant only, she pondered the inanity of them calling each other by their titles, given to them by men now no longer living. Still, the formalities provided distance that she, for one, sorely needed. This was the woman who had taken Hugo from her. Plain and simple, nothing more, nothing less. She took a deep breath and wished it did not feel as though her throat was closed.

'I would like to speak with you. If you have a minute.'

Annabell considered her answer. The last person she wanted to talk with was the woman in front of her. Yet, she could not blame Lady Mainwaring without also laying blame on the woman's partner—Hugo. He had been an active participant in their liaison. While society might wink and turn away from Hugo's involvement, she would not—could not.

'What do you wish to say?' Annabell finally said, suddenly tired beyond imagining.

Lady Mainwaring stopped when she was close enough for her lowered voice to reach Annabell. The full moon sparked off her pale blonde hair and made her skin appear like the finest Limoges porcelain. Her eyes sparkled like sapphires. She was a very beautiful woman.

No wonder Hugo had taken her for his mistress. He was a connoisseur of female beauty even though he had erred when he chose her for his latest dalliance. He had said she was beautiful to him. That had been enough for her.

Pain, tight and breathtaking, took her. She had thought herself past this. She had thought her independence would be enough. Had she been wrong?

'This is not easy.' Hugo's future wife kept her voice low.

Elizabeth Mainwaring's sensual alto penetrated Annabell's agony. She forced herself to let go of what had been. The woman before her was Hugo's past and his future, not her.

Her voice rough, Annabell said, 'Nothing ever is, is it?'

She sighed from exhaustion, wishing this was over and she was in her own room, locked behind a concealing door where she could release her grief and pain instead of holding them in. She did not want this talk, but she would not turn away from it. She was made of stronger stuff, or so she had always believed.

'No, but then life isn't easy,' Lady Mainwaring said. 'I want to tell you the truth.'

Annabell laughed a short, sharp bark that did nothing to conceal her hurt. It was the best she could do.

'What if I don't want to know the truth, Lady Mainwaring?'

Elizabeth Mainwaring looked at her from the corner of her eye. 'Then leave. I won't follow you, and I won't try again.'

Annabell turned away. That would be the simple solution. She could walk away tonight and tomorrow she could leave Rosemont. Susan and her Mr Tatterly were very likely settled, therefore Susan could stay here or not as she chose without jeopardising her relationship with her fiancé. She could go to Guy's London town house. But running away would accomplish nothing, especially on her excavation. Still, she thought she would go anyway. She was tired beyond imagining. She could always return later, hopefully when Hugo and his new bride would not be in residence.

She angled a glance at the other woman. Elegant and beautiful as she was, Elizabeth Mainwaring did not look happy. Bitterness flooded Annabell. The woman had Hugo, but she was not ecstatic. What irony.

Perhaps it would be better to hear her out. If nothing else, one of them might walk away from this encounter feeling better.

'What do you want to say?' She didn't try to keep the resignation from her voice. 'Let us air the dirty linen and be done with it.' She looked at the expanse of grounds, silvered by the full moon, and refused to feel regret. She made a sudden decision. 'I shall be leaving first thing in the morning.'

'You don't need to.'

She shrugged. 'There is no reason to stay. The initial excavation is done. Jeffrey Studivant will be arriving tomorrow afternoon. He was originally going to assist me. Now he can finish it all. He is eminently qualified.'

'Ah. So you aren't running away. I had wondered.'

Annabell felt the heat of anger burn through her chest, easing some of the previous pain of loss. 'No, Lady Mainwaring, I am not.' Then honesty made her add, 'Only a little. I would have left for a while no matter what. My brother and his wife have just had a baby. I would like to spend time with them.'

Only a small white lie. She did want to see Guy and Felicia again and little Adam. The fact that she would not have gone for some time if Lady Mainwaring had not arrived was only a small matter.

The other woman lifted her elegant and rounded white shoulders in a very Gallic gesture. 'I would have left had I been in your place. I have never believed a stoic face worth the effort. Better to leave behind whatever is hurting you.'

The admission took Annabell by surprise. She turned to look at her nemesis. 'I would imagine you have scant experience of being hurt and consequently having to be a stoic.'

'You would have been wrong.' Her voice was ironic.

'How little we know each other,' Annabell murmured.

'True. But we are both women and as such, we both live with our emotions close to the surface.'

Annabell looked sharply at Lady Mainwaring. 'You are marrying Sir Hugo, yet you sound sad.'

'Perhaps I am.' She turned to face Annabell. 'Perhaps I wish things had turned out differently, but they have not. That is why I sought you out.'

A pang of discomfort lodged in Annabell's gut. 'Don'
feel you must tell me anything, Lady Mainwaring. Sir Hug
and I were not engaged, not did we exchange vows of an
kind.'

'No?'

Annabell shook her head slowly. 'No.'

'Then am I mistaken in thinking you care for him?'

Annabell's fingers froze in the act of pulling her shaw
close. She had to pick her words carefully. Lady Mainwaring might speak as though she intended to bare her soul
but so far she hadn't. And Annabell didn't think she coul
make herself more vulnerable to this woman than her lov
for Hugo already made her.

She spoke slowly. 'In the time I have been here, I have
played cards with him, gone on picnics, sat across from
him at the dinner table. He even taught me how to waltz
I would be lying to say that after all that he means nothing
to me.'

'A friend, nothing more?'

Annabell took her time folding the ends of her scar
across her breast, wondering why she was suddenly so cold
The night was nearly balmy. But she knew why. She fel
caught in a situation with no easy solution. It made he
defensive.

'Why are you doing this?'

Lady Mainwaring turned away and leaned over the
stucco railing so that she seemed poised to fly into the nigh
air. 'Guilt?'

'Guilt?' Annabell was certain she had misheard.

Arms still on the railing, Elizabeth Mainwaring looke
at her. 'No matter how you skirt around your feelings, Lady
Fenwick-Clyde—which I call you because I sense you don'
like or trust me—I believe you care deeply for Hugo. I als
believe he cares for you. That is something where Hugo is
concerned.'

She turned back to gaze over the rose bed that spread

from the house nearly to the artificial pond. The scent of its blooms wafted on the breeze.

'I have known him for many years. He knew my husband,' she added. 'After I became a widow, I waited the acceptable year and then approached him.' Her perfectly formed mouth twisted. 'As you can probably imagine, he accepted my offer.'

Annabell sucked in air, but said nothing. She must have made a sound, though, for Lady Mainwaring looked back at her.

'Does that shock you?'

'Should it?' But it did. As independent as she professed herself to be, she did not think she could pursue a gentleman.

'Not if you knew me.' She turned back to her contemplation of the moonlit garden. 'Anyway, he took me up on my offer. That was nearly a year ago. I even went to the Continent when he did. Although, in all honesty, it was not so much for Hugo as for the excitement. Everyone was there.'

'So you and Hugo have been lovers for nearly a year?'

'Yes. But he dropped me when he met you, even though he had made arrangements to return to London when I did and to carry on as we had been doing.'

Another sharp intake of breath. Hugo had been telling her the truth when he said Lady Mainwaring was no longer his mistress. For what good it did now.

'And his action would not have bothered me.' She stopped speaking for so long, Annabell began to wonder if she had finished. 'You see, I cared for someone else.' Elizabeth Mainwaring gave a bitter, disillusioned laugh. 'I was a fool, but I loved him. I cuckolded Hugo with him.'

Annabell seethed with indignation. How dare she treat Hugo like that, betray him with another? She had thought only the married did such things.

Lady Mainwaring shrugged. 'At the time nothing mattered to me but this other man. And, if Hugo knew, he did not let on. However, looking back, his visits did lessen. Yet, he was always careful in what he said, and it was easy for me to be so with him. He is a wonderful lover, but I do not love him so I was never caught in the throes of impatience. When Hugo paused for his protection, it was more than acceptable. I did not want to bear his bastard any more than Hugo wished me to.'

She turned around and leaned backward on the parapet, closing her eyes. Her voice lowered. 'I had already borne someone's bastard, delivered it and given it up to a tenant farmer. A little girl.' Her voice caught. 'My husband did not take lightly to being cuckolded. Charles told me to give up the child or run away with my lover, who would not have me for he was married himself, or find myself turned out with no support.' She opened her eyes, but Annabell sensed she did not see anything but the past. 'I gave up the child.'

Annabell gasped. She could not help herself. But she instantly regretted it. 'What you did is not so unusual in our circles.'

'No,' Lady Mainwaring agreed. 'But, nonetheless, it was not easy to do. I was in a fit of melancholy for at least a year afterward. I vowed that I would never get myself into that position again, and if I did, then I would keep the child.' She gave Annabell an apologetic look. 'That is why I am so very sorry to do this to you, but I will not give up my baby again. Nor will I raise the child as a bastard. Hugo had an easy life of it, but his father was a powerful man at court and in society. No one dared ostracise Sir Rafael or his illegitimate son. I am not so fortunately placed. And society will accept much from a man that it will not condone in a woman.' Bitterness dripped from her last words.

Annabell could do nothing but stare at the woman. Pity mingled with rage in her breast. Pity for the situation Lady Mainwaring was in and the pain she had experienced when giving up her previous child, and rage that the woman had decided to force Hugo into marriage.

'Is Hugo the father of your child?'

Lady Mainwaring's striking blue eyes glowed softly as though tears filled them. 'I don't really know.'

Annabell kept a tight rein on her voice, willing herself to show none of the disgust she felt. 'Yet you are forcing him into marrying you.'

'To provide a name for my child. Yes.'

'What of your other lover, the one who might just as easily be the father? Why don't you make him marry you?'

For the first time since her arrival, Elizabeth Mainwaring faltered. Her elegant fingers clutched tightly to the plaster railing, and her magnificent bosom rose and fell as though she fought for air.

And Annabell knew why. 'You love him.'

'Yes.'

'And he does not love you in return.'

Elizabeth Mainwaring shook her head. Her voice was soft and hurting and lost. 'No, he does not.'

'I am so sorry.'

And she was. After falling in love with Hugo and then losing him to this woman, she understood the agony of not having the person you love. Just a short time ago she would not have understood, but now Lady Mainwaring's pain was an emotion she knew only too well.

Suddenly she understood. 'That is why you won't tell him about the child.'

Elizabeth Mainwaring's breath caught. Annabell sensed the other woman's tension.

'Yes. He…' she turned away so Annabell could not see her face '…he told me from the first that he would not marry. He has been hurt before.'

Annabell did not try to keep the sarcasm from her voice. 'Haven't we all?'

'Yes.' Elizabeth Mainwaring's was just audible. 'And

even should he change his mind and marry for the child… do not think I could marry him, loving him as I do, and have him not care anything for me.' Her beautiful mouth twisted. 'I have not your strength.'

Annabell found herself hating and despising this woman. Elizabeth Mainwaring had made her own situation, and she was ruining another person's life because of her own selfishness and weakness. Yet, she truly understood, now that she had loved and lost Hugo, what it was like to be emotionally devastated.

'Will you tell Hugo?' Lady Mainwaring's voice cracked.

Annabell blinked back tears of anger. Would she tell Hugo? Would she make Elizabeth Mainwaring's child a bastard? Even for her own and Hugo's happiness? Perhaps if Hugo had ever told her he loved her, but he had not. In all likelihood, he would eventually be as happy with Elizabeth Mainwaring as he would have been with her. And she would get over this. Pain was not constant, it faded with time. She knew that from her parents' death. The first days and weeks, even months, she had felt as though a heavy weight lay suffocatingly on her chest. Then slowly it had eased. Now when she remembered them it was with joy and love for what they had meant to her. Eventually that would happen with her feelings for Hugo. It had to.

'No, I won't tell him. It is not my place.'

Rather than stay and hear any more, Annabell turned away. She would walk in the rose garden and delight in the silvered beauty of the blooms and heady scent of their ripening. Tomorrow she would leave.

She descended the steps to the gravel path and began to wander aimlessly. She told herself that in time none of this would matter anymore. In time.

Chapter Sixteen

Dawn barely crept over the late spring sky when Annabell stepped into the travelling chaise that had brought her to Rosemont a few months before. She told herself that in time her chest would no longer feel as though someone had pried it open and ripped out her heart. But not yet.

'Annabell.' Susan's voice penetrated Annabell's misery.

'Yes, dear?' Annabell leaned forward in her seat to look out the window. 'I thought I told you not to bother getting up. We will meet up in London soon enough.'

Worry puckered Susan's pale brows. 'Yes, you did, but I could not help but feel concern. As I told you last night, your departure is so sudden. Are you sure you are not sickening and need me by your side?'

Annabell made herself smile, but she knew it was a poor thing. 'Quite. Guy and Felicia have asked me to visit in London. They have gone there for the Season so Guy can take his seat in Parliament. Besides which, Mr Studivant will be here tomorrow. You will be completely occupied helping catch him up to where we are. And I know he will want you to stay as long as possible to continue your illustrations.'

'Yes, I understand all that,' Susan said peevishly, 'but I still can't help but worry at this suddenness. It is not at all like you. You never leave something unfinished. At least, I have never known you to do so, and I have known you for these many years.'

'Five, dear. Perhaps six. I was much less reliable in my younger days.'

'Faugh! You are being purposely obtuse.'

'Yes, I am,' Annabell said gently. 'I don't wish to discuss my reasons with you, Susan. Please respect that.'

Susan's mouth formed an astonished *O* seconds before her eyes filled. 'I'm so sorry, Annabell. I didn't mean.. don't wish to pry. I just…' She took a shuddering breath. 'I was just worried. You have been different since Sir Hugo's arrival, but it seemed a happy difference. Now you seem distracted and sad.'

Once more Annabell forced a smile that didn't reach her eyes or ease her heart. 'I need to go, Susan. Take care and join me in London as soon as you can. We must plan your wedding. And I shall miss you.'

Susan blushed a rosy pink and started speaking, but Annabell rapped on the carriage roof and the coach lurched forward. She waved to her friend.

Fortunately it was a beautiful day and the trip to London promised to be quick and uneventful. She needed something in her life to go simply.

She pulled the curtain over the window, thought better of it, and hooked the heavy green velvet back. The morning sun would improve her disposition. Consequently, when the carriage drove past the Roman villa, she could not help but see it and the workers she had hired from the village who were rapidly erecting the more permanent awning where the temporary tent had been. She would come back later, perhaps next year, and stay at the village inn.

Hugo would be married by then…and a father. The unhappiness that thought caused was like a rock in her stomach. She hiccupped as she tried to stifle the tears that seemed to insist on falling. She had cried more than enough

ast night, yet here she was doing so again. She was a wa-
ering pot.

She finally gave in to her misery.

Later, she pulled the handkerchief from her reticule and
lew her nose with force. Somehow she felt that if she did
verything with determination, she would manage to keep
oing forward with her life. After all, she had not wanted
o marry Sir Hugo. After Fenwick-Clyde, the last thing she
vanted was to put herself at another man's mercy.

So what if Hugo was nothing like her husband? Fenwick-
Clyde had seemed a reasonable older man when she first
net him. She had not wanted to marry him, but neither had
he feared and loathed him. Instead, she had been young
nd impressionable and had still thought she would find a
rand passion.

What a fool she had been. Was.

She sank back onto the velvet squabs and closed her
yes. Even more recently she had found herself longing for
love that would complete her life.

She had watched Guy and Felicia's stormy courtship with
ll its pain and passion and found herself wanting to care
or someone like they cared for each other. They had defied
he conventions of polite society and now neither was ac-
epted by the sticklers of the *ton,* but they were ecstatically
appy. They had each other and their baby.

She shifted, trying to get more comfortable. Sleep had
luded her last night and exhaustion rode her like a demon.
till, her thoughts would not quit so she could rest.

She was being as silly as Susan so often was. She was
appy. Finding someone would only complicate her life.
articularly someone like Hugo. He was a rake, with every
harm and flaw that epitaph epitomised.

But there is no man more faithful than a reformed rake,
tiny voice said in the back of her mind. That voice had

been more and more persistent as her liaison with Hugo
had progressed. She had nearly believed it.

Then Elizabeth Mainwaring had arrived.

Annabell turned again, frowning at her inability to get
comfortable. She finally gave up, sat up and stared out the
window. The lush Kent countryside passed by her window,
bringing the fresh scent of growing green things. She loved
this time of year. Spring always seemed to promise new
futures. It was the time the Romans had believed Perseph-
one returned from the Underworld, bringing rebirth with
her. She believed they were right.

She was unable to distract herself for long from Hugo.
Her thoughts returned to him will she or nil she. He had
lodged in her heart and remained there no matter what she
told herself.

Her hands clenched the seat cushion, her nails sinking
in. If only it didn't hurt so much.

And what if the child Elizabeth Mainwaring carried
wasn't Hugo's? What if she had left him to the woman
when she might have fought to keep him? What if?

Her decision was made. If Elizabeth Mainwaring truly
didn't know who the father of her child was, then it was
Lady Mainwaring's place to tell Hugo. If she chose not to,
it was not Annabell's right to tell him what had been told
to her in confidence. This situation was between them.
Hugo had slept with the woman of his own free will. Unfortunately for her, she was suffering more from the consequences of that passion than Hugo.

And Elizabeth Mainwaring was hurting as well. Annabell
had to concede that. The woman was in love with one man
and marrying another. It had to be hard. But that was the
way of their world, and, deep down, Annabell admired Elizabeth Mainwaring for doing what was necessary to keep
this child and to raise it as legitimate. That took a lot of
courage.

But the consequences still hurt. She could rationalise all

she wanted. She could tell herself she did not want to marry Hugo, would not have even had he asked. But the fact remained that she loved him and had lost him.

The fact remained that her heart still felt as though it had been ripped from her chest.

Hugo turned from the window, letting the heavy gold-velvet curtains fall back into place. The travelling carriage was long gone, and with it, Annabell.

Annabell of the silver hair and inquisitive mind. Annabell with a passion to match his own. He had lost her before he had even truly had her. And all because of his own actions. He had lived the life he wanted, and had revelled in the pleasures of the flesh. He still did. Only now, he wanted to share those delights with Annabell. And she was gone.

Fury and frustration coursed through him.

He moved to the mantel and swept his hand across the top, sending candelabra and fresh flowers crashing to the floor. The resulting sound of destruction brought no satisfaction.

'Jamison,' he bellowed. 'I'm going riding.'

The valet appeared so quickly it was likely he had been standing on the other side of the dressing-room door. He eyed Sir Hugo with a jaundiced air.

'No use taking your anger out on them gee-gees, Captain. Only cost money to replace them and a maid to clean up the mess.'

Hugo turned on his retainer. 'And what do you suggest I do, Jamison? Drink myself into a stupor?'

The man shrugged. 'Could do worse.'

Hugo's hands fisted, the urge to hit something nearly impossible to resist. Somehow he managed to unclench his hands before he did something he would regret. 'Go away, Jamison.'

'You wanted me to get out your riding clothes.'

Hugo scowled. 'Go away. I will do something else.'

'Ain't like you intended to marry Lady Fenwick-Clyde,' Jamison said as though he hadn't heard the order to leave. 'You was merely amusing yourself. Seen you do it more times 'n I can remember. Do it meself.'

'You are being impertinent.' Hugo's voice was cold enough to frost a frying pan.

Jamison ignored the reprimand. 'You even carried on with Lady Mainwaring off and on for nearly a year. Some would say you gotta pay the piper.'

Hugo's teeth clenched. 'Get out before I forget what we have gone through and throw you out.'

'Some would also say you swallowed Lady Mainwaring's story without so much as a peep. Wonder why?'

'Now.' Hugo's voice was dangerously low.

When in London he practised with Gentleman Jackson weekly and was accounted a good pugilist. The urge to land his valet a facer returned with a vengeance.

'I'm goin', Captain. But I think yer should consider what y'er doin'. Don't seem like you've given it much thought.'

On those words, he quickly moved to the door leading to the hallway instead of the dressing room. He tossed one parting shot. 'Know I went too far, but you needed to hear it and for sure Lady Mainwaring wasn't going to say it. Nor Lady Fenwick-Clyde. I owe you too much to stand quietly by while you ruin yer life.'

Hugo stared at the closed door for a long time before sprawling into a large chair. He ran his fingers through his hair to get it off his forehead and—unbidden—remembered Annabell doing the same thing. She had done so after their first bout of lovemaking. He turned his head to look at the bed. There.

His loins tightened painfully as the memories flooded back. She had been eager and insatiable. She had made him feel like a young buck with his first woman. She had made him feel special. It had been a long time since someone had made him feel special.

Perhaps Jamison was not far off the mark.

* * *

Annabell arrived in London after dark. The mist had rolled in from the Thames and made the going slow. The carriage lanterns cast an orange glow that reflected back. As they progressed further into the city, heading for exclusive Mayfair, the houses began to have gas lighting in front of the doors. Soon the night took on an eerie golden hue. Yes, she was in London during the Season.

The coach pulled to a stop in front of Guy's imposing Georgian town house. Instead of waiting for the servant to open the door and lower the steps, Annabell took a bunch of skirt in one hand, held on to the door strap with the other and jumped into the street. Luckily for her it hadn't rained or she would have soaked her half boots.

The front door opened and Oswald stood haloed by the light from the hall lamps. 'Miss Annabell,' he said in his most proper English butler voice. 'We were not expecting you.'

Annabell mounted the steps. 'I decided at the last minute. Surely Guy is still here. I see the knocker is on the door.'

Oswald stepped back to allow her in. 'His lordship and Lady Chillings have gone to Brighton for the week. His Highness, the Prince of Wales, specifically invited them.'

Annabell stepped further into the hall and instantly felt at home. She had spent more time here during her marriage to Fenwick-Clyde than at her husband's London residence. And the Prince of Wales is not to be gainsaid. Is Dominic here?'

'Yes.' His tone was censorious in the extreme.

'Up to no good, I take it.' Annabell undid the ribbons on her travel bonnet and tossed the confection on to a nearby table. 'I would expect nothing else.'

At that moment, a loud whine came from the door leading to the servants' work area and the steps to the kitchen. Annabell raised one brow in query.

'Mr Dominic's latest waif. A mongrel of less than impeccable blood lines.'

'That is certainly like my brother.'

Annabell laughed for the first time in what felt like ages, although she knew it had not been long since Lady Mainwaring had arrived at Rosemont. It felt good to find pleasure in something as minor as her younger brother's propensity to rescue the underdog—literally.

'Are you referring to Fitz?' Dominic's pleasing tenor demanded.

Annabell turned to see her brother descending the stairs, dressed in formal black satin breeches and coat. He had her height and slimness and high-bridged nose and dark blue eyes, but that is where the similarities ended. His hair was black as pitch and his complexion was swarthy as a tinker's thanks to the inordinate amount of time he spent out of doors pursuing his sporting interests.

'Where are you going rigged out like that?'

He snorted. 'Nowhere interesting, trust me, Bell. Almack's.'

'Almack's? Don't you detest that place?'

He gave a long, exaggerated sigh. 'Immensely. But that is where Miss Lucy wishes to go, so that is where I will escort her.'

'Miss Lucy? As in Lucy Duckworth?'

'The same.'

She frowned. 'I thought Guy warned you away from the chit. She is barely out of the schoolroom and much too innocent for the likes of you.'

He returned her look with a scowl of his own. 'I keep my own counsel, sister, just as you do.'

'Really?' She stood taller and squared her shoulders. 'And what do you mean by that remark?'

Instead of answering directly, he asked sweetly, 'Have you had the pleasure of meeting Fitz? My newest acquisition.'

Dawning realisation made her eye him with ill-disguised ire. '*Fitz,* as in…'

'Exactly,' he drawled. 'Fitzsimmon.'

'How dare you name a dog after Sir Hugo!'

'I dare very well, thank you. After all—' he settled his chapeau at a rakish angle on his ebony curls. '—they are much alike. Roustabouts with a taste for the ladies and less than impeccable antecedents—as Oswald so quickly informed you.'

'The pot calling the kettle black, don't you think, Dominic?' She could barely contain her irritation. 'Yet how like you.'

He made her an elegant, mocking leg, showing a calf any woman would be pleased to admire and any man would long to have. 'If you insist on digging at me about Lucy Duckworth, then I will continue to remind you that Sir Hugo Fitzsimmon is a rake of the first order and someone you should stay well away from.'

She snorted very much in the same way he had. 'I will do as I please. At least I am a grown woman and a widow. Lucy Duckworth is still a child.'

'A delightful one,' he said with a sly grin that quickly turned to disgust. 'Unfortunately, she comes well chaperoned.'

'Ah, Miss Duckworth.'

'Yes,' he said, his tone implying dislike. 'Miss Sourpuss. I swear she criticises everything. Nothing I do pleases the woman.'

'You would please her if you quit pursuing her young sister. Had you thought of that?'

'Ah, but that would not please me.'

'How typical.' She shook her head in resignation. 'But mark my words, Dominic, what you are doing will come to no good.'

He moved past her, turning to look over his shoulder.

'You think so? Then one can only hope it will be interesting.' He sailed out the door to his waiting phaeton.

She watched him with a worried frown. He was such a rakehell and ne'er-do-well, but she loved him. For all his ramshackle ways, he had a heart of gold. Even if he did name his latest charity case after Hugo.

Oswald coughed. 'Excuse me, Miss Annabell, but your luggage is ready to go up to your room. The same as usual?'

'Yes, thank you, Oswald.' In her altercation with Dominic she had completely forgotten that the loyal family servant witnessed it all. She threw caution to the wind and asked, 'Is Dominic getting himself in too deeply?'

Oswald's eyes clouded. 'I believe he might be, miss. It is as though he is driven to chase Miss Lucy, even though Miss Duckworth has been here several times to demand that he stop.' He shook his head in resignation.

'I can see him doing something like that.'

And she could. Something was amiss here, but goodness knew Dominic would never tell her what it was. In the meantime, she had her own concerns to deal with. But she would keep a watch on Dominic.

'So,' Annabell said, sweeping her gaze around the theatre of the Surrey Institution, aware nearly everyone in her audience was male, 'in conclusion, the discovery of a Roman villa in Kent so soon after the discovery of one in Sussex provides further proof that our shores were as fertile and welcoming to the Romans as they are for us today.'

There was a light smattering of applause to which she nodded acceptance before stepping down. Tomorrow she would speak to the Society of Antiquaries. For them, she would be more specific in what she found.

'Excuse me, Lady Fenwick-Clyde.' A gentleman stepped from the group just leaving the bottom row of seats. 'If I may be so bold, would you mind answering some questions?'

A little taken aback, but flattered nonetheless, Annabell stopped. He was a very presentable person. He wore a nicely fitted navy coat over a starched white shirt with points that just barely touched his jaw. His cravat was simple but well done, a point she recognised because of Guy's finesse with the things. And his pantaloons were grey and well-made. Very presentable.

She smiled at him. 'I hope I can answer your questions, sir. I did not stay to complete the excavations, Mr…'

He smiled back at her, showing strong teeth. He had a pleasant face with open blue eyes and a wide, if thin, mouth. His hair was sandy blond.

'I am Mr Daniel Hawks, and I am sure you can answer anything I ask. I know you have been involved in more excavations than this one.'

Her curiosity piqued, she asked before considering, 'How do you know that? I do not think we have met before.'

His face warmed, but he maintained a relaxed yet interested attitude. 'I have heard you speak before at the Society for Antiquities. You seem every bit as informed as your male colleagues.'

She blushed with pleasure. 'Why, thank you.'

He made her an abbreviated bow. 'Fully deserved. But I am wondering if this particular villa had mosaics of the seasons. I understand that another one not too distant does, or did. I believe originally there were depictions of all four seasons but that now only one remains.'

She nodded as she listened. 'Ah, yes. You are speaking of Bignor. I don't believe it has been fully uncovered yet.'

'Correct. I have listened to Mr Samuel Lysons read his second account of the excavation to the Society. I was wondering if you are finding similarities.'

'Some. As must be expected, the coloured mosaics are made from the same materials. And there are a number of rooms that have, or had, heated floors. Of course, we have found what appears to be bathing rooms. Nothing unusual.'

He nodded as he scribbled down her words.

'May I ask, sir, are you an antiquarian?'

He gave her his friendly smile. 'I am an amateur.'

'Aren't most of us?' she said. 'I hope I have helped you, Mr Hawks. I must be going now.'

'I am sorry if I have kept you from an appointment.'

'No, nothing of the kind. But my carriage should have arrived and the tiger hates to have the horses standing for long. They are my brother's and he is very particular.' She smiled to soften her words.

'Yes, yes, perfectly reasonable. Thank you so much.'

He made her a perfect leg, as though he were asking her to dance instead of bidding her goodbye. And if he was more graceful than Hugo, it was of no matter. She nodded and left.

She stepped outside and beckoned Tom, Guy's tiger, who was her tiger for the afternoon. He led the horses up and held them in place while she clambered into the phaeton. Luckily for her, this was not Guy's high-perch phaeton so she did not feel perilously high from the ground.

She glanced back at the elegant portico of the Surrey Institution to see Mr Hawks standing between the Ionic columns. She managed a small wave before Tom released the horses and clambered on to his spot in the back of the carriage. They were in Blackfriars Road and had some way to go to get back to Guy's house. Fortunately it was summer and the sun would be up for some time.

She flicked the reins and off they went.

She was a fair hand with the ribbons and could let her mind wander as she drove. Mr Hawks's attention had been very gratifying, and she wondered for what must be the hundredth time if she should write a paper about this excavation. Up to now, she had decided against it because women did not do that sort of thing. But then, women did not travel to Egypt alone such as she had done. Nor did they choose to live there as Lady Hester Stanhope was doing.

Perhaps she would write that paper after all. It would give her something to concentrate on besides Hugo. She smiled spontaneously for no other reason than she felt a glimmer of happiness. It was the first time in weeks.

With hard work, she might even forget Hugo. Hah!

Chapter Seventeen

'La,' Lucy Duckworth simpered. 'You are so naughty, Mr Chillings.' Suiting action to words, she swatted Dominic on the sleeve with her fan.

He grinned and appeared completely infatuated. If there was a gleam of ennui in his dark eyes, only those who knew him best would see it.

'Only with you, Miss Lucy.'

Annabell thought their inane flirting would make her nauseous, but she still managed to smile and nod and wonder what she was doing at Almack's with them. She had only been in London a week and Dominic had managed to drag her with him in lieu of Miss Duckworth as chaperon for Miss Lucy Duckworth.

Miss Lucy laughed a light trill that sounded straight out of the schoolroom. Annabell turned her attention elsewhere. She had not been to Almack's since her own coming out many years ago. It hadn't changed. The rooms were un-adorned, the food was mediocre at best and the company convinced it was the finest in the land.

Annabell sighed. So much for an enjoyable evening. But she could keep an eye on her brother.

'Bell,' Dominic said, 'Miss Lucy and I are going to have the next dance.'

'Don't monopolise her.' She flashed a smile at the young woman. 'It isn't done.'

'Yes, Lady Fenwick-Clyde.'

Miss Lucy Duckworth flushed with excitement. One would think she had never been here before, which Annabell knew was not so. Dominic had brought her last week. Of course, this was probably the first time the chit had been here without her older sister.

The music began and Annabell watched the couple join the group forming for a quadrille. She noted that a number of ladies followed their progress with envious looks. Her brother, rakehell that he was, was still considered a very desirable catch. He had an air about him of danger and passion that was nearly irresistible.

She turned from watching them to see Mr Hawks before her. 'Oh!'

'Pardon me,' he said, bowing. 'I did not mean to startle you.'

She smiled at him, noting he was once again impeccably dressed. 'No, do not apologise. I was thinking of something else and did not hear you approach.'

'Do you mind?' He indicated the chair beside her.

There was no polite way to tell him no, and she was not sure she wanted to. It would be nice to have company other than Dominic and his silly Miss Lucy. She wondered how the very serious and proper Miss Emily Duckworth managed. But that was none of her concern—she hoped. So long as Dominic behaved and did not go beyond the bounds of propriety, Miss Lucy would continue to be Miss Duckworth's problem.

'Ahem…' Mr Hawks cleared his throat.

'Oh, dear, I am sorry, Mr Hawks. Please be seated.'

'Thank you.' He took the chair and angled himself to look at her. 'Do you come here often?'

She laughed. 'No. I haven't been here for years, but my brother talked me into coming tonight.'

He looked at the closest set of dancers. 'Mr Dominic Chillings?'

'Yes, do you know him?'

She was not sure that knowing Dominic was a good recommendation. He often moved with a very fast and loose crowd. But then so had, did, Hugo, and that had not kept her from falling in love with him. The unbidden memory instantly dampened her spirits.

'Is something the matter?' Mr Hawks's voice held concern.

Annabell realised her emotions were showing on her face. Where was the stoic countenance she had worked so hard to perfect when married to Fenwick-Clyde? She would have to resurrect it.

'No, nothing is wrong.' She forced her voice to lightness and pressed him, knowing the surest way to make someone leave behind one topic of conversation was to insist they answer a question. 'You did not answer my question. Do you know Dominic?'

'No. Merely hearsay.'

'Really?' She lifted her chin, prepared to give him a setdown if needed.

She did not like his tone of voice. It implied that Dominic was unsavoury. She might often think that, but he was her brother. For a perfect stranger to think it was unacceptable.

Mr Hawks reddened and had the grace to look uncomfortable. 'Pardon me, Lady Fenwick-Clyde. I did not mean anything derogatory.'

'I am glad to hear that, Mr Hawks.'

He gave her a rueful smile. 'I seem to be at sixes and sevens with you this evening. Nothing I say or do is correct, which is my own fault. Perhaps I should leave, then come back and try again.'

That made her laugh. 'Don't be ridiculous.' Taking pity on his obvious discomfort, she asked, 'Do you come here often?'

'More than I should, no doubt.'

'Why is that?'

He gazed around the room and Annabell looked where he did. The glittering throng dipped and swayed, simpered and flirted to the rhythm of the music. Some of the finest jewels in the world glittered under the light from massive chandeliers, and some of the greatest minds in the country mingled with some of the most empty.

'I am supposed to be here in London to make contact with Mr Samuel Lysons. I wish to work with him, but so far I have done nothing but listen to him.' He finished with a grin. 'But that is nothing to concern you. May I have this next dance?'

Annabell blinked in surprise. 'Are you saying you wish to be more than an amateur antiquarian?'

He reddened. 'I have ambitions in that direction.'

'How interesting.'

She smiled at him. He returned her smile, his with a hint of interest she did not return. She decided it would be wise to change the subject. A country dance would not be amiss. It would put some distance between them and end this conversation.

'I would be delighted to dance—as long as it isn't a waltz. I am not good at that.'

His face lit with pleasure. 'I am sure you can do anything you set your mind to. However, if the music is any indication, I believe the next dance will be another quadrille. They are popular.'

It was not the dance she had hoped for, but it was better than sitting here and talking. She took one quick look around to locate Dominic and Miss Lucy. They were at the refreshment table talking to several other people. For the moment, she might leave them to their own devices.

Mr Hawks stood and gave her his hand. When her fingers met his, no shock of awareness made her tingle. Nothing. She had reacted to Hugo from the first, even when she didn't know who he was and he kissed her. For a moment she stared at nothing as the memory of Hugo's lips on hers made her ache for what she would never have.

'Lady Fenwick-Clyde?' Mr Hawks's concerned voice finally penetrated her reverie of joy and pain.

She turned her lips up into the semblance of a smile. 'I am so sorry, Mr Hawks. I keep thinking of other things. I believe I am tired.'

His blue eyes filled with sympathy. 'Would you like me to escort you to your carriage instead?'

Her smile turned genuine. 'You are so nice. Too nice for me not to keep my word.' She moved slightly ahead of him. 'We will dance.'

He followed with alacrity.

They took their places, he bowed and she curtsied. The music began. They moved through the steps, touching, then parting, then touching again.

She enjoyed the music and the movement, but there was nothing special when his fingers touched hers or his eyes met hers. Nothing at all. It was as though she was physically numb.

The music ended, he bowed, she curtsied and they returned to her seat to find Dominic and Miss Lucy already there. She still felt nothing for the attractive, nice man who stood at her side. She glanced at him and turned away with regret.

'Dominic,' she said to her brother, who was in the act of signing Miss Lucy's dance card. 'Miss Lucy has already danced with you twice.'

He stopped. 'And what if she has? That is just one of Society's bugaboos.'

She raised one brow.

'Very well.' He gave the young woman a rakish, lopsided grin. 'You will have to make do with this gentleman here.' He indicated Mr Hawks.

Taken by surprise, Mr Hawks did a credible job of concealing any sense of ill use he might have felt. Instead he bowed. 'If Lady Fenwick-Clyde will introduce us, I would be honoured to dance with the lady.'

Annabell's mouth thinned at Dominic's rudeness, but she made the introductions. Lucy Duckworth would be considerably safer with Mr Hawks than with Dominic. After the couple had joined the group forming on the floor, she rounded on her ne'er-do-well brother.

'Dominic, what game are you playing? That was appalling.'

His eyes narrowed. 'I am doing as I please, just as you have since Fenwick-Clyde stuck his spoon in the wall. You, of all people, should understand what that means.'

And she did. A tiny bit of her irritation with him evaporated, but still… 'That is all fine and good and I do understand, but that is no reason to ruin the chit. Unless…' An appalling thought occurred to her. 'You don't wish to marry her, do you?'

Totally affronted, he took a step back. 'Absolutely not.'

'Then stop making her the latest *on dit* with your pursuit. You are sometimes a loose screw, but this is outrageous even for you.'

He stiffened and his hands paused in the act of straightening his cravat. 'If you will excuse me, sister, I see an acquaintance.'

He stalked away without hearing her response. Just as well, she decided. He would not have liked her reply. He was behaving strangely, even for him.

'Lady Fenwick-Clyde,' a deep, honey smooth baritone said from just behind her.

Annabell's skin goose-pimpled and her stomach clenched. The room seemed suddenly hot and close, as though there wasn't enough air. One hand went instinctively to her throat.

She turned to see Hugo.

'Hugo.' She couldn't keep the note of joy from her voice.

When his sombre face lightened into a smile, she was glad she had not been able to.

'I called at your house earlier and they said you were here with your younger brother and Miss Lucy Duckworth.'

He had called at Guy's? In spite of knowing he should not have done so, she found herself happy he had. She was a mass of contradictions, had always been where he was concerned.

'That was very bold of you. An engaged man does not call on another woman, at least not a respectable woman, and I believe I am still considered one.'

The smile fled his face, leaving it harsh and hard angled. 'There is no reason for you not to be. I gave the excuse that I was looking for Dominic.' When her eyes widened a fraction, he added drily, 'We have been known to see each other at some of our haunts.'

'Of course, I had momentarily forgotten how much the two of you have in common. Although,' she added, irritation making her words bite, 'I don't believe I ever heard of you pursuing a chit barely out of the schoolroom.'

He lifted his quizzing glass to one clear green eye and surveyed the room until he found Dominic. 'Not since my salad days at least. Is it Miss Lucy Duckworth?'

Annabell sucked in her breath and bit her lower lip. 'Is it common gossip?'

'Didn't I just hear you tell him it was?'

She scowled at him. 'Were you eavesdropping?'

'You were not whispering. Besides, it is common knowledge. I have only been in town a day and have already heard the comments.'

She would swear there was a look of pity in his eyes. 'Don't pity me for my fool brother.'

'I don't. But I do understand your concern. It is not the thing to dally with someone of Miss Lucy's years—unless he intends marriage.'

Annabell sighed. 'You likely heard him say that was not the case.'

'I did. But if he continues as rumour says he has gone on, then he might find himself forced to it by a duel with the girl's father or brother. They are a ramshackle pair, but even they value their good name.'

Annabell's shoulders drooped. 'Very true.'

'But come,' he said, his voice dropping to a provocative challenge, 'forget Dominic. There is a waltz beginning, and I believe you could use another lesson.'

She eyed him askance. 'I don't think that is wise.'

He shrugged, but there was a hunger in his eyes and in the curve of his erotic mouth that told her he meant to have this dance. 'When have we ever been wise about each other?'

'So true,' she murmured.

'Then why start now, Bell? I want to hold you. It has been too long.'

There was an intensity of longing in his words that caught and held her. She realised with a mingling of fear and happiness and anticipation that she could not deny them both this small pleasure.

'All right.'

She moved to the dance floor, sensing he followed her without having to look. Her blood sang with his nearness. This dance was so little compared to what they had had, to what they had lost. But it was all they would get. She would take and revel in the closeness of his body to hers. She would take what he offered for the next too-short minutes and never regret it.

The music began.

Annabell looked up at Hugo and smiled. He met her gaze steadily with no easing of his sombre demeanour, but the hunger in his eyes burned brightly. He put his arm around her waist and swung her into the waltz.

Unlike their first dance, her feet followed him flawlessly.

It was as though what had passed between them since that time had somehow joined them so her body knew his without hesitation. She became one with him.

'I have missed you.'

His voice was low and seductive, the words full of promises. She responded to him in spite of her better judgement. But this line of unreason would benefit neither of them.

'Don't,' she whispered, her throat tight with regret. 'Don't do this to me, Hugo.'

'Why not?' Anger tinged his voice, lurking on the edges, ready to come forth. 'You know you feel the same way.'

He spun her around and around until she was too breathless to respond immediately to his demand. At the same time, his arm tightened so that she was closer than acceptable. Her breasts brushed his chest and fire, scalding and molten, flowed through her. It was all she could do not to press herself to him.

And the memories. They erupted from the dark corner where she had tried so desperately to bury them. Her face burned. Her body ignited.

'Hugo,' she gasped, her voice deep and raspy, 'take me back.'

A smile that was neither nice nor comforting transformed his face into a mask of desire with an edge of danger. 'No.'

He pulled her closer so that with the next turn, his hips brushed hers. Her eyes dilated and her mouth formed a soft *O* of arousal and need.

'You are remembering, aren't you?' he said. 'Remembering the other times I held you like this.'

She nodded, nearly unable to speak. But she had to. This had to stop. 'Hugo, this is not the place.'

'Then where is?' he demanded. 'Will you come to me?'

She stared at him aghast. 'I can't. You know that.'

'Then this is all I have.'

He twirled her again and again. Cinnamon and cloves

illed her senses. The music filled her ears. And Hugo kept
er close.

Dimly she knew other couples danced around them, but
they were a blur of colour and then they were gone. Nobody
mattered but the man holding her. She revelled in this moment in time. It was one more treasure to add to her memories, one more example of what he could do to her.

Annabell finally noticed they were no longer moving. His
rm remained around her, and their bodies stayed too close
or propriety. Her chest rose and fell in rapid gulps as she
ried to regain her sangfroid.

'Hugo,' she finally managed, 'you are holding me too
close.'

He released her and offered his arm. She wanted to re-
use, fearing that touching him again would only make it
that much harder to let him go in a few minutes. Or worse,
that she would sway towards him, thus telling anyone who
bothered to watch that she loved him. Still, appearances
dictated that she put her fingertips on his forearm. She did
o and he led her back to her seat where Mr Hawks waited.

She was surprised to see the other man. For some reason
he had thought he would leave when he saw her with
Hugo.

Mr Hawks gave her a reproachful look. 'You waltz very
well, Lady Fenwick-Clyde.'

She remembered what she had told him less than thirty
minutes before and had the grace to blush. 'Sometimes I
urprise myself, Mr Hawks.'

'Of course,' he said courteously. He bowed and made his
departure.

'Who is that?' Hugo's voice was low and ominous, noth-
ng like the tone he normally used with her.

Annabell gave him a considering look. 'What is wrong?'

His mouth thinned. 'An upstart makes a comment to you
that implies he has a right to an answer no man should have
right to, and you ask me what is wrong? Don't be naïve.'

Her eyes widened as realisation hit her. 'You are jealous.

He drew himself up ramrod straight as though she had insulted him. 'Think what you please, but answer my question.'

His high-handed assumption that she would kowtow to him was too much. 'I think not, *Sir* Hugo.' She sniffed. 'It is not as though you have a right to know whom I see or speak with. You are—after all is said and done—engaged to another woman.'

His face darkened and his hands clenched and unclenched. 'How convenient for you.'

She fumed. 'And where is your lovely fiancée?'

His jaw clenched. 'She is over by the window.'

For a fleeting moment pain such as she had hoped never to experience again seared through her chest. 'Oh.' It was all she could do to get the single word past the tightness of her throat. She dared not cry here, in front of him.

She pulled in a deep breath, heard it wheeze through the contraction of pain, and looked where he indicated. Sardonic amusement bit between the strands of hurt she felt.

Lady Elizabeth Mainwaring was gazing raptly up into the golden-skinned face of a man who had the bearing and gift of a Greek Adonis. His hair was as gold as the sun, and even from this distance Annabell could see the intense flash of his blue eyes. His shoulders were broad in the formal black coat with tails and his legs were long and well muscled in the black breeches and white stockings. Whatever was going on?

'Who is the gentleman with her?' She turned back to watch Hugo.

'That is St. Cyrus,' her former lover said drily. 'He shared Elizabeth's favours with me for some time.'

Annabell gasped, not certain she had heard correctly. Lady Mainwaring had said he might have known, but for some reason, Annabell had preferred to think he had not.

'What? What did you say?'

His mouth curled. 'You heard me. Elizabeth was bedding him while she was also sleeping with me.'

'And you didn't care?'

After the jealousy he had just demonstrated over her, she found it hard to believe he would countenance a woman of his choosing seeing another man, no matter what Lady Mainwaring had said. He had definitely made it plain he would not willingly allow her to do so.

He shrugged. 'I didn't really care. My liaison with Elizabeth was for one thing and one thing only. I never wanted or expected anything else. If she chose to see someone else as well, as long as it didn't interfere with my pleasure, then she was free to do so.'

'Like a marriage of convenience without the marriage.' It was a bald statement, but his words had been so matter of fact, nearly callous, that her description seemed perfect.

'Exactly.'

'Then it doesn't bother you that they're together now?'

He pinned her with his gaze. 'No, it does not. I'm with you, and even if I weren't, it still wouldn't bother me.'

A shiver ran up Annabell's spine. He was so cold, nothing like the man she had fallen in love with. 'I see.'

'Do you?'

He still would not let her look away; the intensity in his eyes and the aching sharpness of his features held her. 'I don't know, Hugo. I would hope your marriage would turn out to be more than an arrangement to give a child a name.'

His laugh was a harsh sound. 'The child may not even be mine.'

She stilled. Surely Lady Mainwaring had not told him what she had spoken about on the veranda? The woman was not stupid. She tore her gaze away from Hugo to look at the couple. Yet, Lady Mainwaring was obviously hanging on every word St. Cyrus said. He must be the man she loved who did not love her. For a brief moment, she pitied the beautiful Lady Mainwaring.

'Look at me, Bell,' Hugo ordered.

When she did not, he reached for her, but caught himself in time. She finally turned back to him. 'Do you really believe you might not be the father?'

He shrugged. 'It is possible. As you know, I take precautions. Not every man does.'

She flushed. 'Hush, Hugo. There are people around us.'

He glanced around, a haughty look on his face that dared someone to approach them. No one did. 'They are too far away to hear what we are saying, and if you do not give us away with your blushes they will never know.'

She continued to look at him, not sure if his blunt speaking was irritating her or if she was just in a bad mood because of the entire situation she found herself in. She decided it was a combination of everything.

'Very well, Hugo. I will try and control my body better.' She did not try to keep the trace of sarcasm from her tone.

He sighed. 'I am sorry, Bell. I do not like this situation any better than you do. I wish there was some way I could find out if St. Cyrus is really the father but, short of Elizabeth telling me that, I can't. I even—' he looked from her to the couple '—brought her with me tonight, hoping he would be here and she would go to him—as she has.'

Annabell laid a cautioning hand on his arm before she realised it. He looked down at where she touched him and she jerked away.

'This is not the place, Hugo, no matter if no one is near. What you are talking about is too private, too important.'

He sighed in exasperation. 'You are right. What do you suggest?'

She bit her lip. There was no easy answer. No right answer. She wanted to see him, and she wanted to talk this through. More than anything she wished Elizabeth Mainwaring carried St. Cyrus's child and could be brought to admit it—provided the woman even knew. But to see Hugo in private—that was risking much.

'I...' she took a deep breath and let it out in a rush as she spoke '...I don't think we should see each other again. What you are talking about is between you and Lady Mainwaring. I have nothing to do with it. If, by some chance, he calls off your engagement, then...then I no longer know.'

She could see that her answer angered him. His eyes narrowed and his mouth thinned.

'Annabell,' Dominic said imperiously, 'it is time to take Miss Lucy home.' His face hardened as he glanced at Sir Hugo.

She nodded, casting one last look at Hugo. His face was stony, but he said nothing. She followed Dominic and Miss Lucy from the rooms.

Hugo watched her go and wondered that it could bother him so much to see her and not possess her. He had never felt this way. And now, he had lost her and all because of past indiscretions.

He watched his fiancée with the man he knew she preferred and wondered if Elizabeth had approached St. Cyrus and been denied. From the look on her face and the way her body swayed toward him, she wanted him.

He turned his attention to St. Cyrus. The man was a dandy, but had also been a soldier and done well from all reports. He was considered a man of honour. Then why would he not take on the burden of marriage to Elizabeth? Because she did not think he was the father. That was all he could think of.

He no longer wanted to stay. It was hot and too many dowagers with their wagging tongues watched him. He made his decision.

He sauntered toward Elizabeth and her companion, nodding to acquaintances but keeping his expression closed. The last thing he wanted was to be approached and forced into conversation. That was not his purpose for being here.

He reached the two and drawled, 'Elizabeth, St. Cyrus, I

believe it is time to leave. Anyone who is anyone alread
has.'

Elizabeth's violet eyes sparked and she opened her mout
in what Hugo knew would be a protest. St. Cyrus laid hi
hand lightly on her arm for a moment, no longer, and sh
composed herself. Interesting.

'I believe you are correct, Sir Hugo,' the other man said
'I was just telling Lady Mainwaring that I must be leaving
I have another engagement.'

Elizabeth's cupid-bow mouth thinned, but that was th
only sign that she was not happy. Hugo found himself ad
miring her ability to keep her feelings to herself. It was
skill he had always prided himself on possessing. Now i
seemed he was slipping. He did not like that.

He extended his arm. 'If you will, Elizabeth? My carriag
should be brought 'round shortly.' He nodded to St. Cyrus
'I hope to see you around.'

St. Cyrus bowed to Elizabeth and nodded to Hugo. 'I an
sure of it. We do frequent the same clubs.'

Hugo studied the other man for a long minute, wondering
if there was more to his words. When St. Cyrus remained
sanguine, he decided the man meant exactly what he said
Apparently he had shared Elizabeth's bed simply for th
pleasure with no emotional ties. Just as he had. Hugo almos
found it in himself to feel sorry for her. And he might have
if she had not picked him to be her sacrificial goat.

He nodded curtly to St. Cyrus, put a palm to the smal
of Elizabeth's back and escorted her outside to his closec
carriage. He helped her into the carriage but, instead o
joining her, closed the door and rapped on the side of th
vehicle, telling the coachman to take her home. Here i
London, Elizabeth stayed in her own town house.

She stuck her head out of the window the instant she
realised what he was about. 'What are you doing?'

He looked at her beautiful face, so perfect in every detai
even though she was pouting. 'I am doing as I please, Eliz

abeth. We may be engaged, but that does not require me to squire you everywhere.'

It was obvious from the pinched look around her mouth that his words did not make her happy. Instead of replying, she dropped the curtain back into place and closed the window with a snick of the latch.

Hugo watched the coach until it turned the corner and was lost to sight. There was nothing for him at home and he was not sleepy. Nor did he intend to share Elizabeth's bed, even though she had indicated that he would be welcome. Of course, her invitation had come before she had met St. Cyrus again.

He would go on to Brooks's. Of all the clubs he belonged to, it was his favourite. And the walk to St. Timothy's Street would do him good. He was still tense from the encounter with Bell.

He set off, swinging his ebony cane with an occasional swat at nothing simply because he needed to do something or he would explode. She was the only woman who had ever made him care if he never saw her again. And he'd be damned if he wouldn't. Even if he did end up married to Elizabeth, he would see Bell. It would be better if he could find something to link St. Cyrus to Elizabeth's current state, but he had a feeling that information would have to come from the man.

Watching Elizabeth with St. Cyrus had told him much about their relationship. St. Cyrus was the dominant one. He would be the one to determine if there was more to their liaison than shared passion.

Rain started and Hugo picked up his pace.

A night ending with gambling and drinking. It could be worse. He could be in his bed alone.

Tomorrow he would call on Bell whether she liked it or not. He would also arrange to meet up with St. Cyrus.

Chapter Eighteen

Annabell sat stiffly in the carriage and wished she had never agreed to accompany Dominic and the simpering Miss Lucy to Almack's. And from the look on her brother's face, he was going to set into her as soon as they left Miss Lucy on her doorstep. Well, he had another thing coming if he thought anything he said would make a difference. Dominic was everything he accused Hugo of being, and he was younger.

In the meantime, she had to sit and watch the two. The chit blushed and giggled. Dominic barely skirted the edge of propriety. No wonder Emily Duckworth was beside herself. Annabell wasn't sure if she wanted this spectacle to end so she would not have to agonise over what was going on or if she dreaded the end of this little trip because then she would have to listen to Dominic's tirade.

Either way, they arrived at Miss Lucy's London residence and Dominic helped the chit from the carriage and walked her to the front door. Annabell winced when he raised the girl's gloved hand to his lips and instead of kissing the back of her hand, turned it over and kissed her wrist. Very Continental and calculated to further ensnare a girl as susceptible as Miss Lucy appeared to be.

As soon as the chit was in the door and he turned around,

he smile left Dominic's face. Annabell was tempted to signal the coachman to drive away. It wouldn't hurt Dominic to walk home. But she hesitated and the chance was lost.

He climbed in, then sprawled across the seat opposite her, his relaxed pose at direct odds with the look on his face. She knew him well enough to know he was ready to explode with fury.

'What did you think you were doing, dancing with that man?'

She kept her countenance bland. 'Do you mean Sir Hugo? Or Mr Hawks?'

Through clenched teeth he said, 'You know exactly whom I mean, Bell. Don't try my patience.'

'Don't try yours?' She leaned forward. 'What about you trying mine? What I do is none of your business, Dominic. I don't care that you are my brother. I am a widow and older than you. And...' she paused ominously '...my reputation is considerably better than yours.'

He wagged one finger at her. 'Don't drag my reputation into this, Bell. It has nothing to do with your association with Sir Hugo Fitzsimmon. The man will ruin you—you won't be accepted anywhere in polite society.'

She sniffed. 'I don't see that it has harmed Felicia not to be accepted by the sticklers. Nor would it bother me. I never go about in society as it is. I only went tonight to give poor Emily Duckworth a reprieve from seeing you seduce her young, silly sister.'

'Don't bring Miss Sourpuss into this either,' he retorted.

'I can't imagine why you call Emily Duckworth such an uncomplimentary name. She has done nothing to you.'

He scowled. 'Don't change the subject. This discussion is about you and Sir Hugo. If you don't value your reputation, then at least show some pride. The man is engaged to be married. Rumour says Elizabeth Mainwaring is carrying his child. If that is so, and I don't doubt it since the two have been lovers for at least a year that I know of, then the last thing you should be doing is throwing yourself a him.'

Her scathing reply died before she could even think wha it was going to be. She turned away from her brother's all too-discerning gaze. The last thing she wanted was to cr in front of Dominic. She had become a watering pot an what for? A man she could never have and wasn't eve sure she would marry if she could have him. Not that h had asked. But... Damnation, she was a mess.

'Bell?' Dominic's voice had softened. 'What is the mat ter?'

She took a deep steadying breath. 'Nothing, Dominic. am merely tired...from being out later than usual and fron arguing with you.' She pushed back a strand of hair tha had come loose from the elaborate braid circling the bacl of her head. 'Please, no more talk. You are perfectly righ about Sir Hugo and I know that. All right.'

He sat up. 'You agree?' His voice held incredulity.

She sighed wearily. 'Yes, I agree. Can we let it go?'

'Then you won't see him again, and you definitely won' dance with him again?'

She would have smiled at his persistence if she hadn' been so tired of it all. 'I very likely won't see him again and I'm positive I won't be in another situation where th opportunity to dance with him will arise.'

He opened his mouth to say something, but she held he hand up to stop him. 'No, Dominic, some promises ar better not made.'

He shook his head. 'You always were stubborn to a fault Bell.'

She raised one slashing black brow. 'And you aren't?'

He laughed. 'I believe it is a family trait. If I remembe correctly, both our parents were burdened with it.'

'At least we come by it honestly, as the saying goes.'

Fortunately the carriage pulled to a stop in front of Guy' town house before Dominic could start berating her again

She slid to the door, opened it and clambered out before he or a servant could help her. The last thing she intended to do was give him the opportunity to take her arm and keep her captive while he continued his rant.

The next morning, Annabell entered the sunlight-flooded breakfast room with less than her customary appetite. Oswald stood near the sideboard, waiting to hear whether she wanted tea or hot chocolate, but instead of his normal welcome, he looked uncomfortable.

'Good morning, Oswald.' She smiled at him and took the chair held by the footman. 'I won't be needing ser— What is this? An old copy of *The Times?*'

Oswald cleared his throat. 'Mr Dominic left it for you.'

Unease settled into Annabell's shoulders. She picked the paper up and realised it was only a page showing the engagement announcements. One of them was circled. *Sir Hugo Fitzsimmon announces his engagement to Lady Elizabeth Mainwaring.*

Ten simple words.

Annabell closed her eyes and felt the tension move to her stomach. She took a deep breath. This was not the time or the place. Please, don't let her cry.

She placed her hands flat on the table and pushed herself to a standing position. She felt like an old woman, aged before her time.

'I believe I will have tea in my rooms, Oswald. Nothing to eat.'

To give him credit, the old family retainer merely said, 'Yes, Miss Annabell.'

She couldn't even look at him for fear she would see pity on his face and that it would be her undoing. She walked from the room, back straight.

She managed to reach her rooms.

Why seeing the announcement had bothered her so much, she couldn't say. It was nothing but words. And she had

known about the engagement. Had known about it for fa
longer than the announcement had been public. But there
was a finality to the written word that the spoken word di
not share. Perhaps that was it.

Either way, it did not matter. Seeing the announcemen
in black and white negated any hope she had sustained th
night before. Hugo might find out that Elizabeth Mainwar
ing's child was not his, but it was too late. He had alread
placed the announcement in *The Times*. Only a scoundre
would cry off after that, and whatever else Hugo was—an
he was many less than savoury things—he was not a scoun
drel or a loose screw. He would not break the engagement

Lady Mainwaring would have to do that.

The following afternoon, Hugo knocked at Viscoun
Chillings's town house. The door was opened by a ver
proper butler who looked him up and down.

'Yes, my lord?'

Hugo handed over his card. 'Please let Lady Fenwick
Clyde know Sir Hugo Fitzsimmon is here to see her.'

The butler's eyes widened a fraction, but his voice re
mained completely noncommittal. 'Please come in, m
lord.'

Hugo entered the hall and handed his beaver hat to th
waiting servant. 'Come this way, please, my lord.'

He followed the butler to the drawing room where h
was left. There was a portrait over the mantel of Annabel
and her brothers. There was a marked resemblance betwee
her and Viscount Chillings. He vaguely remembered hear
ing they were twins. The younger man also had a likenes
of them, but where their hair was silvery blond, his wa
black as night. And there was a mischief in his eyes tha
was missing in the others.

'Damn if it isn't you,' a male voice said.

Hugo turned to see the younger man standing in the door
way. His black brows were drawn together.

'Dominic Chillings.' Hugo kept his voice pleasant even though he sensed the man's anger. 'Pleased to see you again.'

'Well, I am not pleased to see you. Nor do I intend to let you see my sister. She is better off without you.' Dominic paced into the room, his very posture a challenge. 'Go back to your fiancée.'

Hugo stood his ground. 'I am here to see your sister, not you. And I believe she is old enough—and independent enough—to do as she damn well pleases.'

'Well, she won't wish to see you or even hear from you when she learns what's been written in the betting book at Crooks's.'

Surprised, Hugo asked, 'What do you mean?'

Dominic scowled. 'Don't play the innocent with me, Fitzsimmon. It doesn't sit well on a man of your ilk.'

Hugo took a deep breath and reined in his rising temper. 'I have only been in town two days. I stopped briefly at Crooks's last night, but did not stay late. I didn't look in the betting book and no one mentioned it to me.'

Dominic sneered. 'Then the bet must have been placed some time between when you left and this afternoon when I was there for lunch. Not much time.'

'And just what bet are you referring to?'

Dominic's voice lowered ominously. 'The one that reads: *What knight is engaged to one woman who carries his child while in love with another? A monkey he jilts the one to save the other.*'

'You jest.'

'Not about my sister.' Dominic's voice was as cold as Hugo's.

There was a cold pit in Hugo's stomach. That was exactly what some cur who imagined himself to be a wit would write. And it was close to the truth. Too close.

'Bloody cur,' Hugo growled.

'My sentiments exactly,' Dominic said. 'And it is all be cause of you.'

'Perhaps no one knows who the blackguard is referrin to.' Even as he said the words, Hugo knew it couldn't b true. The bet was too precise.

'Not after the way you behaved at Almack's last night

Hugo had never before regretted any of his actions. N even having Elizabeth Mainwaring for a lover. But he re gretted this. And the realisation surprised him.

'So,' Dominic continued, 'I want you to leave this hous and I don't ever want to see you near my sister again or will be forced to call you out. Do I speak plainly enough Fitzsimmon?'

'Perfectly.'

Hugo bit the word off, wondering who infuriated hi more, the worthless cad who had placed the bet or th young man who stood defiantly before him. Both had ma it impossible for him to continue pursuing Annabell, som thing he knew he should stop. If only he could. Nor coul he duel with this young hothead. Annabell would nev forgive him if he hurt her brother. But he could find o who had written in the betting book.

'Whatever is going on here?' Annabell demanded fro the drawing-room door.

Hugo spun around. He had not heard her come in an from the look on his face, neither had Dominic.

'Nothing,' both men said at once.

Annabell came nearer, a suspicious look on her fac 'Then why do both of you look like little boys caught wi your fingers in the biscuit tin?'

Hugo looked at Dominic, who was looking at him. F once they both had a common goal, to keep the sordid tru from Annabell.

'I was telling Fitzsimmon to be off,' Dominic said. 'To him you didn't wish to see a man who was engaged another woman.'

Much as the words irritated him, Hugo had to admire Dominic's quick thinking. She would believe that and it was the truth.

'And I was telling him that I wanted to hear you dismiss me yourself.'

She looked from Dominic to him. 'He is right. I don't wish to see you.'

Her words hurt more than he would have expected. He had thought the musket ball in his thigh had been painful, but it had been nothing compared to this. This went deeper than physical agony. But he knew she was right. He needed to leave her alone. If he continued this, someone would notice and her name would eventually be dragged through the worst the *ton* had to offer.

He kept his gaze on her as he bowed. 'I won't bother you again, Lady Fenwick-Clyde.'

Her eyes widened slightly as though she had not expected him to agree so readily. His mouth twisted. She did not know about the bet. Were it not for that, he would not have accepted her dismissal so quickly. He would not have accepted it at all.

He took his leave before she could pry deeper. Better to never see her again than to drag her through the gutter. A nearly impossible decision to make, but a necessary one for her sake.

Hugo made his way to Brooks's. It was early, but the betting book was always there. Perhaps there was a clue that would tell him who would do such a despicable thing. And there would undoubtedly be members there just to get away from home.

He signalled his tiger and jumped into the seat of his high-perch phaeton. With an accomplished flick of the wrist, he set his pair in motion. At St Timothy's, he pulled to the curb and waited for the tiger to go to the horses' heads before getting out.

'I probably won't be in very long, John. Don't go far.'

'Yes, sir.' He took the reins and started walking the team up the road. He would continue to do so until Hugo returned.

Hugo entered the cool, dark club and handed his beaver and cane to a waiting footman. 'Brandy.'

'Yes, sir.'

The man left and Hugo went into the central room where the bulk of the gambling was done. The long crimson curtains were closed. The chandelier provided enough light for gambling and reading the papers.

He found the betting book and opened it to the last page. The bet was even uglier in writing than it had been coming from Dominic Chillings's mouth. He set the book down and his fists clenched till the knuckles turned white. He looked around, wondering if any of the people here were responsible. A few men watched him surreptitiously. No one came over.

The servant found him sitting in one of the corners, his feet stretched out in a pose of seeming nonchalance. He was far from it.

'Thank you,' Hugo said, pouring a generous measure.

Someone was going to lose a great deal of money. Much as he didn't want to marry Elizabeth Mainwaring, he was going to. As for Annabell, he hadn't asked her to him marry even before this fiasco, and she would have told him no he had.

He downed the brandy and poured more.

'Mind if I join you?'

Hugo looked up, starting at the interloper's immaculately polished Hessians, past a perfectly fitted jacket that even Beau Brummell could not have found fault with, to the intensely brilliant blue eyes of St. Cyrus. He did mind, but shrugged.

St. Cyrus took that as permission. 'Mind if I share?'

Hugo took another drink and eyed the other man. 'Yes

St. Cyrus's chin jerked a little, but he waved to a servant.
?ring me a bottle of whatever this is.'

'Brandy,' Hugo said.

'Brandy.'

Hugo waited St. Cyrus out. They were not friends, nor
?d they served together during Waterloo. In short, with the
?ception of Elizabeth Mainwaring, they had nothing in
?mmon.

The second bottle of brandy arrived and St. Cyrus poured
? glass and drank the contents in one gulp, his Adam's
?ple bobbing behind the intricate folds of his cravat. He
? the empty glass down and turned to face Hugo.

'Your engagement to Lady Mainwaring was sudden.'

Hugo took another drink, wondering where this was go-
?g. 'It depends on how you look at it.'

St. Cyrus took a sip of his brandy. 'Perhaps. She had
?rely returned from Paris when it was announced.'

'True.' Hugo angled to look at the other man. 'However,
? is none of your business.'

St. Cyrus set his glass down sharply. 'Are you sure?'

'The lady assures me that it is so.'

'And you believe her?'

Hugo looked away, checking to ensure no one was close
?. Their discussion was private and, if overheard, dam-
?ng to Elizabeth's good name, or what she had of one.
?ill, in spite of the situation, he did not want her hurt. He
?rned back.

'Shouldn't I?'

St. Cyrus's perfect features reddened. Hugo eyed the man
?rdonically, wondering how indiscreet he would be.

St. Cyrus cleared his throat. 'I think the lady might have
?ted in haste.'

Hugo's heart lurched. Surely he had not heard what he
?ought he had heard. Elizabeth had led him to believe she
?d already spoken with St. Cyrus.

'Really?'

It was hard to keep his mounting interest out of his voice, but if St. Cyrus was about to admit to something, he did not want to scare him off by seeming too eager. He took another drink.

St. Cyrus had stopped drinking. 'It is very possible.'

Hugo chose his next words with care. 'Then what do you intend to do about it?'

'I have arranged to speak with her this evening. At the theatre.'

Hugo started. 'I am taking her there.'

St. Cyrus had the grace to look uncomfortable. 'I know, but…'

She had sent St. Cyrus a note. Hugo's mouth twisted. '**I** see. That is not a very private place.'

'No, it is not.' St. Cyrus's hands clenched on his thighs. 'That is why I wanted to speak with you. It is a stroke of luck to find you here.'

'It is the stroke of a very malicious pen,' Hugo muttered.

'I beg your pardon?'

Hugo eyed him with dislike. 'The betting book. Perhaps you even wrote it.'

St. Cyrus drew himself up straight. 'I am not in the habit of writing in the blasted thing.'

Hugo snorted. 'From what you have hinted at these past minutes, you would certainly stand to gain if the bet came true.'

St. Cyrus's eyes turned frosty. 'I will see what you are talking about.'

Hugo shrugged. 'As you wish.'

He watched the other man make his way to the infamous book, and wondered what was going on. From the implications of the conversation, St. Cyrus was not happy that Elizabeth was engaged to someone besides himself. Interesting.

St. Cyrus read the last page, and Hugo saw his elegant body stiffen. The other man swept his cold gaze around the oom. No one looked at him. So, Hugo decided, St. Cyrus was not the target of the bet, nor was he the perpetrator—unless he was a superb actor.

St. Cyrus stalked back to the seat beside Hugo. 'When I find out who wrote that, I will see to it that he does not write anything else.'

'My sentiments exactly.' Hugo was mildly surprised to see that he and St. Cyrus could agree on something besides wedding Elizabeth Mainwaring.

'But for different reasons, I would wager.'

Hugo watched the other man through narrowed eyes. 'For the nonce, my reasons are my own.'

'Understood.' St. Cyrus stood. 'I will be calling at your box tonight.'

Hugo nodded. He had a season box at Covent Garden. Juliet used it more than he, but he got it every year.

He watched St. Cyrus leave, wondering what would come of this. And what would he do if St. Cyrus did ask Elizabeth to marry him? Would he ask Bell to wed him? He didn't know.

That evening, Hugo sat in his box and looked casually round the theatre. As usual, all the *ton* had come to Covent Garden Theatre. The boxes were full and the pit was crowded. The women were in evening gowns and masses of jewellery. The men had their quizzing glasses raised. At least, a quizzing glass was one affectation he did not aspire to.

He heard Elizabeth flick open her fan. 'La, Hugo, it is hot in here. Would you get me something to drink?'

He turned to her. As usual, she was stunning. She wore a black evening dress with white trim of some sort. The neck scooped low to show her milky breasts. And there was a brightness in her eyes and a flush on her fair complexion. His mouth twisted sardonically. She was excited about St. Cyrus's visit. Far be it from him to interfere.

'Of course, Elizabeth.' Hugo rose to leave.

She nodded graciously. 'Take your time.'

Even as she spoke to him, her eyes scanned the nearby boxes with an eagerness that was almost painful to watch. He was not accustomed to seeing her expose her emotion openly. For the first time since this fiasco began, he felt sorry for Elizabeth. She might have created this intolerable situation, but she was no more happy than he.

Hugo bowed and left, swinging his ebony cane jauntily. With luck and another man's jealousy, tonight might see him a free man.

With that thought, Hugo searched to see if Annabell was here. There was no reason to believe she would be since she was not at all interested in society and where it congregated. Still, he would like to see her, and if she was here he would go so far as to visit her. Nothing ventured, nothing gained.

He found her. She was across the theatre in a box with a group that included Dominic Chillings, Miss Emily Duckworth, who looked as though she had just eaten a lemon, and her sister, Miss Lucy. He would wager the tension in that box could be cut with a knife.

Without pausing to consider his actions, Hugo made his way to the box and knocked. Dominic Chillings came to the door and stepped out.

'You are not wanted, Fitzsimmon.'

'By you or your sister?' Hugo asked coolly.

'Both.'

Hugo looked the younger man in the eye. There was a belligerent set to Dominic Chillings's jaw that spoke of determination. If he forced the issue, Annabell's brother would be glad to help him cause a scene. That was the last thing any of them needed. Nor was it fair to Annabell. She had already told him to leave her in peace. It was not her fault he was unable to do so.

Hugo took a deep breath and made himself do the right

thing. 'I will leave for now.' He didn't bow, but pivoted on his heel and sauntered away, working to keep the simmering irritation he felt from showing. It was bad enough that anyone watching had seen him turned away. Now the gossip-mongers would have a feast, but at least it was no worse. There would be no challenge to titillate everyone.

He paused and looked at his own box, which was in the first circle. St. Cyrus was there. He and Elizabeth had their heads together. She even had her hand on his forearm. They were so obviously a couple that Hugo decided to leave. St. Cyrus would see Elizabeth home—his or hers. It didn't matter. All he wanted was a note telling him the engagement was off because she was to marry St. Cyrus.

Nothing else mattered.

Chapter Nineteen

Hugo found it impossible to sleep after the theatre. He paced his room and dozed, with more pacing than dozing. Morning couldn't come soon enough. Having never really slept, when morning finally arrived Hugo found himself even more impatient, if that were possible.

Now he had to wait until afternoon when Elizabeth would be up. He knew from the past that she was not an early riser. And then he would have to be patient and see if she would send for him.

And what if she didn't?

He wouldn't think about that. She would or she wouldn't. If she did, then he would be free to go to Annabell. If she didn't, he would marry a woman he didn't love because of a child he might or might not have fathered. Simple, no matter how the second action would hurt.

Half past noon, Butterfield knocked on the library door. 'Excuse me, sir, but there is a message for you.'

'Thank you.'

Hugo jumped up from the leather wing chair he had been lounging in, trying to read and being unsuccessful. As at Rosemont, the library here was also his favourite room. He liked books and maps. Always had.

He picked up the sheet of paper, which was sealed with red wax. The scent of tuberose engulfed him. Relief eased the tension in his shoulders.

Opening the note, he read: *Dearest Hugo, please call on me immediately. I have something of great importance to tell you. EM.*

He tore the sheet into pieces and threw them on the grate. When the fire was lit this evening, the paper would be ashes. He trusted his servants, but this was a private matter.

'Butterfield, have my carriage brought 'round.'

'Yes, sir.' There was only a hint of curiosity in the old retainer's eyes.

'Don't worry, old man, you will know soon enough.'

Hugo could no longer go to Butterfield with his trials and tribulations, but he still cared for the man. And he knew Butterfield had been troubled by his engagement, although the butler had never said a word.

'Yes, sir.'

Hugo smiled. 'Where is Jamison? I need a coat at the very least.'

'I believe he is upstairs, but he could also be out.'

'True,' Hugo said, more amused than irritated at the possibility. 'He does like London and all the possibilities it provides.'

He went up the stairs two at a time. He should have put a coat on first thing upon dressing, but it was hotter than normal today and he liked his comfort before he cared for fashion.

He entered his chamber. 'Jamison.'

When the valet didn't appear, Hugo went to the dressing room and found a bottle-green coat. He shrugged into it, thankful he did not believe in tailoring to the point that he needed help to dress. He didn't always cut a dash, but then his lack of polish had never hurt him either.

He went down the stairs as quickly as he had gone up

them. His phaeton waited. He jumped up, took the reins and signalled the tiger to get into position.

He found himself more anxious by the minute. What if he was mistaken and Elizabeth had not summoned him to release him from their engagement? What would he do then? He would deal with that if and when it happened. There was no point in borrowing trouble.

He consciously relaxed his shoulders and made himself pay attention to his driving. The streets were busy as usual at this time of year, and he did not want to cause an accident or be in one of another person's making.

He reached Elizabeth's town house and gave the reins to his tiger. 'Walk them. I might be a while.'

Not waiting for a reply, Hugo ran up the front steps and rapped. Elizabeth's butler was prompt.

'Good afternoon, Sir Hugo,' the butler said. 'Her ladyship is expecting you.'

'Hello, Edwards.'

He followed the butler in and was shown to the drawing room. It was done in the Egyptian motif of several seasons before. He had always thought the drama of it was the perfect foil for Elizabeth, who could be quite dramatic if she felt it suited her.

'Sir Hugo Fitzsimmon,' the butler announced.

Hugo walked in and immediately saw Elizabeth by the window. She sat stiffly in one of the very uncomfortable settees. She was obviously as unsettled as he was. But there was a glow about her face that told him she was either excited or happy—probably both.

'Elizabeth,' he said, coming to a halt in front of her. 'Is something the matter?'

He sounded inane, but he was afraid to say anything that might worsen the situation. He was suddenly very aware that he wanted her to break their engagement more than he had ever wanted anything in his life—with the exception of Annabell. Nothing had prepared him for what Annabell had come to mean to him.

Even now, the realisation stunned him and he missed Elizabeth's first words.

'—so, you see, I think it for the best.' There was such hope in her eyes that Hugo's hopes soared.

'Pardon me, Elizabeth, but I was not paying proper attention. Would you please repeat what you just said?'

He had never been this gauche, and he would have been ashamed if he were not so nervous. But he wanted this so badly.

She gave him a cold look. 'Do you need to sit, Hugo?'

'No.'

She licked her full, red lips. 'Well, I just told you St. Cyrus has asked me to marry him.'

Hugo sat. It was either that or shout for joy. He was a free man. But he did his best to keep his spirits under control. It would not be right to parade his relief in front of her.

'And what did you say?' he asked, careful to keep his voice pleasantly curious only.

She tilted her head to one side. 'Hugo, aren't you happy? I thought you surely would be.'

'That depends on what you told him, Elizabeth. If you remember, you told me I am the father of your child.'

He couldn't keep a slight tinge of irony from his words. Happy as he was to know his freedom was in sight, he still harboured a little bitterness about the situation her demands had created. Annabell had been hurt. She might refuse to take him back, and he couldn't blame her.

'You are not making this easy, Hugo.'

'Should everything be easy for you, Elizabeth?'

She had the grace to blush. 'I suppose not.' She took a deep breath and determination settled over her like a mantle. 'I told St. Cyrus yes.'

'Is he the father of your child?'

Why he was pursuing this, Hugo didn't know, but he was piqued that she had nearly ruined his life and Annabell's and now she acted as though nothing had happened.

She shrugged. 'He might be as easily as you. Probably more so for the reason you and I have previously discussed.' Her blush deepened.

'Ah, protection,' Hugo said softly.

'Hugo!'

He eyed her. 'Does he know the situation?'

She nodded. 'He is willing to raise the child as his.' Her face took on a blissful look. 'He loves me. I didn't believe so when we parted on the Continent.' Now she looked the tiniest bit sorry. 'That is why I sent for you.'

Hugo just looked at her. His joy at being released was like a balloon that threatened to explode if he wasn't careful. But at the same time, his irritation with her was not easily put aside and it made his voice crueller than it should have been.

'I was your ace in the hole.'

'To put it crudely, yes.'

'Then you will send a retraction to *The Times*.' He made it a statement.

'Yes. You are free to marry your Annabell, Hugo.'

He stood and looked down at her, ignoring her last words. What he intended to do was none of her business. 'I wish you the best.'

'Goodbye,' she said softly to his back.

Hugo did not look back.

Annabell sat by the front window, watching the pedestrians: men in beaver hats and spotless coats, women in walking dresses. Occasionally a maid scurried on her mistress's errand. Sometimes a nanny with several children in tow passed.

The last reminded her of Joseph and Rosalie. She wondered how they were doing, and Juliet. She smiled, but it was melancholy. She would very likely see them again. Unless she missed her guess, her stepson intended to wed Lady Fitzsimmon.

She sighed and rose. It was time to dress for the lecture at the Society of Antiquaries. Mr Jeffrey Studivant was presenting his paper on *her* Roman villa, a follow up on the first paper she had presented several weeks ago.

She moved slowly, determined not to think about what had been in yesterday's *Times*. Dominic had shown her.

She stopped and her heart thudded painfully. Lady Mainwaring had announced that her engagement to Sir Hugo Fitzsimmon was broken. Hugo was free. But he had not come to tell her even though the separation had to have happened several days before.

Had all his words, all his pursuit been nothing? She feared so.

She blinked, realised she had stopped moving, and forced herself to continue to the door. She needed to dress. She needed to go out so she would not sit here and descend into melancholy.

And to think she had wondered if she could have brought herself to marry Hugo, should he ever ask. She was a fool, a self-delusional fool. She loved him. It seemed she had loved him her entire life.

But he had not come for her.

The drawing-room door opened and Oswald stood there with a very pleased look on his face. 'Sir Hugo Fitzsimmon.'

Surely he jested. But, no, Hugo was right behind the butler. Her former lover strode into the room, and she wondered how she could have ever thought she would not have him if he offered. But he hadn't, so her fall from independence was immaterial.

She dredged up all her pride. 'Good afternoon, Sir Hugo.' She smiled, knowing it was thin and unwelcoming. 'I fear you have come at a bad time. I am just on my way out.'

He did not return her smile. 'What I have to say won't take long, Bell.'

She started at his use of her family name. 'Lady Fenwick-Clyde.'

He took a step nearer. 'Bell. My Lady Spitfire.'

She blanched and tried to walk around him, but he shifted so that she could not pass. Nor was there anyone to call for help. Coward that he was, Oswald had already left and closed the door behind him. He had known something was afoot. Where was Dominic when she needed him? Gone out with Lucy Duckworth.

She threw caution to the winds. 'Why are you here, Hugo? The announcement was yesterday.'

Nor could she keep the hurt and disappointment from her voice. That shamed her. She had fought for her independence and now she would gladly give it up. No, she would beg to give it up to Hugo. She shook her head and made herself stand tall and proud.

He closed the distance between them.

She edged away, not wanting him to touch her. Whenever he touched her she lost all resolve, no matter what her reason for resisting him might be. She had learned that lesson well during her stay at Rosemont and, later, here in London, that night at Almack's.

He moved with her. 'I couldn't come sooner, Bell.'

She frowned. 'Couldn't or wouldn't?'

The look he gave her was tender and loving. She wondered if her brain had gone soft as her body was threatening to do. Surely he was not looking at her the way she thought he was. If he were, he would have rushed to her as soon as he knew he was free—days ago.

'Wouldn't, Bell.'

She stared mutely at him, unable to speak. The last thing she wanted to do was cry in front of him. What had happened to all her independence, her determination to make a life without a man's hand on her? Gone. Lost the first time he kissed her, only she hadn't realised it then.

She lifted her chin. She could still be independent. She was strong. 'Please leave.'

She was proud her pain didn't show in the clipped words. She would get through this, just as she had gotten through his engagement to Elizabeth Mainwaring.

'Not until I ask you to marry me.'

'What?' Surely she hadn't heard him correctly.

'Marry me, Bell.'

His words were soft, almost hesitant. If she didn't know him better, she would think he was unsure of himself. Yet, there was that determined gleam in his green eyes.

She gaped at him, then anger came to her rescue and stiffened her resolve. 'Your jest is in poor taste, Sir Hugo.'

He shook his head, the too-long hair framing his sharp cheekbones. For a second he looked wild. 'No jest, Bell.' His magnificent lips curved. 'I have never jested with you. And I have never lied to you.'

She looked long and hard at him, searching for the truth of his words. She didn't think she could stand to be hurt by him again. She had only survived the last time because of her determination and strength. If he failed her again...

She sucked in air, wondering what would happen if the dizziness overtaking her won. She would fall to the floor and awaken later, remembering this only as a dream. She had longed so much for him to come to her like this.

'If you truly mean what you say, why did it take you so long?'

Now a little bit of her agony was in her voice. She flushed at the realisation that she was so vulnerable to this man, and she had let him know.

'Because I wanted you to have this when I proposed.'

He held out a velvet box. She shuddered.

'Another piece of jewellery?' Bitterness tinged her words. She drew back.

'Yes.' He closed the distance between them and fell to one knee, wincing.

Concern swelled up in her. 'Don't, Hugo. Your injury doesn't do well when you kneel. Please stand.'

He looked up at her and opened the box. Inside was a ring. A star sapphire, large as a pigeon's egg, surrounded by diamonds, winked up at her. It was large enough to span one knuckle.

'The Garibaldi engagement ring, my grandmother's gift to me. I want you to have it.'

She gasped, her left hand going to her throat where her pulse beat rapidly. The first words from her mouth were unintentional, but came from the depths of her hurt soul.

'That isn't the ring you gave Lady Mainwaring.'

'No,' he said, taking the ring from its satin bed. 'I would have never given it to her. She is not the bride of my heart. The ring is always given to a true love. That is why I'm giving it to you.'

The tears she had tried so hard to hold back welled up and over. They spilled silently down her cheeks. She couldn't stop them.

'Hugo.'

He caught her unresisting left hand and slipped the ring on to her finger. It fit perfectly.

'I love you, Bell,' he said simply, but there was such a wealth of emotion in the words that she could not doubt him.

She sank to her knees beside him.

He smiled tenderly at her. 'The sapphire came from India back in the late sixteen hundreds. It was given to one of my Garibaldi ancestors by a Maharaja as a token of esteem. Legend says that as long as the gem goes to a true love, that union will be blessed with happiness and many children. My ancestor had it made into an engagement ring.' He cupped her cheek with his hand, his thumb rubbing her bottom lip. 'I could have never given it to anyone but you, Bell.'

She kissed him gently at first, then more passionately. 'Hugo, I love you so much.'

He pulled away just enough to say, 'I know.'

Their wedding was a small affair, held in the small chapel at Rosemont. They had invited immediate family only, and Susan Pennyworth and Tatterly.

The minister beamed at the couple before him. 'You may place the ring on her finger.'

Hugo looked at Annabell as he slid the sapphire-studded wedding band on to her finger. 'I love you.'

The minister closed the Bible. 'I pronounce you man and wife.'

Annabell smiled at her husband. 'I love you forever.'

'Hear, hear,' Dominic Chillings's voice rose above the hearty clapping. 'Kiss her like you mean it, Fitzsimmon. No pecking. You put her through enough to get here.'

Hugo felt Annabell stiffen. He lifted his head enough to look at his brother-in-law. 'You are a reprobate, Dominic, but occasionally you do have a good idea.'

The other guests cheered.

Hugo turned back to his bride and smiled. 'Shall we show them how it's done?'

She blushed, but there was a glint in her eyes. 'By all means.'

He placed his mouth on hers and forgot the initial challenge as he fell into the passion and love they shared. Her lips opened and he plunged inside, wishing he could do more than kiss her. His body ached to do more.

When they came up for air, she was flushed and he was aroused. He buried his face in her hair and whispered, 'Thank goodness we are home and can go upstairs. I am about to embarrass myself.'

Her laugh was throaty and full of promise. 'We don'
want that, love.'

He nipped her ear. 'No, we don't.'

He turned her to face their guests. Guy, Viscount Chillings, had given Annabell away. He stood to one side with
Felicia and their very healthy baby son, Adam. Dominic
was now heckling Susan Pennyworth, the future Mrs. Tatterly. Tatterly stood nearby, watching the byplay with a
besotted look on his face. Juliet and the children beamed
at him. Timothy, Lord Fenwick-Clyde, stood close. They
had not announced their engagement, but Hugo sensed they
would do so soon. He hoped they would find the same joy
together that he had found with Annabell.

Hugo guided his bride through the well-wishers. Annabell glowed with happiness.

She turned to him, 'I am so glad we had our wedding
here.' She looked around the chapel, decked out in the last
of the summer roses. 'Rosemont has been like a home to
me since I first came here.'

'Since you found that Roman villa here, you mean,' he
teased.

'That too.' She smiled up at him.

'Here, here, you two,' Dominic said, closing the distance.
'Don't forget you have guests and we still have breakfast.
Then you can show us around.'

Hugo shook his head. 'Not this time. We are too old to
stand by society's practices.'

Dominic raised both brows. 'Really? Then what do you
intend to do, leave us to our own devices? Hardly gracious.'

Hugo laughed. 'Too bad.'

'For that is exactly what we intend to do,' Annabell finished for her husband.

She wanted him as badly as he did her. They had remained chaste since their engagement, knowing the self-
denial would make their wedding night all that more mem-
orable.

Everyone had heard her words, but she did not care. There was clapping and a few indiscreet remarks followed.

'Not done, old fellow,' Dominic continued to press. 'The same to you, Annabell. You should be blushing from the top of your gown to the roots of your hair.'

She laughed. 'But I am, little brother.'

'Wait until you are wed,' Hugo said to Dominic. 'I venture to guess you will be even more impatient than we are.'

Dominic turned brick red as though Hugo had caught him in the act of something forbidden. Hugo gave him a speculative look, but said nothing. His brother-in-law would do whatever it was he intended to do. He knew the man well enough to know there would be no sense in prying.

Besides, he had other interests. He turned to Jamison, who had been his groomsman. 'Lady Fitzsimmon and I are retiring. See that no one disturbs us.'

'Yes, sir,' the valet replied, a twinkle in his eyes. 'I'll stand guard outside the door.'

'You don't need to go that far,' Annabell protested before seeing the mischievousness in Jamison's smile.

'Yes, my lady,' Jamison said, barely able to suppress his guffaw.

Hugo shook his head and propelled Annabell through the door and up the stairs before anything else was said. When they reached the door to his chambers, he stopped her.

'I intend to carry you over the threshold.'

She laughed. 'Absolutely not, Hugo. The last thing I want on our wedding day is to injure your leg.'

He dipped his head to kiss her. 'If I hurt that, it won't stop what I have in mind for this afternoon, evening and all day tomorrow.'

Her blush returned and her grin was wicked. 'No, but that would make it painful for you, my dear, since I intend to see that you live up to that boast.'

He opened the door, then swung her into his arms and carried her into the room and to the bed. He dumped her

in the pile of silk and satin cushions where she lay ver
still, gazing up at him.

'I love you,' she said quietly, all of her previous humou
gone. 'I love you so much it hurts.'

'And I you,' he said, meaning every word more than h
had ever meant anything else in his life. 'Now and always

She sighed and reached for him.

He went to her.

When they lay naked in the sheets, he caught her bottor
lip with his thumb and rubbed. 'I want to remember thi
for the rest of our lives.'

She twinned her arms around his neck. He meant s
much to her. 'We will, love. We will.'

He gazed at her with more love in his heart than he ha
ever imagined himself capable of. Then he kissed he
deeply and passionately. She opened to him.

Annabell revelled in the desire he always ignited in he
With him she felt that anything was possible. She stroke
the unruly hair from his face and dug her fingers into th
silken strands to hold him to her.

He drank in her bounty, his hands cupping her breast
His fingers stroked her swollen flesh until her nipples hard
ened and she gasped. He ached for her, ached so it hurt.

She rubbed one hand down the back of his neck to hi
shoulders, marvelling in the muscles that rippled beneat
his skin. Her fingers raked gently down the ridges brack
eting his spine. He was so strong and so beautiful in hi
masculinity.

He broke away from her lips and gave her his rakis
smile. 'You are mine.'

When her slumberous eyes opened and her moist mout
smiled, he thought he would lose control. His manhoo
strained against the slight swell of her stomach. But h
wasn't ready to enter her yet.

Annabell saw the passion in his eyes and felt her stomac

wist as sensation started radiating through her. She was
nore than ready for him. She moved her hips suggestively.

'Not yet,' he murmured, kissing her chin lightly in pass-
ng.

He nuzzled the sensitive skin on the side of her neck and
own to the hollow at the base of her throat. His hands
hifted downward, skimming over her ribs and abdomen.
Ie felt her nails dig into his hips and knew he was exciting
er. He chuckled low in his throat.

Then his mouth was at her breast and he sucked pow-
rfully so her back arched and a small whimper came from
eep in her chest. He continued to pull and nip while his
ingers moved inexorably lower. When he entered her, she
vas moist.

Pleasure filled him. He wanted her to remember their first
ime together since being wed. He wanted that so badly that
e could postpone his own release until he had completely
atiated her.

Annabell felt his fingers inside her and thought she would
xplode. She gasped and tingles started at the small of her
ack and rushed outwards. She gripped him tightly, urging
im deeper. Her mind grew fuzzy and the only thing that
nattered was what he was doing to her.

She was on the brink when he withdrew. She gasped,
Hugo.'

'Easy, my love. I won't leave you like this. I promise.'
Ie kissed her mouth lightly, then deeper. 'I want you to
emember this time for the rest of your life.'

Tears welled up and she did nothing to stop them. 'You
nake me so happy.'

'Don't cry, my love,' he murmured, licking one salty
rop from her cheek. 'This is only the beginning.'

She nodded and pulled his lips back to hers. 'Always.'

He sank into her embrace, his body over hers. When her
egs opened, and his hips settled, he was lost. 'I am sorry,

Bell,' he gasped. 'I had wanted this to last longer, but
can't hold out.'

She hooked her ankles around his hips. 'Pleasure m
now, Hugo. I cannot take any more.'

He kissed her long and hard as her hips rose up to mee
his. He wanted her so badly he hurt.

For one last moment of sanity, he held himself back. '
am not protected.'

She smiled at him, her lips swollen and moist. 'I war
your baby, Hugo.'

He thrust forwards until he thought he would die from
the tight heat of her. Her gasp of pleasure joined his as sh
rose to meet him. Their hot, wet skin met and slipped to
gether in a passion that mounted with each penetration.

Her moans filled his mouth, her nails dug into his shoul
ders, urging him to greater heights. He withdrew, thrus
forward again and again. Their bodies moved together a
though they had been made for one another.

She sucked his tongue deep, and he felt her contraction
start. She pulsed around him, pulling him inside so deep h
thought he had died and gone to heaven. Then he joine
her. The ache in his loins became such exquisite delight h
was not sure where he ended and she began.

Only much later, still sheathed inside her, did he com
back to himself. Propped on his elbows, he gazed down a
her. 'I thought you were going to take me so deep insid
yourself we would become one,' he murmured, hi
breathing rapid.

She smiled. 'I wanted to consume you,' she said, he
voice deep and raspy. 'I wanted to have what you wer
doing to me never end.'

He shifted and realised he was ready again. 'It won't en
just yet, love.' He moved so that she gasped and the sma
of his back tightened in pleasure.

She moaned and matched the motion of her hips to his

* * *

Later still, exhausted but happy, he rolled to her side and pulled her into his arms. 'I love you, Lady Spitfire.'

She smiled at him. 'Lady Fitzsimmon.'

He watched her. 'What happened to your independence?'

'Nothing. I finally realise I can be independent and married. It took me a long time to understand that.'

He smoothed a strand of silvered hair from her forehead. 'I didn't help with my own situation.'

She caught his hand and turned her head to kiss his palm. 'You are a man of honour. You did the right thing.' Her smile broke through. 'And we were fortunate enough that St. Cyrus was also a man of honour.'

More cynical than she, he added, 'And in love with Elizabeth.'

'That too.' She put a finger to his lips. 'But enough of that. Make love to me again.'

He gave her a mock look of shock. 'Again?'

She pressed her lips to him. 'How else am I to get pregnant with your child before we leave this room?'

Joy and love filled him so that tears sprang to his eyes. 'You are my life, Annabell. I love you more than I ever thought possible. If we have a child, then I will be doubly blessed.'

Smiling, he pulled her on top and entered her safe haven.

She bent to kiss him, this man who meant more to her than life. 'Just love me, Hugo. Just love me.'

* * * * *

Published 17th December 2004

TESS GERRITSEN

BARBARA DELINSKY

Two emotionally compelling novels by international
bestselling authors in one special volume

Family Passions

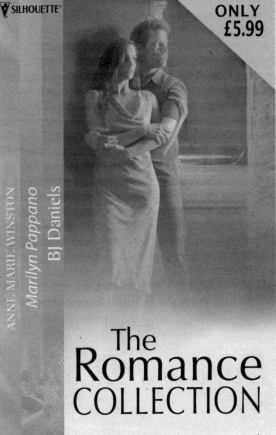

No. 1 *New York Times* bestselling author

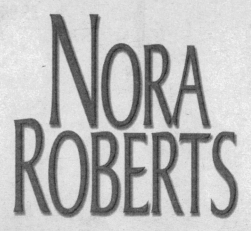

NORA ROBERTS

presents two classic novels about the
walls people build around their
hearts and how to break them down...

Love by Design

Available from 21st January 2005

FREE!
2 Books
and a surprise gift!

We would like to take this opportunity to thank you for reading this Mills & Boon® book by offering you the chance to take TWO more specially selected titles from the Historical Romance™ series absolutely FREE! We're also making this offer to introduce you to the benefits of the Reader Service™—

- ★ FREE home delivery
- ★ FREE gifts and competitions
- ★ FREE monthly Newsletter
- ★ Exclusive Reader Service offers
- ★ Books available before they're in the shops

Accepting these FREE books and gift places you under no obligation to buy. you may cancel at any time. even after receiving your free shipment. Simply complete your details below and return the entire page to the address below. You don't even need a stamp!

YES! Please send me 2 free Historical Romance books and a surprise gift. I understand that unless you hear from me. I will receive 4 superb new titles every month for just £3.59 each. postage and packing free. I am under no obligation to purchase any books and may cancel my subscription at any time. The free books and gift will be mine to keep in any case.

H4ZEF

Ms/Mrs/Miss/Mr ....Initials ....

BLOCK CAPITALS PLEASE

Surname ....

Address..

....

....Postcode ....

Send this whole page to:
UK: FREEPOST CN8I, Croydon, CR9 3WZ